Murder at Monte Carlo

E. Phillips Oppenheim

Murder at Monte Carlo

The present edition is a reproduction of previous publication of this classic work. Minor typographical errors may have been corrected without note, however, for an authentic reading experience the spelling, punctuation, and capitalization have been retained from the original text.

ISBN: 978-1-64799-673-4

CHAPTER I

Paul Viotti tapped with the tips of his finger nails the five cards which lay face downwards before him upon the green baize table. His four companions took the hint and prepared to listen. This was no ordinary card room in which the five men had met. It was the Holy of Holies in the most famous gambling club of New York. He would be a brave man who sought entrance there while a séance was being held.

"To-night," he said, "we are to speak of serious things. Perhaps I am more careful of my health than you others. Anyway, I know when the going is good. One gang against us was dangerous enough. We had all we could take care of when Tim Rooney brought his boys out. Now there are two. I am for fighting when I think that we'll win. Now I am sure that we shall lose if we go on, I say let us get away."

His four companions listened in absorbed interest. The game was momentarily forgotten. The cards lay untouched, the chips uncounted. Each seemed to have adopted a different attitude. Marcus Constantine—he was known under a different name in Paris and on the French Riviera—a long, graceful-looking youth, pale of complexion, with dark eyes and a curiously sensitive mouth, slouched across the table, his head supported between his hands, his eyes fixed upon his chief as though afraid of missing a single word. Matthew Drane, a good-looking, elaborately dressed man with smoothly brushed brown hair, pink-complexioned, with a

1

humorous mouth and a right hand which was reputed to be the quickest in the world at drawing a lethal weapon from the obscurity of a hidden pocket, listened with equal interest but more geniality. Tom Meredith, his neighbour, the flamboyant beau of the party, a pudgy-faced, narrow-eyed man of early middle age, dressed in imitation Savile Row cut tweeds, a shirt of violent design and a shameless tie, grunted his impartial approval of the scheme, whilst Edward Staines opposite, a tired-looking man who had the appearance of a successful but hard-working lawyer, listened with the slightly cynical air of one predisposed towards pessimism.

"That's all very well for you, Paul," the latter remarked. "You've got a country to go to where you can buy a mountain or two and an old castle and live like a lord for a few dollars a year. What the hell are we going to do, fussing about Europe? I'll admit we're up against a tough proposition here with this gang of Tim Rooney's hanging about after our territory, but what about lying low for a few months?"

"No damn' good that," Tom Meredith objected. "While we are lying low, Tim would be organising and we should never get our feet in again. Seems to me we're about through with this racket. We've got to either split up or find some place where the Star Spangled Banner doesn't flutter. We've had the cream. Let's leave the slops for Tim."

Paul Viotti, a swarthy, black-haired Corsican, expensively dressed, clean-shaven and perfumed, shook a fat forefinger at them all, a forefinger upon which flashed a wickedly assertive diamond.

"I've got a hunch for you," he announced. "There's only one place for us in the world. Money there for the picking up and a clear field."

Marcus Constantine looked swiftly across the table.

"Where's that?" he demanded.

"The South of France," was the prompt and triumphant reply. "Listen, I got a brother there and I know something. Cannes, Nice, Monte Carlo—why at the baccarat there there's millions, millions you can handle, mind, in good *mille* notes, changes hands every night. Suckers there by the thousands and not a nursemaid to look after them. Hauling liquor round here has been a good-enough job while it lasted, but the shooting's getting a bit too free and easy for me."

The long young man, Marcus Constantine, tapped a cigarette upon the table and lit it. There was a gleam of excitement in his eyes.

"I'll say that Paul is dead right," he declared. "As you fellows

2

know, I'm over there every year. I've got crowds of friends and I know the runs. Matthew isn't exactly a stranger there, either."

Paul Viotti smiled upon them all beneficently with outstretched hands.

"You hear Marcus?" he exclaimed. "He knows what he talks about. My brother over there, too. He knows. He's not in the game, but he knows. What I say is that we wander over there separately, take our time about it, mind; look at Paris and London first. Wait until people have forgotten what they may have heard about us out here. Time enough if we begin in, say, twelve months. My brother, he can get ready what we need. It won't be much. Just a place where we can meet and no one guesses—like here.

"There is one thing," Matthew Drane remarked. "I guess we'll have to take care of Luke Cheyne. Last we heard of him, he was out that way."

There was a moment's silence. Paul Viotti was stroking his black moustache.

"A pity about Luke," he sighed. "He should not have left us. Luke will have to go. Only a few days ago I had a pleasant little chat with Inspector Haygon down at Police Headquarters. I am afraid there is no doubt it was Luke who tipped Conyers off. He didn't clear out for nothing."

"What about the stock?" Edward Staines demanded.

"Never been so low," Viotti confided. "And listen, boys, I've an offer for the lot. Four hundred and fifty thousand cash. The stuff's worth more, but it would clean things up nicely."

"I'm for making the move," Tom Meredith declared. "I'd sooner find myself alive at the Ritz Bar this time next month, taking one with Charlie, than feeding the worms up at Woodlawn."

"Disgusting fellow," Marcus Constantine drawled. "I take it we're all agreed upon the move. We've drunk many a highball to our luck in this little room before we've gone out into the hard world. We'll drink one now to 'La Belle France'!"

They all crowded around the sideboard and helped themselves, for no waiter ever crossed the threshold of their sanctum whilst their session was in progress. Paul Viotti alone remained at the table. He had made a million dollars by bootlegging, but it was his boast that he had never yet touched a drop of hard liquor in his life.

"Come along, you boys," he called out presently. "Let's start the game. I ante five hundred. Very cheap to see me. Come along, all of you."

They took their places. The heavily curtained windows

3

reduced the roar of the avenue beyond the square to something stifled and monotonous, but the rattle of the overhead railway and the sirens from the steamships and ferries on the river came as reminders that they were in the heart of the great city.

"I guess," Tom Meredith remarked thoughtfully, "it will seem quiet at first in Monte Carlo."

"Maybe we'd soon all be quieter," Paul Viotti grinned, "if we stayed on here."

* * * * *

That was the afternoon when it was decided that the most dangerous gang of liquor dealers in the United States should disband and enter upon a fresh sphere of operations in Europe.

Certainly Roger Sloane's environment was all right. He was seated in a wisteria-wreathed arbour with his back to the snow-capped Alpes-Maritimes and before him the most enchanting landscape in the world. Little wafts of perfume floated up to him from a grove of orange trees just below, and beyond, the mellowing meadows and flower farms faded downwards to the blue streak of the Mediterranean. The Estérels made a silvery background on his right. The ancient hill town of La Bastide hemmed him in on the nearer left—a village so ancient that it was almost impossible to tell the inhabited dwellings from the crawling masses of grey stone. The sunshine was a live thing that morning, dancing and gleaming through the trees and amongst the flowers which stocked his garden. Without a doubt his environment was beyond reproach, yet before him on the rude Provençal table was a neat pile of manuscript paper clipped into a leather case, it's pages virgin of even one disfiguring scrawl. For three successive mornings he had lounged in this miniature paradise, had soaked himself in the sunshine, been sung to by countless sweet-throated birds, had feasted his eyes upon this mass of colouring and absorbed the perfume of an everchanging nosegay of delicious scents. Not a line written. And he called himself an author!

Along the stony footpath which fringed his domain came an unusual sight, a pedestrian tourist. His attire was strange and his gait peculiar. He walked with a loping slouch, a staff in his right hand, and although more than fully grown, he wore what seemed in the distance to be the undress uniform of a Boy Scout. As he drew nearer, he paused in the middle of the path to stare at Sloane—a little rudely, the latter thought. The occupant of the arbour rose to his feet and sauntered to the wall. The newcomer was, at any rate, a

4

curiosity worth looking at. Besides, there was something familiar about his slouch.

The two men scrutinised one another in perfunctory fashion, perhaps at first a little insolently. Then came almost simultaneous recognition.

"Holy Jupiter!" the pedestrian exclaimed. "It's the poet!"

"Erskine!" the other young man gasped. "Pips Erskine!"

They babbled a few senseless commonplaces. They had been at a preparatory school and Oxford together, but during the four years since they had slipped into the larger world they had not met.

"How are things with you, Pips?" Roger Sloane asked.

"So-so. And you?"

"I keep free from debts and melancholia. What," he continued, "for the love of Mike, is the meaning of that musical-comedy costume of yours? Have we gone back to the days of Drury Lane? Are you Dick Whittington searching for the Lord Mayor of these parts? You won't like him when you find him. He's a small fruit farmer and seldom sober. He comes of a Corsican family, his name's Viotti, he hasn't got a gilliflowers and carnations and even the wild roses, which had taken root in its moss-encrusted interstices. His climb had been long and strenuous. He had always possessed the gift of concentration and his eyes were fixed thirstily upon the villa. His friend struck a gong.

"Gin and tonic, whisky and Perrier or country wine?" the latter enquired.

"Gin and tonic," was the prompt response. "A double, if you don't mind. I have walked from Nice."

Sloane gave the order to the white-coated butler who had hastened out from the house. Then he established his friend in a comfortable wicker chair, pushed the cigarettes across to him and filled his own pipe.

"So you really are a lord," he exclaimed, with a touch of the young American's curiosity toward an inherited title lurking in his tone.

"I certainly am," Erskine assured him. "Only a baron, I regret to say. But, after all, I've always had a lurking weakness for barons. Ancient history is full of the records of their deeds. Runnymede, for instance—"

The drinks were brought and served. Sloane gave orders for luncheon.

"What, then, is your full designation nowadays?" he enquired of his guest.

5

"Reginald Phillip Erskine, as before, but I am commonly known now as Lord Erskine. The baronry—"

"That will do," Roger Sloane interrupted. "I shall continue to call you Pips."

"How flows the inspiration?" Erskine enquired. "Seems to me a pretty tidy spot for ink-slinging."

Sloane pointed ruefully to the untouched sheets of manuscript paper. Leisure, environment, opportunity—all favorable. Not a line written.

"I seem to lack mental energy out here," he complained, stretching his muscular limbs. "I wake up in the morning brimful of ideas and by the time I settle down I can do nothing but listen to the bees, smell the flowers and warm myself in the sunshine."

"The highest forms of literary effort," Erskine began. "I mean, the best sort of stuff in your line, was never turned out by any one leading a life of contemplation. The very atmosphere here is soporific.... How did your investments withstand this Wall Street débâcle?"

"Gallantly," Roger Sloane admitted. "Besides, my uncle's popped off since our college days and I've touched again."

"There you are," Erskine pointed out. "You lack the incentive for mental exertion. The stories may form in your brain, but in this atmosphere they will never materialise.... Just a drain more, thanks."

"What do you suggest, then?" Sloane enquired, having ministered for the second time to his friend's thirst.

"A breaking away from this life of æsthetic indolence, a life of travel and action," the visitor urged.

"You are not suggesting," Sloane shivered, "that I should come out to Ceylon and watch tea plants growing and hang little cups on rubber trees?"

"Certainly I am not suggesting anything of the sort," Erskine assured him. "I doubt whether you have the moral stamina for a life of real hard work and privations."

"What about those week-ends at Kandy or Colombo?"

"You have been fed up with false information," Erskine declared coldly. "Besides, I myself have finished with Ceylon. In course of time I must settle down in England and look after my property and interests. I was referring to the free life I am leading nowadays, wandering about where I like, sleeping where I like, making friends or not as I please. Join me, Roger. Let us explore this part of the world."

"Not if you're going on wearing those clothes," Roger insisted.

6

"You probably have a car," his friend observed. "In which case these garments, eminently suitable for pedestrian exercise, will not be necessary. I will humour your whims. I can still assure you, though," he added, glancing down dispassionately at his stained wide khaki shorts and hairy legs, "that this is the everyday costume of the Singhalese planter."

"Very healthy and manly and all that," Roger admitted doubtfully, "but in these parts—well, you have to wear a tie to get into the Casino."

"I am a broad-minded person," Erskine declared. "I have other costumes for other pursuits. To-day I am mountaineering."

CHAPTER II

On the way down the winding road after lunch Roger Sloane drove his Packard at almost a walking pace. The flower gatherers were at work and the drowsy air was sweet with a tangle of perfumes. After the second corner the road became little more than a gully with orange trees on either side. Women and girls and a sprinkling of older people were everywhere busy on ladders, over the tops of which they disappeared into a green-and-white obscurity. Petals were falling everywhere like snow. Roger was surprised to find that even his companion, leaning back in the car, was entranced into silence. His lips were parted, his eyes half-closed. He had the air of one travelling in Paradise. Roger contemplated him in benign approval. Notwithstanding his uncouth attire and mundane luncheon conversation, it was obvious that the joint enthusiasms of their Oxford days might easily be reawakened. He found himself speculating as to the thoughts which might be framing themselves in his friend's brain.

"Damn' good smell," the latter murmured drowsily.

Roger opened his lips but his sharp word of rebuke was never spoken. He was suddenly conscious of a brisk tap on the top of his skull and a slowly fluttering waterfall of exquisite blossoms upon his cheeks and head and around his feet. He stopped the car and glanced upwards. Lying upon her stomach on the overhanging branch of a veteran orange tree was a wisp of a girl, long-legged, long-armed, with a mass of chestnut brown hair blowing about her shoulders, eyes so light a hazel that they seemed almost yellow as they laughed into his, and a face like the face of an elf born of a fairy grinning down upon him.

"Mademoiselle!" he protested. "I am blinded."

He gained nothing by his expostulation. Seeming literally to be hanging through space, she leaned across and reached a neighbouring bough, plucked another branch laden with blossom and, leaning once more perilously downwards to ensure a correct aim, she dropped a shower of petals upon him so that he was again enveloped. Then she laughed and he fancied that a bird must be singing in the tree.

"You little devil!" Roger exclaimed. "Wait till I can get at you."

He had no idea of any definite purpose. He obeyed apparently some sort of a hunter's instinct, some subtle response that stirred within him to the challenge of those brown eyes. He jammed the hand brake a little tighter and swung himself out of the car. He had taken one step towards the trunk of the tree—it was probably in his mind to climb or pretend to do so—when one of the most thrilling sounds he had ever heard in his life clamped the soles of his feet to the ground and sent an icy chill, even on that day of hot sunshine, through his veins to the very pulses of his heart. It was the cry of a child in terror—but the soul of the child had found its way to her lips....

There was a flutter of commotion everywhere. The small crowd of flower gatherers, mostly girls and mostly of the same peasant type, deep-bosomed, black-eyed and bareheaded, came creeping out of unexpected corners. From the higher part of the orchard descended the disturbing object and as soon as Sloane had seen him he scented trouble. Here was a man in a passion, a black-browed, heavily built man, cutting the air with a switch as he moved, an ugly protruding jaw reminiscent somehow of the dragon in a child's story. Sloane could almost imagine the red fire gleaming from the newcomer's eyes as he loped along through the daffodil-starred long grass. Then his somewhat indifferent curiosity changed to a more poignant emotion. He felt his pulses quicken and a sense of crisis precipitated itself. The strange child above was swaying on the bough and moaning to herself. He looked up. There were no tears in her eyes, but she went on moaning and her fingers were digging deep into the bark.

"Do not be afraid, little one," he called out encouragingly. "He can't reach you."

"There is a ladder," she sobbed.

Roger saw that she was right and the object of the child's dread seemed indeed about to use it. He planted it against the tree

8

but, as he placed his foot upon the first rung, Roger realised what was about to happen. The child above him had crawled in her terror an inch or two farther along the bough and that inch or two was just a trifle too far. The limb of the tree sagged and cracked. She swung for a moment in mid-air, a strange medley of struggling arms and legs, a shape of grace and phantasy. Then the bark fell away, the white wood split. Already in the road beneath her Roger stiffened his back, preparing for the inevitable happening. With the final crashing of the branch, she came warm and fluttering into his arms.

A moment before the incident had seemed trivial—an ugly interlude in a pleasing but unexciting hillside pastoral. Now, to Roger Sloane, the seconds seemed stabbed with some magic fire. He was caught up in a blaze of incredible and incomprehensible sensation. This half-dressed, probably unwashed brat was clinging to him with all the abandon of her long supple limbs and pulsating body, her strange-coloured eyes aflame, her breath sweet as the flowers themselves falling hot upon his cheeks. She was nearly mad with terror. Her sobs told him that and the frantic rise and fall of her small bosoms.... The man's voice—he was only a yard or two away now—broke the silence, ugly with curses, terrifying with threats. The girls and women, even the few older men, gave way before him like scared rabbits. He jumped into the road and paused for a moment to recover his breath. A sudden silence seemed to have fallen upon every one, one of those silences which precede a storm. The man eyed Roger evilly. He had dropped his switch and began to swing his fists. There was mischief in his bloodshot eyes, murder in the leer of his grinning mouth. The girl who, in obedience to his gesture, had unwound herself from Roger's arms, crept towards the car which was standing by the side of the road. Erskine opened the door and pulled her in, but all the time her eyes were fixed in agony upon her protector. A brave old woman, toothless and decrepit, with a shawl around her head, called out from the other side of the ditch.

"Let him alone, Pierre Viotti. You have drunk too much red wine. The young American has done no harm. That little devil, Jeannine, she pelted him with the orange blossoms. *Au temps de 'la fleur' ils sont tous en folie!"*

Pierre Viotti took no notice. He went blundering on to his doom. He struck savagely at the usually good-natured, but now stern face of the young man, only to find that he was beating the air. A moment later he was lying in the dust of the road, partial oblivion clouding his murky senses. Roger bent over him for a moment, listened to his stertorous, but regular breathing, then stepped back into the car.... The attitude of the crowd was somewhat uncertain. Some of the young women were dancing for joy. The older people were whispering together. One lad was slouching off towards the village. After all, the man lying in the road was a *rentier* and their mayor and the man who had struck him was a foreigner. They hung together like leeches, these French village folk.

"If you take my advice," Erskine observed, with a glance around, "you will get out of this, Roger. Pity you could not have let the fellow know what you did at Harvard and Oxford in boxing."

"No time to tell him anything," Roger replied, thrusting the gear shift into reverse. "I couldn't even warn him. He came at me like a mad bull."

They backed noiselessly to the corner, swung around and crawled up to the entrance of the pink-and-white villa on the hillside. The girl seemed to have got over her terror and was making queer little noises in her throat. Roger glanced at her questioningly. Suddenly he realised that she was laughing. Her eyes were dancing with happiness, her brown face had puckered up into creases of mirth, her soft, delicately shaped mouth was quivering, no longer with fear. She was clasping and unclasping the long fingers of her scratched but shapely brown hands and swaying from side to side in rhythmical content.

"What the mischief are you going to do with her?" his friend demanded.

"Heaven knows," Roger answered.

* * * * *

Madame Vinay, *cuisinière* and housekeeper, summoned from the kitchen, was inclined to take a gloomy view of the situation.

"He is a bad man, Pierre Viotti," she declared, "but he is the mayor and he owns all the land, the *épicerie* and the café. He does what he pleases with the girls and all the people about the place. If Monsieur has touched him, he will probably go to prison."

"Oh, la, la," the girl laughed gaily. "Has Monsieur seen Henri our gendarme? He is no bigger than I am. Monsieur Viotti—he is the strongest man in the village and *voilà, Monsieur l'a battu.*"

"Where are your father and mother?" Roger asked.

The girl shook her head. Madame Vinay explained.

"The child's father and mother never lived in the village, Monsieur. Her mother taught in the school and her father was a foreman at Molinard's, the perfume factory in Grasse. They died within a few weeks of one another and her grandmother brought

10

her here. Now the old grandmother is herself dead since last week. What is to become of the child no one knows. The Curé has concerned himself in the matter, but Monsieur le Maire wishes her for his house. Just now there is work for all in the fields, but afterwards—well, Pierre Viotti is the mayor and what can one do?"

The child calmly stretched out her long arm, helped herself to an apple from a dish on the sideboard and began to eat it. "I will never work for Monsieur Viotti," she declared firmly. "He is a bad man. All the children in the village are afraid of him and so am I. I will pick the blossom for Monsieur here," she added, her eyes laughing into Roger's.

"The Curé is in the kitchen," Madame Vinay observed. "He might have advice to give. After what has happened, the child would be better away from the neighbourhood altogether."

"By all means let us consult him," Roger agreed. "Fetch him at once, Madame."

Madame Vinay rustled out and the Curé presently made his appearance in her company. He was an elderly man, rotund in shape and with few of the graces of life, but his expression was pleasant and he was at once helpful.

"Monsieur," he said earnestly to Roger, "what you have done may indeed turn out to be a fortunate action. We are all bound to respect Monsieur le Maire, who is a hard-working man and has amassed much money. Nevertheless he is not a fitting guardian for the child."

"He is a beast!" the latter declared vehemently, her white, beautifully shaped teeth crunching once more into the apple.

"What I should like to do," Roger Sloane explained, "is to find the child reputable employment and a safe home until she is old enough to decide for herself what she would like to do. I will be responsible for any money that is necessary and if you will help me in this matter, Monsieur le Curé, I will with pleasure give a donation to your poor."

"I wish to remain with Monsieur," the child begged. "I will work for him. I will be obedient. I will do what I am told."

Madame Vinay, who was standing in the background, coughed.

"In the village," she said severely, "they say that you obey no one."

"In the village," the child scoffed. "But that is different. Here I will obey you, Madame Vinay. I will obey Monsieur."

"What do you think, Monsieur?" Sloane asked.

The Curé hesitated.

11

"Jeannine is a strange child but I believe that she has good qualities," he pronounced. "They say in the village that she fights all the time."

"I only fight if I am touched," she cried. "I will not be touched by those others. When they leave me alone, I behave."

The Curé scratched his chin thoughtfully.

"If Monsieur would try her for a week," he suggested.

The girl sprang suddenly to her feet and danced around the room, her arms waving, her legs moving to some strange measure. They stared at her in astonishment. Madame Vinay sighed and shook her head. The Curé only smiled.

"They say that her mother once wished to be a *danseuse*," he confided. "The child is difficult but I have found her truthful."

She came to a sudden pause in front of Sloane, dropped almost on one knee, seized his hand and kissed it. Then she stood up again.

"I will obey you," she promised. "I will pick your blossoms faster than any one has picked them before. I will do everything that Madame Vinay tells me."

Roger Sloane drew a deep sigh of relief. He found himself wondering why he was so persistently anxious to avoid looking into the depths of those questioning brown eyes with their strange lights.

"That's all arranged then," he said, in a matter-of-fact tone. "You and I can get on our way to Nice, Pips."

* * * * *

In Nice the two young men spent an evening of masculine, but restrained hilarity. Upon their arrival Roger strolled upon the Promenade des Anglais and watched the sunset while his companion went to his hotel and changed his attire. Afterwards they visited the Casino, drank cocktails and amused themselves playing midget golf. They dined at a famous restaurant, gambled for an hour or two at the Palais de la Mediterranée, supped at Maxim's and even danced. At three o'clock Roger dropped his friend at his hotel and drove homeward through the velvety darkness. For the last ten kilometres the road wound its way through the flower-growing country and already the carts were crawling along the lanes to pick up their cargoes of blossoms. Once or twice Roger paused by the wayside to listen to the nightingales and to feel the queer fascination of the silence before the morning. The first pencil shaft of light was creeping into the sky when he reached the villa. He drove his car into the garage, locked it up and mounted to his room by the back stairs. He walked with light footsteps and a smile upon his lips. After the meretricious and somewhat futile straining after pleasure of a night spent in crowded rooms, of gambling, noisy music and overheated atmospheres, the coolness and perfume of his own home delighted him. He felt like the boy Marius on his way to his bed in the mountain monastery, with the life of the cities far behind and the purity and sweetness of the country already like a sweet tonic in his blood.... Then, during his last few steps, his fingers outstretched towards the handle of his door, he came to a sudden standstill. There was an old-fashioned Provençal bench outside which looked as though it had been made from a discarded refectory table. Seated upon it, wrapped in an old dressing gown of flaming red, probably a loan from Madame, was Jeannine!

Her eyes shone up into his, her quivering lips parted expectantly. He was astonished to find how sternly he could speak.

"What are you doing here?" he demanded.

"*Je ne fais pas de mal,*" she faltered, a little frightened at his tone. "*Je vous attendais.*"

"But why?"

Her lips became almost pathetic.

"Monsieur Viotti—"

"What about him?" Roger interrupted, speaking with fierce anxiety but keeping his voice low.

"He told me that if I served him in the house and he spent the evening out, that I must wait up till he came home. He told me that any one I served would expect that. I was waiting for you."

He met her eyes, frankly this time. There was a stern but kindly light in his own and a sense of great relief in has heart. It was not for the child to know that his knees were trembling.

"Forget everything that such a beast has told you," he enjoined. "Go to your room at once and stay there."

She rose obediently to her feet, but she was shivering as though his words had hurt her. He laid his hands upon her shoulders and kissed her lightly upon either cheek. He could almost feel the warmth of her inviting lips as he passed them by.

"Now run," he ordered.

He entered his room, closed the door and listened to her departing footsteps. As soon as there was silence, he turned the key very softly and threw wide open both his windows. Already the streak of light had grown broader and the moon paler. There was only one nightingale left in the valley, still singing faintly. Here and there, along the lanes, the carts with their swaying lanterns were

13

moving—ghostly, obscure objects. And all the time the perfume of the orange blossoms. He thought of the old woman's speech—

"Au temps de 'la fleur' ils sont tous en folie!"

The two friends lunched together a few days later under a striped umbrella upon the terrace of Juan-les-Pins Casino. Already the early heat had drawn the crowds to the sands below. There was a fair sprinkling of bathers, a great many more lying about enjoying a sun bath. The suggestion of a mistral had given a faint tang to the sea breeze. The Estérels had thrown off their silver mantle, their sharp outline was firm and vivid against the crystalline background.

"What about the little protégée?" Erskine asked.

"I've scarcely seen her during the last few days," Roger replied. "Madame Vinay's latest report was that she was restless and didn't wish to work outdoors. She thought of trying to get a job for her in a flower shop in Nice or Monte Carlo."

Erskine watched the serving of a mostelle with an air of reverent admiration.

"Do you know, Roger," he confided, "I shouldn't be surprised if that girl didn't turn out damn' good-looking some day."

"She's quite attractive enough now," Roger said calmly.

"No, but I mean a real tip-topper," Erskine persisted. "She's got something about her, I don't know what it is, that these Frenchmen describe so well in the memoirs of all their famous courtesans. Write a novel about her, old chap. If you've got the right touch, you might achieve immortality."

"I'm off work," was the rather terse reply. "Look here, Pips, I've been thinking—one's got to clear out of here presently. I've been here six months on end and that's pretty well long enough. I'll make a bargain with you, if you like. I'll do as you suggested and go back to England with you, look up a few old pals and get some golf while you settle up your affairs and—what is it you have to do?—stick a coronet on your head and strut across the Palace yard and get turned into a bona fide Lord. I'll see you through this if you'll come across to the States with me for a month or so and get back here in say, November or December. How does that appeal to you?"

"It's a bargain," Erskine declared emphatically. "Nothing I should like better, old chap. We'll get back, as you say, about October or November and I'll have a real season here. I always thought I should like to, if I could get hold of a little of the ready. When do you think you could make a move? The only trouble is, I really ought to get over to London at once, you know. I got off at Marseilles and I was doing a tramp around here to sort of get my bearings, but the lawyers are getting a bit sniffy now. They can't understand a chap who's come in for a title and a decent spot of the ready not being anxious to get his hands on it."

"I'll start to-morrow, if you like," Roger promised.

"Capital," Erskine exclaimed. "We'll make it the day after, if you don't mind. Or let's say the first day we can get seats on the Blue Train; or there may be a steamer calling at Monaco."

"Agreed."

They lunched lazily but with excellent appetites. The food was good, the wine and service perfection. Erskine was thoroughly content. Now and then he looked at his friend curiously.

"I should think you're right in what you say, old chap," he remarked. "Six months might be enough for any one without a move, and you look a trifle fagged. We'll have some golf up in Scotland, but by Jove, the one thing I'm going to look forward to is our next season out here."

They raised their glasses and drank to it. A few thousand miles westward five men, including Paul Viotti, the illustrious brother of the Mayor of La Bastide, were doing very much the same thing.

* * * * *

Down the mountainside, a week later, in snakelike fashion, through the vine-growing country and the stripped flower farms crawled the dilapidated grey motor omnibus which plied between the out-of-the-way hill villages of the Alpes-Maritimes and Nice.

Jeannine, with Madame Vinay on one side and the Curé opposite, felt herself so well guarded that she indulged in a derisive grimace at Monsieur Viotti, the Mayor, who was leaning against his grey stone wall looking steadily seawards. Madame Vinay reproached her charge severely.

"Manners such as that are not for the town," she declared. "In Nice one must forget such peasant ways."

Jeannine made no reply. There was something in her eyes, however, and the quiet smile upon her lips which made her guardian just a trifle uncomfortable. More and more every day she was getting to realise that this charge which she had undertaken at Roger's earnest request was likely to be no sinecure. When they turned the corner, from which was a fine view of the sea below, Jeannine leaned out and her eyes travelled westward. That way his ship had gone—the man whom some day she hoped to make suffer....

Behind them, and some distance above them now, Monsieur Pierre Viotti was also gazing at the sea, a cunning smile of self-satisfaction upon his lips. Halfway across the Atlantic, bound straight for Cherbourg, came the great three-funnelled steamer bearing his famous brother and his friends. He gloated over the thought of their arrival, made plans, indulged in mischievous fancies. What strange instructions these were which he had received. Never mind, they should all be carried out. In time, perhaps, he might become as rich as Paul....

That little devil of a Jeannine! So they were going to try and cheat him out of her. Not a chance. What did Monte Carlo matter? He would be there himself in a few weeks. The leer of the village satyr parted his thick red lips.

CHAPTER III

The season to the success of which Roger and Erskine had drunk on the terrace at Juan-les-Pins, the season which Pierre Viotti had awaited so impatiently, had arrived at last, and on a certain evening early in December the round table in the centre of the Sporting Club bar at Monte Carlo was crowded with a gay little company of habitués. There were the Terence Browns—Franco-Americans and globe-trotters known in every resort in Europe, but finding in Monte Carlo, as Terence Brown frequently confided, their spiritual home. There was Lady Julia Harborough, elderly and autocratic, but exceedingly popular and still one of the leaders of the social life. There was Luke Cheyne, an American banker, a very pleasant fellow and also popular, but with the appearance of a man who was suffering from nerves or dyspepsia. He was talking to Prince Savonarilda, a tall, elegant young Sicilian, who was reported to have enormous, but unprofitable estates in Sicily and who made periodic but mysterious visits to New York. Maggie Saunders, the most sought-after young woman in the Principality, was retailing one of her marvellous stories to Lord Bradley, an English newspaper peer, who was clutching six plaques of a hundred thousand francs each which he had just won at *trente et quarante*. Under cover of the general buzz of conversation, Luke Cheyne was talking very confidentially indeed to Prince Savonarilda.

"What I'd like to know," he whispered, "is just this. How do I stand with the boys? You could tell me, Prince. Don't mind giving me a bit of a scare, if it's coming to me. I just want to know."

16

Savonarilda tapped a cigarette upon the table and lit it. To all appearance he was sublimely indifferent to the gossip of the little group from whose circle they had slightly withdrawn their chairs. All the time, however, from under his veiled eyelids he was watching—and listening.

"I think you're all right, Luke," he replied. "They didn't like your quitting, of course. But we've quit ourselves now, so you were only anticipating. The game was getting too dangerous and you were never a fighting man, were you?"

"I never pretended to be," Luke Cheyne reminded his companion. "That wasn't my part of the show. Tell me, then—it seems odd to be calling you Prince—you think I'm all right to stick on here? They're not sore with me?"

"You're all right to stick on here till doomsday," Savonarilda drawled, "even if some of the others are having a look at Europe. That doesn't mean that they're here on serious business. You should sleep at night, Luke. No one has anything against you."

Luke Cheyne called for another drink. His spirits had risen visibly. He responded with alacrity when Lord Bradley beckoned him to draw his chair a little closer.

"We're all wondering," the latter observed, "how long it would take a disciplined band of criminals, such as you have on the other side, Mr. Cheyne, to break down the police of this country as they seem to have done in the States. Those little pets in the gay uniforms outside, for instance, I wonder how some cold shooting in the streets would strike them."

"You may get it," Cheyne rejoined grimly, "and then you'll find out. The profession is becoming overcrowded in New York and Chicago and I shouldn't be a bit surprised to hear any day that a band of American crooks had made this place their headquarters. Did you read about that Englishman who disappeared last week in Marseilles?"

"Nothing in that," Terence Brown intervened, breaking off his conversation with Lady Julia. "He was a poor man and he wouldn't have been worth robbing."

"That just shows you don't read your own newspapers," Luke Cheyne replied. "In this morning's *Eclaireur* they announced that he had been paid over seven hundred thousand francs for a big land deal the day he disappeared and there is not a trace of the money in either of his banks."

"Personally," Lady Julia remarked, "I can't think why Monte Carlo is such a law-abiding place. With all the money there is about,

I shouldn't be surprised any day to hear of one of you rich people being murdered in his bed."

"We don't carry our wealth about with us," Bradley pointed out. "You women always have your jewellery in evidence. I would sooner insure a millionaire's life than that of a woman who wears such diamonds as yours."

She made a little grimace.

"How horrid of you," she exclaimed. "You've probably spoilt my night's sleep. Anyway, I'm not one of those careless women who leave their things all over the dressing table. I keep—"

She paused. Terence Brown had struck the table in front of him lightly but firmly so that the glasses jingled. He leaned toward her.

"Lady Julia," he begged, "do please forgive a hint from an elderly person of experience. Don't talk about what you do with your jewellery."

"I suppose you are right," she admitted. "Still, we are all friends here."

"That doesn't amount to much," Luke Cheyne observed. "It's generally our friends that rob us."

"The point of the matter is this," Savonarilda explained. "We happen to be all friends at this particular table, but there are others in the room and unless I'm very much mistaken one or two of them, at any rate, are listening to what we are talking about. This is a club in name only, you must remember. Even murderers belong to clubs and all they have to do here is to plank down their hundred francs."

"And yet the trouble I had," Lady Julia sighed, "to get my dear little protégée from Prétat's a *carte*. First she was too young, then they objected to her because she has done a stroke or two of work now and then in the Principality and then, at last,—"

Lady Julia never finished her sentence. There was a little chorus of welcoming exclamations from the table. Every one was waving their hands and calling to a tall, sunburnt young man who had just entered the room.

"Why, it's Roger!" Lady Julia exclaimed.

"Roger Sloane, by all that's amazing!" Terence Brown called out.

The young man came up to them, smiling pleasantly. He was overwhelmed with greetings. A valet brought him a chair, another a glass. Lady Julia, who was his aunt, presented her cheeks. Every one else insisted upon being shaken hands with. Maggie Saunders passed her arm through his and clasped it.

"The only man I ever cared for," she cried, "and he went away

18

like that—" she snapped her fingers. "Vanished! Over a year ago. Not a line. Not a word. People last season got tired of asking one another—what's become of Roger?"

"Quite right," Terence Brown agreed. "Give an account of yourself, young man."

"There have been several most alarming rumours," Lady Julia sighed.

"One,'" Savonarilda observed, "was that you had murdered a peasant near your villa and been obliged to go into hiding."

"After having abducted his daughter," some one else murmured.

"Your character would have been torn to shreds," Lady Julia declared, "if I had not been here to protect you. Still—what did happen?"

Roger drank his wine and smiled upon them. He was looking a trifle older but the slight lines in his face were not unbecoming. He had lost all signs of easy living.

"I got rather fed up with the life here," he explained. "One day Erskine, Pips Erskine—some of you know him, I expect; he was at Oxford with me—came along, also at a loose end. We had a night in Nice together and I suddenly felt that this atmosphere was too enervating for me to stick it any longer. Pips and I left for England a few days later by a steamer that was going direct from Monaco to London. We were going to the States after that, but Pips had to go back to Ceylon to settle things up there and I went back with him. He'd been tea planting there, poor devil. Pretty sick he must have been of it. Afterwards we went on to India and wound up in Abyssinia."

"Good sport?" Bradley asked.

"Wonderful, and every sort of it," Roger replied. "Snipe shooting between Colombo and Kandy, and a couple of tigers and several cheetah up North. In India I had some of the most marvellous duck shooting and three days of driven peacock. Beats all your pheasants. Then I had some good days after tiger at Hyderabad. Abyssinia was difficult and the climate pretty beastly, but I didn't do so badly there."

"Well, it's good to see you back again, anyway," Lady Julia declared.

"Where are you staying?" Terence Brown asked.

"Pips and I are both staying here for a day or two," Roger answered. "We picked up the *Franconia* at Port Said and she brought us to the door. The villa will want restaffing, so I shan't be able to go there for a few days."

"Any work?" Bradley asked. "I could do with a good strong serial for one of my North Country papers."

"My stuff wouldn't suit you," Roger assured him. "Altogether too high class! Besides, I'm beginning to lose faith in serialisation. Seems to take the gilt off the gingerbread, somehow or other."

"You'll refuse my good money?" Bradley grumbled.

"I daresay I sha'n't, after a day or two in the rooms. What's the news here?"

"Nothing much, except that we're all shivering with terror and apprehensions," Terence Brown confided. "Cheyne here has been warning us that crime has become an overcrowded industry in his country and that they are sending missionaries over here!"

"That's a fact, all right," Cheyne admitted. "The trouble about you folk in this part of the world is that the Press doesn't help. If you have a good he-murder, you suppress it instead of advertising it."

"What about starting a newspaper here, Bradley?" Terence Brown suggested.

"I should have as much chance of being allowed to do that as of being elected Dictator of this Principality," Bradley remarked drily.

"Is that all the news? Is there nothing else fresh to tell me, after all these months?" Roger enquired.

"A few choice pieces of scandal," Lady Julia confided. "They must keep though. Christos is here to-night."

Every one was rising to their feet. There was a movement towards the door.

"What's happening?" Roger demanded.

"The baccarat has started," Terence Brown announced, looking back over his shoulder. "Christos is here. Christos, the philanthropist, with a few millions to distribute. Look at us all hurrying off for the crumbs!"

"All very well to laugh," Maggie Saunders grumbled, "but they won't keep a place for a minute."

They trooped out. The magic name of Christos seemed to be a call to their blood. Christos was the one great banker at baccarat who had his spells of bad luck. They were all of them thirsting for his money. The home-coming of an old friend whom no one had seen for over a year had already slipped into the background of their thoughts. Gambling was in the atmosphere. It was gambling that counted. Human beings and human emotions shrank back into their proper places. Roger was back again—*tant mieux*! A pleasant fellow, a distinguished companion, a fine golfer and tennis player, but Christos was seated in the coveted place dominating that long

20

green baize table, and presently the fingers of Christos were going to deal cards which meant—well, thousands, or hundreds of thousands, whichever you would. The money was there.

Roger, leaning back in his chair, found himself deserted by every one except Cheyne. The latter settled down by his side and they ordered another drink.

"Playing polo?" Roger asked.

"I played a few times at Cannes last month," the other replied. "It didn't go so well with me as it used to."

"You put in a pretty good spell of work in New York, didn't you, the last three or four years?"

Luke Cheyne nodded.

"Great city, great country," he observed. "But no good for any one with nerves. I'm not the man I was, Sloane, when I used to play outside right against you."

Roger yawned. Polo didn't interest him very much these days.

"What's all this talk about some of your bad boys from New York paying us a visit over here?" he asked.

Cheyne was silent for a moment. Turning to glance at him, Roger was sympathetically disturbed at the change in the man. He could scarcely be over thirty-five, but he had lost his poise, his directness of vision, his complexion. He looked like a man who was feverishly seeking middle age.

"To tell you the truth, I got a bit mixed up with some bootleggers myself in New York," he confided. "Nothing serious, of course, but there was big money in it and a certain amount of sport to start with. I soon got cold feet, I don't mind admitting it, so I cleaned up and came over here. But I get news sometimes from the other side. There are too many of them on the job there. I haven't heard anything definite, of course," he went on, "but I sometimes fancy that if they realised the loose money there is floating about here and the careless way people treat it, it wouldn't be long before we had some kind of visitation."

Roger tapped a cigarette upon the table and lit it.

"The French police wouldn't stand for that sort of thing," he observed.

"Wouldn't they?" his companion answered drily. "I don't know what they would do about it, if the right men got over. Then there's another thing. We're in the Principality of Monaco here and they're very jealous of outside help."

Roger suddenly abandoned the conversation in which he was not greatly interested.

"Luke," he said, "you have been here for some time. Who is

that plump little Frenchman with the pink cheeks and smooth face and villainous-looking eyes on the stool at the bar there? He's done nothing but watch us in the looking glass and if ever I saw a man trying to listen, he's doing it. I'm certain I've seen him somewhere before, but I can't remember where."

Cheyne glanced carelessly at the person whom Roger had pointed out.

"He's a Niçois who's made a lot of money. Gambles a bit sometimes, but I've never even heard his name. Aren't you going to try your luck at baccarat?"

Roger shook his head. Somehow or other his thoughts had wandered away, back to his villa on the hillside. The sweet half-drugged perfume of orange blossoms was disturbing his senses.

"I don't feel the urge yet," he confessed. "I think I shall watch the people for a time. Don't let me keep you, though."

Cheyne sauntered off but his mind was not immediately set on gambling. He accosted Savonarilda, who was standing in the doorway and drew him a short distance down the passage.

"Marcus," he said quietly. "Tell me. Is Viotti here?"

Savonarilda paused to take out his cigarette case. There was a curious but significant change in his manner.

"If I were you, Luke," he advised, "I should not ask any questions. Not any questions at all. I should forget that you know a person of that name. With us, it is different. We meet as a matter of course. Let it remain like that."

"Be frank with me, Marcus," Cheyne begged. "I know Viotti hates any one to quit. I can't help remembering," he added, with a shudder, "what happened to the other two who broke away. How do I stand with him and you others? There's no bad feeling, eh? Viotti must know that I'd as soon put a gun to my forehead as squeal. He must know that."

Savonarilda smiled slowly and lazily. They had reached the spot where the passage branched into the Nouvel Hôtel and he swung around again, his hand upon Cheyne's shoulder.

"Do not be foolish, my friend Luke Cheyne," he recommended. "We're in Monte Carlo, not on Sixth Avenue. Besides, Viotti has no ill feelings against any one. If you come across any of the others except me—you have done so already, I daresay—I should fail to recognise them. Otherwise, we are still all friends. We are taking a vacation. You have nothing to fear. Why, I should not be surprised if Viotti sent and asked you to come and see him. You were always rather a favorite of his."

The idea of a visit to Viotti evidently made no appeal to his late colleague.

"We are better apart," the latter said doubtfully. "Much better apart. Let me ask you one more question, Marcus. That brother of Viotti's, who is always hanging about here—little fat man, looks like a peasant out on a fête day—what's he doing here? Is Viotti using him for a spy?"

Savonarilda paused at the entrance to the Baccarat Room.

"You should know better than to ask me a question like that, Luke," he remonstrated, with a certain amount of smothered irritation. "It is not discreet. It is foolish of you. Come and see if there is room at the baccarat table."

* * * * *

Roger, after the departure of Luke Cheyne, was kept fully occupied for the next half-hour or so by greeting acquaintances and exchanging reminiscences. At the end of that time, a little bored with it all, he strolled into the gambling rooms, which as usual at that time of night were crowded. The greater part of the people were standing three or four deep around the baccarat table. One heard rumours everywhere of high play. A Frenchman, a noted gambler, was reported to have lost a million. A young English duke had won even a larger sum. Lady Julia beckoned to her nephew from the divan where she was seated alone.

"I have lost my *mille*," she confided, with a tragic gesture. "It was most unfortunate. I followed Luke Cheyne, who had been winning heavily, and directly I put up my money he lost!"

"A *mille*," Roger reminded her, "is not an irrecoverable sum."

"It is as much as I permit myself to lose in an evening," Lady Julia declared. "Everything is so expensive nowadays and the taxation is dreadful. Did I ever tell you about my protégée, Roger?"

"Not a word," he replied.

"When I come to think of it, I haven't had much chance, have I?" she went on. "Now I shall show her to you. She has only been here once before and she's rather stupid about it. She prefers to go to bed early. Still, perhaps her profession—Here she comes! What do you think of her?"

Roger turned around. A girl was crossing the room towards them, accompanied by a voluble Frenchwoman, Madame Dumesnil, his aunt's *dame de compagnie*. The latter was gesticulating and talking fast. The girl seemed scarcely to be listening. She was wearing a white dress—the fashion of the moment—designed by the cunning brain which knows how to glorify simplicity. She was without jewellery and her shining light brown hair had obviously never been touched by a coiffeur. Roger, who had known the savour of life during his last twelve months of voluntary exile, who had more than once found himself evenly balanced between life and death, felt in those few seconds such a thrill as he had not experienced since the night in his villa when he had thrown open his windows to the song of that lonely bird and the perfumes of the night. The habitude of crises, however, kept him motionless, notwithstanding his amazement. There was scarcely even gladness in his eyes.

"Jeannine," Lady Julia said. "This is my nephew, Roger Sloane. Roger, I thought I wrote to you about my protégée, but if I didn't, here she is. She's a dear child but she must not be spoilt."

Jeannine lifted her eyes. There was a gleam of subtle reminiscence in them.

"I do not think," she said, "that Mr. Sloane will spoil me."

"I expect he has forgotten what all you modern young women are like," Lady Julia observed. "He has been away for a year killing wild animals—I can't imagine why. It seems to me an incredibly brutal pastime. Madame Dumesnil, you remember my nephew? I am not very pleased with him because he suddenly deserted a charming villa here and went away without a word to any one last season. However, he is a nice lad. Sit down with me, Madame. My nephew will take Mademoiselle Jeannine for a promenade. In a quarter of an hour, Roger, please bring the child back."

CHAPTER IV

The young people moved off together. Of the two, the little flower picker was by far the more composed. Roger scarcely recognised his own voice.

"I don't understand this," he said.

"If you choose, we will sit down somewhere," she suggested.

They found a corner in the inner portion of the bar.

"I thought you knew everything," she went on. "Your *gouvernante*, Madame Vinay—"

"I only arrived home to-day," he explained. "I came by

24

steamer from Egypt. Every mail lately has missed me. I was obliged to change my plans more than once."

"I see," she murmured. "Is it possible, perhaps, that you remember a night and the morning that followed when you suddenly tired of life in your villa and the flowers and of trying to write books, and decided to travel away with your strange friend and say good-bye to no one?"

"I remember," he admitted.

"You may also remember that you left me in charge of Madame Vinay and the Curé. Madame Vinay will tell you that she could do nothing with me. I was, in fact, very troublesome. Then Madame had an inspiration. Flowers, it seemed, were the only things I cared for. Very well. She took me to a cousin of hers—a *fleuriste* in Nice. She found me a post there. I unpacked the boxes of flowers in the morning and I arranged them for the shop window. The people seemed pleased with what I did. We made much business. Then, one day a woman came in who was a famous dressmaker. She asked to see the person who arranged the colouring of the flowers and their grouping—Does this weary you?"

"Please go on," he begged.

"You have shown so little interest," she continued quietly, "that I thought perhaps—well, *n'importe*. She gave me a post in her dressmaking establishment in Monte Carlo and Madame and I moved in here. I pleased her. I do not know why, except that I did my best. Lady Julia is one of her valued clients and between them they have been almost too kind to me. My *patronne* permits me to come to these places with Lady Julia and Madame Dumesnil, to wear her frocks in the evening and I wear them at the establishment in the daytime. I am what is called a mannequin—a living peg upon which beautiful clothes are hung. The only thing is that it does not please me to be out very much in the evening. This is the first time for a long while. I asked to come to-night. I wanted to know whether you were real or only just a dream."

"You knew who I was then?"

"I knew."

"And with the rest of your life?"

"I study. I have learnt this little English I sometimes speak. I have learnt to make fewer mistakes in my own language. There are many things I have tried to teach myself. I have tried to understand the different ways people have of looking at life. For that I have read books and Lady Julia is very good. She talks to me."

He was beginning to feel dazed.

"I see that you are no longer a child," he ventured.

25

"Would that be possible?" she asked gravely. "I was always older than you thought me, but I still have not very much understanding outside my work. There is one thing which has been in my mind every moment since that great pain came in the early morning when I awoke."

"Tell me about it, please," he begged.

"I mean when you went away without a word. I did not understand. I do not understand. I think that I never shall understand. Why did you do that? Was it to hurt me? Were you afraid of anything?"

He looked at her long and searchingly. Her eyes met his without tremor or embarrassment. He suddenly realised that there were no words with which he could make her understand.

"I left because I was afraid," he told her.

"Afraid—of me?"

"Of what might happen between you and me."

"But you were my god," she persisted. "No one had ever been kind to me before. You stood up against the man whom I hated, the devil who was filling my days with black terror, who but for your coming would probably have had his way with me and dragged me down into the mud. You carried me away to safety. You lifted me to heaven and then you snapped your fingers. Why?"

"I just can't tell you that, Jeannine," he answered. "There are some impulses and some thoughts behind them which don't lend themselves to explanations. But believe one thing, please. I left because you were a child and I was afraid that I might forget."

A softer look came into her face, a smile almost of happiness played upon her lips.

"You liked me?" she asked, with a queer little shyness.

"I think I might say that I loved you."

"And yet you went. Men are not like that—such men as I have read and heard of. You did not mean to hurt me—"

"I went away for fear of hurting you...."

Lady Julia, a little annoyed, leaning on the arm of Madame Dumesnil, presented herself.

"I said quarter of an hour," she declared. "It is now twenty-five minutes. Jeannine, Madame is waiting to see you home. I am a stern duenna of my charge, Roger," she went on. "I allow no young man, not even you, to be her escort."

"I regret that I have stayed so long," Jeannine apologised, rising to her feet.

"What has that young nephew of mine been saying to make you so pale?" Lady Julia asked curiously. "He's a clumsy fellow. He never learnt the art of talking to women. His father knew all about it—more than any American or Englishman I ever met in my life. Say good night to him, my dear. I have an irritable chauffeur and I'm a little later than my usual time."

Roger escorted them to the steps, then very slowly climbed the stairs into the club once more. A man brushed past him, the pink-cheeked, stout little Frenchman with the malicious eyes whom he had seen seated at the bar. Suddenly Roger remembered. A Niçois who had made money! It might seem to be a miracle, but without a doubt this was the *rentier* whom he had knocked down in the orange grove on the day when Jeannine had fallen into his arms!

* * * * *

Wandering a little restlessly about the fast-emptying Salles de Jeu, Roger came to the conclusion that except in so far as they had provided him with a certain amount of sport and enjoyment, a slice of his life had been sacrificed. He had scuttled away into safety to escape from what he looked upon as a poisonous thought which was urging him on to a poisonous action. He was back again after a period of many adventures to find the fever still in his blood, even though the danger of yielding to it might have lessened. What a development!... In a certain way he found a measure of justification for his own temporary insanity in Jeannine's present success. That strange unwashed creature of legs and arms, of mocking lips and laughing eyes, a *gamine* of the flower fields, had something in her which had proved itself. It was no gross impulse which had assailed him. On the contrary, for a young man whose traffic with women had been of the slightest, he had shown a perfect genius of perception. She was off his hands now. She could have no better protectress than his aunt. She was safe, so far as she desired safety. For the rest she must choose her own life.... What a humbug he was, he reflected angrily, when he knew that the one dominant idea in his mind was when he could see her again.

He threw some plaques upon the roulette table and gathered up his not inconsiderable winnings with indifference. Erskine, who was with a party, tempted him downstairs for half an hour, where he ate sandwiches and danced to the music of an amazing band. When he came back to the gambling rooms they were almost deserted. The bar was empty save for one man—Luke Cheyne—who called to him eagerly.

"Come here, Sloane, there's a good fellow," he begged. "Come and sit with me for a moment. I've got the jimjams."

27

"What about?" Roger asked, accepting the invitation. "Been losing?"

"You bet I haven't. I've half a million of the best in my pocket just cashed in!"

"Too many highballs?"

"The first since we parted. I just came in to get one. You'll join me?"

"A last one, then," Roger stipulated. "You're looking all in, Luke."

"It's just nerves," the latter replied. "I've rather played the fool with the crowd I was mixed up with in New York and I'm not quite sure that I'm exactly in their good books."

"I don't understand," Roger confessed. "You're not under any obligation to any one, are you?"

"Not financially," was the doubtful reply, "but I gave you a hint before, if you remember, Roger. I was mixed up with rather a roughish crowd in the liquor business there. I came away to get clear of it. They never complained. I've never had any message from them, but I've always had an idea that they meant getting me."

There was a crash of breaking glass close at hand. Cheyne swung around on his stool just as the barman stood up from under the counter.

"What the hell are you doing there?" the former demanded.

"I stooped down to pick up the broken glass, sir," the man replied.

"How long have you been there?"

"Scarcely a moment, sir."

Cheyne looked at him suspiciously. He was a new employee, a Monegasque who had worked for some time in New York. He had bright, ferretlike eyes and a somewhat furtive manner. He picked up the broken pieces of the tumbler and disappeared.

"I'll swear that young fellow was listening," Cheyne muttered.

Roger was inclined to be incredulous.

"You're all nerves, my friend," he said. "This crowd you were speaking of in New York—they've got nothing definite against you, have they, except that you quit? You didn't give them away to a competitor or the police?"

The other laughed scornfully.

"I didn't," he replied, "or I should never have got to Europe alive! It's not that exactly, but the boss was a curious sort of fellow. He was as clever as hell but he hated any one to quit. He hated the idea that any one alive who had played for safety himself had the power to squeal. This is all rubbish, of course. It only comes into my head at odd times. But to-night, curiously, I was talking—"

He broke off in his speech. The barman was back, industriously polishing the counter with a serviette. Cheyne scowled at him and dropped from his stool on to the floor.

"Time we were getting along, I think," he suggested. "Where are you staying, Roger?"

"In the Nouvel Hôtel, just along the passage here.... You weren't going to tell me that you met one of the gang in here, were you?" he added, lowering his tone.

"Never mind," Cheyne replied. "There are times when I wonder myself if I don't talk too much."

"I should have thought we were far enough away from New York," Roger remarked. "Where are the others? Maggie and the Prince and the Terence Browns and Thornton?"

"They've gone up to the Carlton," Cheyne replied. "With half a million in my pocket, I thought I'd better get back. The streets of Monte Carlo may be safe enough at night, but I should like to see a policeman about now and then."

The head barman emerged from his sanctum, lifted the flap of the counter and came over to them. He leaned confidentially over the table at which the two men had seated themselves.

"You will excuse me, Mr. Cheyne," he said, "but why don't you let me get you a draft for the money you have won and lock it up here? You can have it at any time after eleven o'clock to-morrow morning and send it up to the bank. You'll forgive my mentioning it, but it doesn't seem a very wise thing to carry five or six hundred thousand francs about with you at this hour of the morning."

"What's got you talking this way, George?" Cheyne demanded.

The man hesitated.

"Well, the chief here dropped us a hint to warn our good clients, sir," he confided. "There hasn't been any trouble to speak of, over here, but one never knows. Just as well to be on the safe side."

"Has there been any trouble anywhere else on the Riviera?" Roger asked curiously.

The barman hesitated again.

"Well, I believe there was a little unpleasantness at Cannes one night, sir, and there have certainly been some rough doings at Nice. The police seem to have an idea that some crooks from the other side have found their way over here."

"Well, I'm much obliged, I'm sure, George," Cheyne said. "If I were going out, I would do as you suggest, but I'm not. I'm going straight back to my room in the Paris along the passage."

"You will be sleeping with it in your room, sir," the man reminded him.

Cheyne smiled.

"With my servant in the next room and the best Smith and Wesson that was ever made under my own pillow. Don't you bother, George; I shall be all right. If I'd joined that frisky party and gone up to the Carlton, it would have been a different matter."

"You will excuse my mentioning it, sir," the barman begged, as he took his leave.

"Sure," Cheyne agreed, rising to his feet. "Are you coming, Roger?"

The two men strolled along the passage. The archbishop with the chain around his neck at the farther end bowed his *adieux* and accepted with becoming gratitude Cheyne's not inconsiderable tip. They passed through the swing door and turned to the left. Roger paused before the lift and stifled a yawn.

"Would you like me to come on with you to the end of the long passage?" he asked.

His companion scoffed.

"What sort of a pussy do you think I am?" he demanded. "So long as we're indoors, we're perfectly safe. Good night, Roger. See you for a cocktail to-morrow morning?"

"I'm not sure," was the doubtful reply. "I may go up and have a look at my villa. See you before long, anyway, though."

The two men parted. Luke Cheyne went on to the end of the passage, stepped into the waiting lift and made a brief descent. He tipped the boy and glanced towards the empty chair where the fireman generally sat.

"Where's Tom to-night?" he asked.

"Off duty, I expect, sir. It's past four o'clock and there's scarcely any one left in the club."

Cheyne nodded and walked on. A few yards and he was around the corner. He could see now to the end of the passage and he noticed that the lift was not there in waiting. Somehow or other, the journey down the carpeted way seemed longer than usual to-night. It came to an end, however, in due course. The lift was still absent and Cheyne pushed the bell. Nothing happened. As a rule, one heard almost immediately the banging of the gate upstairs and the rattle of the lift on its way down. This time there was no response. Cheyne glanced at his watch and yawned. Perhaps the boy had gone to sleep. In any case, it was only a couple of flights up the winding stair. He turned to the left and began to climb. He had swung around the first curve and his foot was on the next when suddenly the lights behind him and in front went out and he found himself in complete darkness. Almost simultaneously there was a terrible pain in his left side, a sharp sound no louder than that of a child's popgun, another spasm of pain. His knees crumpled up beneath him....

The electrician found him about a quarter of an hour later, lying like a man who had fallen backwards and broken his neck. There were two small holes in his shirtfront exactly over the heart and his pockets were empty.

CHAPTER V

It was Roger Sloane who gave the luncheon party at the Hôtel de Paris on the morning of Luke Cheyne's funeral. Lord Bradley, however, did most of the talking. The guests consisted of Mr. Terence Brown, a Major Thornton introduced by the former as liaison officer between a certain branch of the Foreign Office and Scotland Yard, who had come down to Marseilles in charge of some Indian princes and was having a few weeks' holiday in Monte Carlo before returning, Prince Savonarilda, Erskine and Bradley. The latter would have liked to have made a more formal affair of the gathering but was overruled.

"After all, you know," Roger pointed out, as he tasted the vodka which was being served with the caviar, "there's no harm in talking over anything we want to at luncheon. The police here might get raw with us if we held anything in the shape of a meeting."

"The lad is right, without a doubt," Terence Brown observed, making secret signs to the waiter to indicate an unsatisfied appetite for caviar. "The authorities here are touchy. Very touchy sometimes."

"That's all very well," Lord Bradley commented guardedly, "but we're the people who keep the place going and we've got to have a word or two to say sometimes. For instance," he went on, "we none of us want to find fault with the laws of the Principality or the policy of the Casino, but we have to look after ourselves. The policy of the Casino dictates that every crime which happens should be covered up, so far as possible, and given as little prominence in the news as may be. The police and the Press are hand in glove with the administration."

"That's all very well, so far as regards suicides," Terence Brown pointed out; "but when it comes to the case of the murder of a friend like Luke Cheyne, something has got to be done about it. It's an ugly thought that a man can be murdered and robbed of half a million francs in this very hotel and that the murderer can get away with it. What do you think, Major Thornton? You're the man who has had experience in such matters."

Thornton was lean and grey, slow of speech, with steely blue eyes and a strangely shaped mouth, owing to his long upper lip. His voice was soft and pleasant. He had the air of an absent-minded man—which he certainly was not.

"Well, there isn't much to be said just now, is there?" he remarked. "I can tell you this, if it is of any interest. We know for a fact in London, and they know it in Paris too, that a larger number of criminals than usual—mostly internationals—are working along the coast between Biarritz and San Remo. The French police are on to them in Nice and Marseilles. This little spot we're in at present always seems to me a trifle unguarded. I don't like their police methods and I tell you so frankly."

"Tell us what you find fault with chiefly, Major Thornton?" Terence Brown enquired.

Thornton sipped his wine and found it of a pleasant flavour.

"Well, I'll tell you," he confided. "The murder, as most of us know, took place on the stairs by the last lift, but the body was discovered by the police, when they arrived, in Mr. Cheyne's bedroom, with a revolver lying upon the carpet, from which the shots might have been fired but certainly were not! This, I suppose, was done to suggest suicide. It was a clumsy effort and, of course, makes the discovery of the criminal more difficult."

"What about the half million francs?" Erskine asked.

"There wasn't a *mille* note left," Thornton replied. "Although, when enquiries were made, it transpired that Mr. Cheyne had a large balance at the bank here and a larger one still in Paris, not a word of this appeared in the Press."

"Going a trifle too far, you know," Lord Bradley muttered.

"Furthermore," Thornton continued, "the lad who was chloroformed whilst asleep in the chair by the side of the lift was summarily dismissed by the hotel authorities for inattention to duties and has disappeared. I make no comment upon that fact, but he has disappeared."

"Disgraceful!" Erskine exclaimed.

Terence Brown leaned across the table. He was a handsome, elderly man who had once been a great beau, American by birth but a thorough cosmopolitan. He was probably amongst the most popular visitors to the Principality.

"As I daresay you all know," he said, "I am a great supporter of the administration here. I know intimately most of the officials of the place and I admit frankly that I love Monte Carlo. Ugly things happen here sometimes. Suicides, for example. When they do happen, I am all for the policy of the authorities. I believe in keeping them quiet. I believe in hushing them up. In my experience, the class of person who commits suicide here would be just as likely to do it anywhere else, if he had losses on the Stock Exchange or horse racing."

"I'm inclined to agree with you, Terence," Lord Bradley admitted.

"It's a very reasonable point of view, anyhow," Erskine observed.

"But," Terence Brown continued, shaking his forefinger, "when it comes to a murder like this—of a man we all knew, too—it's a horse of a different colour. I disagree with the official attitude altogether and I don't mind telling you gentlemen that I have called upon some influential friends of mine this morning and told them so."

Prince Savonarilda dropped his eyeglass and abandoned with reluctance his admiring contemplation of a planked *loup*.

"The murder of a man like our friend Cheyne in the most important hotel of the place gives one unpleasant thoughts," he remarked. "If no arrest is made, one cannot but believe that other crimes will follow. We shall have to go about in threes and fours for the sake of safety. They speak of the brigandage and the *crimes passionels* in the villages and mountains of my own country but indeed I begin to wonder whether there would not be greater safety there."

Terence Brown, who had been favoured with a sight of the *loup*, helped himself plentifully.

"I am bound to confess," he said, "that my country stands behind much of this increase in ruthless crime. Bootlegging started it, of course. Here was a law one felt justified in disobeying. And from that one moved onwards. Crime began to appeal to a different sort of mentality. At the present moment, I am perfectly convinced that some of the most dangerous criminals in the world are men of brains and position. Explorers who used to shoot lions, bully and kill natives, and hoist the flag of their country in the far-away places are indulging in very similar instincts nearer home. ... Jean," he added, turning to the *sommelier*, "another glass of that delicious white wine, please."

"I don't like Mr. Terence Brown's theory," Thornton remarked grimly. "The one thing we dread at the Yard is the educated criminal. The Bill Sykes type scarcely exists any more."

A messenger boy from the hall approached the table and handed a note and card to Terence Brown. With a glance of apology towards his host he tore open the envelope and read.

"My dear Sloane," he said, lowering his voice a little. "This comes in the nature of a coincidence. The note is from my friend Monsieur Pleydou, the *commissaire* of police here on whom I called this morning. He desires to impart some information at once. May I invite him to join us?"

"By all means," Sloane agreed.

Monsieur Pleydou was ushered in, a grave-looking man with black beard and imperial, dark clothes and a general air of solemnity. He shook hands with Terence Brown, bowed to the others to whom he was introduced and accepted a glass of wine. He took the *déjeuner* always, he explained, at midday.

"Gentlemen," he announced, "I bring you news. The murderer of Luke Cheyne has confessed. The mystery is solved."

There was a murmur of interest. Monsieur Pleydou continued.

"A letter was brought to the Police Station this morning signed by a certain Samuel Crowley, confessing to the crime and giving particulars as to how it was executed. It was apparently partly an act of personal vengeance on the part of this man who had had unfortunate business transactions with Mr. Cheyne in New York and partly an ordinary robbery. Our police at once visited the small ketch upon which Crowley had been living in the harbour and found that he had disappeared. His body was discovered only an hour ago."

There were a few moments of curious silence. Somehow or other to one or two of the auditors at any rate the story seemed to lack substance.

"Did the confession which Mr. Crowley left," Roger asked, "contain any particulars as to how he committed the crime?"

"They were scarcely necessary," the police commissary replied, "but as a matter of general interest he did leave some particulars. He entered the hotel by the front way, muffled up, and walked straight ahead. It was a perfectly simple thing to do as it was past four o'clock in the morning. A great many of the guests are in the habit of coming home at that time from the night clubs and naturally the members of the staff who were about were sleepy. He

34

found the lift boy, for instance, fast asleep, which made his task easier. He chloroformed him, pulled him out of sight and sat just at the bend of the stairs with his hand upon the electric switch waiting for Mr. Cheyne, of whose impending departure from the Club he had been advised by a confederate."

"And the money?" Erskine enquired.

"A certain amount of it—quite enough to confirm Crowley's story—was found in his cabin. The remainder will doubtless be recovered later. That is an affair between us and the administration. It is a sad story, gentlemen, and the only satisfactory part of it is that it clears up the mystery of Monsieur Cheyne's death."

Every one seemed to feel that there was little else to be said. Monsieur Pleydou accepted coffee, a liqueur and cigar and the conversation drifted away to the always interesting subjects of the unreported suicides and robberies in the Casino. When the luncheon broke up Thornton, who seemed to have taken a fancy to Roger, walked with him and Erskine to the courtyard where the latter's car was waiting to take them to the tennis courts.

"You own a villa in the neighbourhood, I understand?" Thornton enquired of his late host. "When are you leaving?"

"I'm not quite sure," Roger confided, "that I shall leave at all for the present. Things seem to me as though they might become too interesting down here. I am returning to my villa for luncheon to-morrow, but I am keeping my room here and I shall probably stay on for some time."

"I am not sure that you're wise," Thornton reflected. "If there is any gang work going on down here, you would probably be a marked man after your luncheon to-day. You'll be safer at the villa, Mr. Sloane."

"That may be so, but I don't think I shall stay there. Am I allowed to ask you one question?"

"Just one," was the rather grudging reply, "and I think I can guess what it will be."

Roger clambered up to Erskine's side in the car and waved the porter away. He leaned towards Thornton.

"You are not accepting whole-heartedly this solution of Luke Cheyne's murder?"

Major Thornton smiled frostily. His voice had sunk almost to a whisper, although they were alone in the courtyard.

"I am not," he admitted. "I am wondering whether the police here are trying to be very clever indeed or whether you are up against a gang of criminals with new ideas."

35

CHAPTER VI

Roger, with Jeannine by his side, stood on the terrace of his villa the next day after luncheon and gazed with a shudder at a flamboyant new château, fortunately half hidden by a turning in the road.

"Who on earth has built that atrocity, Bardells?" he asked his butler, who was serving the coffee.

"Monsieur Viotti, who was Mayor of the place last year, sir," the man replied. "He has come in, people say, for a great deal of money. A wealthy brother in America. At any rate, he has become rich. He has a large apartment in Nice, an hotel on the Corniche between Eze and Mentone; he has left all the farm and flower lands here and visits the place but seldom. His mother and sisters occupy the château."

"God help them!" Roger muttered. "You mean, of course, the man I—"

"Precisely, sir. The man you knocked down the day you brought the young lady up."

Roger nodded.

"I've seen him in the Sporting Club," he said. "He looks just as disagreeable as ever, but opulent. By the by, Bardells, I am going to stay on at the Hôtel de Paris for a few weeks. Wisden has a list of the things I shall require. Tell him not to forget everything necessary for golf and tennis, two bathing suits and both my automatics."

"Your automatics, sir?" the man repeated.

"The habit of living in wild countries, I suppose," Roger remarked carelessly. "Anyhow, I like to have them. No liqueurs, thanks."

"Very good, sir."

The man disappeared. Roger led his companion down to the arbour.

"This is where I was sitting," he told her, "when Pips Erskine came along and we started off to Nice and—you happened."

"Yes, I suppose I happened," she meditated. "What about Lord Erskine? He is by himself all this time. I think I shall go and talk to him."

"You will do nothing of the sort," he told her. "You will stay and entertain your host."

"I failed once before in doing that," she observed with a strange smile.

36

"You have learnt a great deal since then," he retorted.

"I think that I have learnt nothing that changes me very much."

"Could you climb along the bough of that tree now?"

"Of course I could," she assured him, "if I took off my skirt. On the other hand, Madame does not like her skirts taken off. I have to be careful even how I sit down. It is a strange feeling, always wearing clothes that do not belong to you. I am happiest when I get home and put on an old crêpe de Chine frock which I bought with my first month's salary."

"Does any one ever offer to buy you frocks?" he asked, with a sudden twinge of jealousy.

"Dozens of people. Generally gentlemen who have been in with their wives the afternoon before and make some pretence to come back again. Laurette is the fortunate one, because she sometimes very discreetly goes out to dinner with one of them, then she wears a frock of the establishment and she does not have to return it. Myself," she sighed, "no one makes me offers now. They have decided that I am a foolish girl."

He beamed upon her.

"You are a very wise one," he declared. "Shall I give you a frock?"

She looked at him curiously.

"Would you like to, Monsieur Roger?"

"I'd love to! My aunt and I between us, if you like."

The smile left her lips.

"A frock is not necessary for me," she confided. "I can always wear what I choose and I do not go out in the evenings unless it is for the Maison. We must go and talk to Lord Erskine. He looks very lonely."

"Not so lonely as I shall be if you leave me," he complained.

"Then you can come too. You observe that I am wearing a white gabardine skirt and your garden seats are not very clean. One has to remember things like that when the skirt belongs to the Maison! I shall make a promenade."

"Very well," he assented sulkily. "Go and find Erskine."

She laughed and held out her hand.

"Come with me," she begged. "It is a neighbourhood full of dangers, this. Another wild man may appear. Did you know that Monsieur Viotti had reformed? He has approached Madame Vinay. They are great friends and they go to the cinema together. He has demanded my hand in marriage."

Roger rose to his feet.

37

"Look here, you little devil—" he began.

"I am not a little devil any longer," she interrupted him. "I am a grown-up young lady, second mannequin at the great house of Prétat. It is not in the least extraordinary that Monsieur Viotti should ask for my hand in marriage. I am old enough to be at least fiancée."

"How the mischief old are you?" he demanded.

"Ah, no one has ever told me that," she regretted. "That is what comes of being born a ragamuffin. Only I know that I was old enough to be hurt when you found me...."

Lady Julia came out of the house in great good humour.

"I have had a very pleasant sleep," she announced, "and your excellent Mrs. Bardells has given me a cup of tea which I could drink. We will lunch with you again, Roger. You are quite ready, Jeannine?"

"Quite, Lady Julia," the girl answered. "Will you take my arm?"

"I rather thought," Roger suggested, "that I might drive home Mademoiselle Jeannine in the Packard and you could take Erskine in the limousine. You can tell him more stories about how you used to flirt with his father."

"I shall do nothing of the sort," Lady Julia replied. "You have seen quite enough of Jeannine for one day. She is a very sweet girl and she pleases me very much, but she must not be spoilt nor must her head be turned."

Roger Sloane sighed as he handed Lady Julia into her car.

"And I once thought that you were my favourite aunt!"

"So I ought to be. Don't forget that if you finish your tennis in time, I like to be taken into the Sporting Club bar and given a cocktail at seven o'clock."

"We're not playing this afternoon," Roger told her, "so I shall be there."

"A thousand thanks for the delicious lunch," Jeannine murmured, leaning forward.

"And you ate nothing," he reminded her.

She waved her hand.

"I must remain slim enough to wear the frocks of the Maison Prétat!"

Lady Julia suddenly changed her mind. After all, Erskine was a pleasant youth and there were a few family questions she had forgotten to ask him.

"A wave of good nature has come over me," she declared. "You can take Jeannine, but drive carefully and don't loiter. Send Reggie along at once. It is time I started."

Jeannine dismounted demurely.

"You like to take me?" she asked Roger.

"I'll say so," he answered, as he handed her into the Packard.

* * * * *

Roger seemed smitten with an inexplicable dumbness that afternoon, and Jeannine herself appeared to be curiously content with his silence. They stopped for a few moments in Nice and he bought roses at the shop where Jeannine had served her apprenticeship, and chocolates next door. Then they mounted to the Moyen Corniche and paused once or twice to look down at the marvellous view.

"You are happy in this new life of yours?" he ventured.

"It is far more wonderful than anything I could have dared to hope for," she replied.

"But you are contented?"

"Is any one contented with life?" she asked a little restlessly. "It never gives with both hands and it never gives precisely what you want."

"What is it you want?"

She smiled.

"Your questions," she complained, "they are like bombshells. A year ago I could have answered you. Now life has become more confused."

"I believe," he said, "that you would have liked me better if—if I had—"

She broke into her old laugh. Roger felt himself more than ever a bungler.

"You are a great cavalier," she mocked him. "Do you mind if I tell you that you make me think sometimes of that strange knight who went about with a lance and a fat steward? They made an opera about him."

"A half-baked idiot he was," Roger declared angrily. "Supposing I drive on and take you across the frontier into Italy."

"It would annoy your aunt very much," she pointed out, "and Prétats would probably issue a procès against me for going away in their precious clothes!"

"And you," he persisted. "How should you feel about it?"

She smiled in puzzling fashion.

"I've left off feeling," she confided. "Once I felt too much."

39

They passed through La Turbie and swung around to the right. He brought the car to a standstill in front of the café and raised his hat in greeting to two strange-looking people—a man and a woman—who were seated side by side at one of the outdoor tables. The man was toying with a guitar. The woman was seated with her hands in front of her, apparently dreaming. They were both old, they were both dressed in rusty and shabby black.

"My friends from the Vistaero," Roger greeted them, throwing up his arms.

They recognised him with enthusiasm. Madame rose to her feet and attempted a curtsey. Monsieur, with the memory of many a fifty-franc note in his mind, abased himself joyfully before his wealthy young patron.

"What are you doing so far away from home?" the latter asked them.

The careless question seemed to produce some embarrassment.

"In the afternoons and evenings sometimes we visit here," the woman explained. "Business at the Vistaero is always in the morning. When the sun goes behind the hill, the visitors shiver."

"But are there any visitors here?" Roger asked, looking around him in surprise. "And what is all that building at the back?"

"There are people who call here for tea and an *apéritif*," the woman explained. "They have built an hotel there. It is connected with the café."

"An hotel up here?" Roger repeated. "What an idea. Jeannine, would you like some tea?"

"Must it be tea?" she asked. "I should like an orangeade and I should like your strange friends to sing to me—a Neapolitan song if possible."

They descended from the car. Roger pushed open the door to summon a waiter. To his surprise, the place was fitted up in the most modern and tasteful fashion. A white-jacketed barman stood on the other side of a polished counter. A man whom Roger recognised with astonishment was seated upon a stool, talking to him. The latter swung around at Roger's exclamation.

"Hello, Thornton!"

"Hello, Sloane! What are you doing up here?"

"Just what I was going to ask you," was the smiling reply. "I'm driving a friend back to Monte Carlo and the look of this place rather intrigued me. Can I have two orangeades outside, please," he went on to the barman.

"Certainly, sir," the man replied civilly, but without enthusiasm.

"Seems very smart here for an out-of-the-way place," Roger remarked, looking around. "Tremendous lot of men at work, too, round at the back."

Thornton nodded carelessly.

"The hotel's rather a hobby of a rich Niçois, I'm told. Shouldn't think it will ever pay. By the by, when could I have a few words with you to-night?"

"Not at all, unless it's really urgent. I'm dining with the tennis people at Cannes and I shall stay on until pretty late. What about luncheon to-morrow?"

Thornton nodded.

"That'll do," he agreed. "Meet you in the hotel bar just before one."

"That's a date."

"Haven't I seen you somewhere before?" Roger asked the barman, as the latter served his order.

The man, sturdily built, middle-aged and with the curiously inscrutable expression of his class, smiled faintly.

"Very likely, Mr. Sloane," he assented. "I know you quite well. I was at the Racquet Club in New York for five, and at the Manhattan Club for ten years. Since then, I've been at Le Touquet and the Ritz."

"Of course! You're Sam," Roger exclaimed. "What on earth are you doing in an out-of-the-way place like this?"

"I received a good offer," the man confided. "The place will grow some day, sure. Wonderful air up here."

Roger pointed to the two musicians.

"Serve Monsieur and Madame with what they desire," he directed. "And, by the by, ask the gentleman inside if he would like a lift down."

"The gentleman came in his own car. He pushed it through the gate at the back."

"I see," Roger murmured thoughtfully.

Wine was brought to the two musicians, toasts were exchanged and a song. In the midst of it a large automobile turned off the main road and came to a standstill in front of the café—a powerful Voisin, but hideously painted in a violent shade of lilac. A fat little man descended from it, a man who wore tight, glossy clothes, over-elaborate linen and a beflowered tie. He wore gloves, he was smoking a cigar and he carried a cane. His thick lips pursed

41

themselves into a whistle as he recognised Jeannine. He took off his hat with a sweeping bow.

"*Bonjour*, Mademoiselle Jeannine," he said.

"*Bonjour*, Monsieur Viotti," she answered coldly.

The newcomer looked across at Roger and seemed about to attempt some sort of greeting. Roger's eyes met his, however, stonily. The two musicians made obeisance. The ex-Mayor of La Bastide passed on into the bar.

"*C'est le patron*," the woman musician confided.

Jeannine set down her glass.

"Let us go," she whispered.

As they dropped down the hill, Roger looked at his companion curiously.

"You are still afraid of Monsieur Viotti," he observed.

"I shall be afraid of him until my dying day," she confessed.

He held out his hand and for once she yielded hers quickly, almost impulsively.

"Promise me," she begged, "that if ever you have anything to do with him, you will remember that he is bad and you will be careful."

He had the intention of answering differently but he was suddenly aware of the almost passionate appeal in her eyes. It was the child again who was afraid.

"I promise," he said simply.

CHAPTER VII

Roger lunched with Thornton the next day and a very angry man he discovered his host to be.

"I am strongly inclined," the latter declared, "to go back to London this afternoon. No sort of vacation here is likely to do me any good."

"Just what do you mean?" Roger asked.

"Mine," Thornton explained, "is one of those professions that get into your blood. If there are things stirring around you, up goes your nose to the breeze and you smell 'em out. You can't help it. We are being made fools of down here, Sloane."

"In what way?"

"Well, that Crowley confession, for one thing. It's a faked

business from beginning to end. The man was a perfectly harmless person who loved his life of adventure. He had kept his log for the last six months and the one place he had never been near was the United States of America. He had heaps of letters in his locker—all from people of a most respectable class in England."

"But surely you don't suspect the Monaco police of forging his confession and planting four hundred thousand francs in his locker just to save their own faces? Isn't that just a little thick?"

"I don't suspect anything of the sort," Thornton rejoined. "Of course not. What I do complain about is that the Monaco police were only too pleased to get hold of the confession and they didn't take the trouble to verify it. It suited them to have it accepted as a genuine affair and so they accepted it as such."

"What is your idea, then?"

"I believe that this man, Crowley, poor devil, was murdered by the same people who murdered Luke Cheyne and that the confession was a faked document written by the murderer."

"What are you going to do about that?" Roger asked.

Thornton waited for a few moments while the principal dish of their luncheon was served. The restaurant was crowded, and with the excitement concerning the two murders the chief subject of conversation, the two men who were known to be greatly interested were themselves the subject of many comments. Thornton continued in a slightly more casual tone.

"I went to see the authorities this morning," he confided, "and explained my point of view."

"Did they tumble to it at all?"

"They did not. I wasn't any too popular before but this time they practically turned me out. They don't want foreigners upsetting their people and they certainly don't want to foster the idea that there are dangerous criminals at work in the Principality."

"That's the Casino influence!"

"I told them I should appeal to—well, to a certain person who shall be nameless, and I was met with a shrug of the shoulders, a whiff of cigarette smoke and a polite gesture towards the door."

Roger rose to greet a passing acquaintance and the conversation was interrupted for several moments. When he sat down again, he remembered the question he had been intending to ask Thornton.

"What were you doing up at that strange café yesterday?" he enquired.

"Nothing of any consequence," was the brief reply. "I must confess that this affair is bothering me. The supposed suicide's letter is to be published in the Monegasque and Nice evening papers. The Luke Cheyne murder is considered solved. Meanwhile, the next affair is brewing and we can do nothing to stop it."

"Have you any suspicions at all?" Roger asked.

"No sane ones. If only the Monegasque people would throw overboard this Crowley business, even for a few days, and start the Luke Cheyne official enquiries again from the very beginning, we might have a chance. Now all we know is that there is a dangerous gang at work in whose existence the police profess, at any rate, to absolutely disbelieve. They, on the other hand, can get at us at any time they want, if they think we are dangerous. By the by, has Prince Savonarilda or Terence Brown or any of you got any influence up at the Palace?"

"None whatever."

"There's nothing to be done then except to deal with these wooden-headed officials," Thornton remarked, with a touch of irritability.

"They are not wooden-headed," Roger protested. "They are playing their own game. It is not ours, but that can't be helped. They have got out of this Luke Cheyne murder and they want to stay out. Well, I don't blame them. Catching criminals is not their business. Keeping Monaco free from them is. You don't happen to have seen Bradley this morning?"

"Not a sign of him," Thornton answered. "I was up at the Royalty and he wasn't there."

"He promised to come down to the tennis but he never turned up. I meant to ask him to stay to lunch and hear what you had to say."

The page boy from outside approached the table and handed a note to Sloane. On the back of the envelope was printed the name of Bradley's yacht. Roger tore it open. Its contents were insignificant but somehow or other the substance of it was intriguing.

My dear Sloane,

If this reaches you in time, will you lunch with me? If it does not, will you come as soon as you can afterwards. Bring Erskine along if you care to, and keep your eyes open on the quay.

Sincerely, BRADLEY.

"That looks as though something fresh were being started," Thornton reflected, "In his own handwriting, I see. Not too steady, either. I should say that note was written by a man who was in a funk. I thought Bradley was a man without any nerves."

"No millionaire likes even the suggestion of danger," Roger observed, a little cynically. "It seems to him perfectly reasonable that a man in moderate circumstances should be wiped out. Not a tragedy at all, really. But a millionaire—a man who is able to wield the greatest power in the world—to be launched into eternity by the same bullet that would destroy a mendicant doesn't seem right somehow. Oh, I quite sympathise with Bradley."

"Go along and see what he wants, then, as soon as you can pick up Erskine," Thornton begged. "I will stay in for a couple of hours. If the man were not an idiot, he would have asked me to come instead of young Erskine."

"I'll risk taking you, if you like," Roger suggested.

"No, thanks," was the terse reply. "I don't fancy Bradley has much of an opinion of me, anyway, and I won't run the risk of offending him. All the same, if there's anything doing that looks like linking up, get back as quick as you can."

* * * * *

Roger refused to indulge in his favorite penchant for riding in a *voiture à cheval*, neither did he send for his own car or allow Erskine to do so. He ensconced himself in the corner of a taxicab from which he scanned every corner of the quay as he made his way along it. He noticed no suspicious persons of any sort. The few men who were about appeared to have business and to be attending to it. At the gangway of the *White Lady*, as Bradley's yacht was called, were four sailors, one of whom took the cards of the two young men before they were permitted to pass along. Bradley, instead of being seated on deck as usual, was lounging rather disconsolately in the smoking saloon.

"Glad you've come, Sloane, and you Erskine," he greeted them. "See many loiterers on the quay?"

"Not a soul," Roger replied. "The few people who were there seemed to have jobs."

Bradley handed across a letter. It was typed on notepaper of good quality and apparently upon an excellent machine.

To the Right Honorable Lord Bradley, S.Y. "White Lady."

Milord,

We can find a use for those six hundred thousand francs you were flashing about in the Sporting Club the other night. You had better make a parcel of them and leave them in mille notes at the Café Regent at Beausoleil this evening, addressed to Monsieur Monet.

Now, read the rest of this communication carefully. If you attempt to communicate with the police, or if you fail to send the notes, or if you endeavour to have the recipient watched, you will be a dead man before midnight. You can take our word for it that these threats can easily be carried out. Adopt your own counsel to others and be a philosopher. Say to yourself that the life of the great Lord Bradley is worth more to the British public than six hundred thousand francs.

"Pretty cool," Roger remarked, as he passed it back.

"Almost insolent," Erskine agreed, "but intensely interesting."

"What are you going to do about it?" Roger asked.

"I'm going to pay," was the terse reply. "I've thought it over carefully and I've decided to part with the money."

Bradley, for a famous man and a man who had spoken vociferously in the Sporting Club during the last four nights on the subject of crime, appeared somewhat sheepish. Roger's expression was imperturbable but Erskine was plainly surprised.

"It's all very well," Bradley defended himself irritably, "but after all, what's the use of running any risks for a sum I could give away for a tip to a *maître d'hôtel* if I wanted to? If I felt certain that this was a dangerous gang at work, if I felt certain even that they were the same gang that murdered poor Luke Cheyne, it might be worth while risking something for the sake of routing them out."

"My belief is that it is the same gang," Roger declared gravely.

"How can it be?" Bradley expostulated. "The man who murdered Luke Cheyne was an eccentric fellow named Crowley who has drowned himself in the harbour and left a confession behind him."

"Thornton and I have both come to the conclusion," Roger pronounced, "that the confession was a fake and the suicide a murder, probably by the same gang."

"You're not serious!" Bradley gasped.

"Come and talk to Thornton and you'll soon be convinced," Roger suggested.

"I can't leave the damn boat," was the angry reply. "There's another note on the table there, typed on the same machine. I am told that any visitor I have will be watched and that I myself am not to leave the boat until I go to the Café Regent at a quarter to seven. I understand that I am to have an unseen escort right to the door of the damn place and back again. In Monaco Harbour, mind you. What do you think of that?"

Roger was almost inclined to laugh. Bradley, like many other men of real power and genius, was terribly impatient of any form of control. To think of him as prisoner on his own boat for fear of getting a bullet through his lungs was quaint.

"I can't telephone," Bradley went on. "All the company can say is that the line's been disturbed. The devils have cut it! Here I am a prisoner allowed to leave at a quarter to seven on sufferance and carry my ransom money myself in broad daylight to some disreputable café!"

"I wonder who told them that you had that exact sum in plaques in your hand the other night," Erskine meditated. "There were barely half a dozen of us in the room."

"That's what I've been asking myself," Bradley replied. "There's some one in this gang connected with either the Sporting Club or the Casino. No doubt about that. We could almost have counted the people in the bar. As you say, I don't believe there were more than half a dozen, and they've got the exact amount. Don't forget, either, that they knew exactly the minute that Luke Cheyne left the Sporting Club that night and that he'd taken his money with him."

"Well, what do you want us to do about this?" Roger asked. "Terence Brown, I'm sure, would join in; there's Savonarilda—a lazy sort of fellow but a deadly shot—and Erskine and myself. We're ready to take any risk you like. We'll sit round in the Café Regent till some one claims those notes, if you say so, or we'll think out something more subtle."

"You won't do a damn thing," Bradley insisted. "You are to keep right away from the Café Regent at seven o'clock. I shall deliver the notes and then consider the whole affair. Whether I shall send the police up there afterwards or not, I don't know. Just at present, it doesn't seem to me to be worth the risk."

"Very well," Roger agreed, "we won't interfere. I tell you what you might do, though; come in to the Hôtel de Paris bar on your way down afterwards. You may have been able to pick up an idea."

"I'll do that," Bradley promised. "All the same, I'll tell you frankly—you needn't go spreading it about—that I've got the wind up. I feel rather inclined to beat it out at midnight. There's an air about the place this season that I don't like. If a really ugly crowd got together here, there wouldn't be anything to stop them. Have a drink, you fellows, before you go."

The young men refused and presently took their leave. The taxicab was still waiting on the quay but Roger fancied that the chauffeur looked curiously at him as he took his place inside. They drove off, however, quite uneventfully. The only people in sight were a few newcomers fishing in the harbour waters and one gendarme at the corner, perambulating a brief space of the dock. Yet, Roger had a feeling all the time that they were being watched, the most profound conviction that if there had been a note for the chief of the police in his pocket he would have felt the whistle of a bullet through the window. Something of the sort he confided to his companion. Erskine only laughed at him.

"Your condition, my dear Roger," the latter declared, "proves to me that it's time you started writing again. Your imagination is brimming over. You need the typewriter to take care of some of it. Maybe you think our plump friend there on the sea wall with the carnation in his buttonhole is watching us with murderous intent."

"I shouldn't be in the least surprised," Roger replied calmly. "If you look at him again, you'll see who it is. Whatever he's doing here, I'll bet it's no good."

Erskine recognised the saunterer with a little gasp.

"It's the Mayor of La Bastide!" he exclaimed.

"It is," Roger agreed, "and you may take my word for it that the ex-Mayor of La Bastide, whatever he's up to in life just now, is a very bad man."

CHAPTER VIII

Outside the famous establishment of Prétat, on his way up from the quay, Roger saw his aunt's car waiting. He took leave of Erskine, who was on his way to the tennis courts, entered the establishment, and in response to her gestured invitation slipped into a chair by Lady Julia's side.

"Frocks?" he asked.

"Just the usual mannequin show. I come for half an hour most afternoons. It does me good to watch Jeannine."

"That child seems to have fascinated you," he observed.

"She is no child. To me she is ageless. As a matter of fact, as far as she can tell, she is eighteen years old."

Roger was conscious of a queer, internal disturbance. It seemed incredible to him to reflect that she had actually been on the threshold of womanhood when he had first seen her sprawling in the boughs of an orange tree making fun of him with the true *gamine's* love of mockery. It was more bewildering still to recall that same night when he had seen her waiting patiently on the hard seat outside his room.

"I should have thought she would have been too young for this job, anyway," he muttered.

"Jeannine has an abnormal intelligence," his aunt pronounced. "At the rate she is educating herself and developing her mental outlook, she will be a very clever woman before she is twenty. Can you tell me—you have written some queer short stories and profess to understand something of life—can you tell me how a girl brought up in a hill village amongst peasants, climbing trees to pick blossoms for the scent factories, learnt to be so magnificently devoid of all self-consciousness?"

Jeannine was passing down the room towards them now, showing off an afternoon gown to some newcomers. There was none of the gesturing or posturing of the ordinary mannequin about her deliberate movements. She looked once or twice, as she passed before them, at the girl on whose account she was wearing the frock; otherwise it was clear that no one else, not even her patroness, existed. Monsieur Prétat, who had paused to pay his respects to Lady Julia, watched his employee for a moment thoughtfully.

"That girl," he confided, "is either one of the greatest artists at repression or she is the most perfect mannequin in the world."

"She is much too good to remain a mannequin," Lady Julia declared. "You will lose her some day."

Monsieur Prétat frowned.

"I hope your Ladyship won't encourage her to do anything foolish," he said. "I pay her already a high salary but I would pay her more than any other mannequin in the world sooner than lose her."

Lady Julia raised her lorgnettes.

"She's nothing extraordinary to look at," she remarked thoughtfully.

Monsieur Prétat shrugged his shoulders.

"None of the women who have turned the heads of the world have been very wonderful to look at," he reminded Lady Julia, as he obeyed the summons of another patron.

"Prétat knows what he's talking about," Roger remarked, rising to his feet.

"Why are you so restless?" his aunt asked.

Roger muttered something about an appointment. He knew very well why he was restless. Lady Julia looked at him keenly. Perhaps she too guessed.

"I will come with you," she decided. "There is nothing I can afford to buy to-day. The sooner that girl gets a lover or a husband," she added, "the better."

* * * * *

49

Precisely at quarter past seven that evening Bradley descended from a *petite voiture* and entered the bar of the Hôtel de Paris. He crossed towards the table where Roger, Erskine and Thornton were waiting for him and sat down a little heavily. His manner was disturbed, his cheeks were bereft of colour and he was breathing rather more quickly than is usual in a man of good health. In his eyes, too, there was a look of trouble.

"Anything gone wrong?" Roger asked quickly.

The other shook his head.

"Everything went according to plan," he announced. "I drove up to the place in a horse carriage, found quite an ordinary café with several decent-looking men of the shopkeeper type sitting about and two or three women. No one at all remarkable. I went to the counter, laid down the packet and covered it with a newspaper exactly as I had been told. Then I ordered a *Fine*—a very good *Fine* it was too—paid for it and left the place."

"Who served you with your drink?" Thornton asked.

"He seemed to be quite an ordinary barman, rather above the usual type, if anything—clean white linen coat—spoke English perfectly. I didn't hurry over my brandy. I was trying to make up my mind about the people. When I left I bade the barman good evening. He replied quite pleasantly and made no reference at all to the parcel I was leaving behind. As I was stepping into my carriage I looked back. The newspaper had gone from the counter and my packet with it!"

"And you drove straight here?"

"I drove straight here."

Roger called the barman and gave an order. Thornton was tapping a cigarette thoughtfully upon the table.

"I suppose you have still made up your mind to sacrifice the money and let it go at that?" he asked.

Bradley frowned.

"I don't think I went quite so far as that," he replied. "I may have hinted as much to Erskine and Sloane here this afternoon, but the point I was definite about was that I didn't want any outside interference."

Thornton was suddenly grave, his tone almost inquisitorial.

"Lord Bradley," he said, "you strike me as being an amateur who may be trying to measure his wits against some very experienced professionals. You have had this demand made upon you and you have paid these men the money they insisted upon. I daresay you have been wise, but I want you to tell me this—are you keeping anything back?"

Bradley made no direct answer. He felt in his hip pocket and produced a well-fitted *portemonnaie*. From it he drew a *mille* note and laid it upon the table.

"Do either of you see anything unusual about that?" he asked.

Roger took up the note and examined it carefully. He spent some few minutes over his investigation before handing it back.

"Seems to me all right," he admitted.

"What about you, Erskine?"

The latter also subjected it to a close scrutiny.

"I should like a thousand of them," he observed, as he returned it.

"And you, Thornton?"

Thornton adjusted some rarely used spectacles and went over the note inch by inch.

"Seems to me O.K." he acknowledged finally. "Wait a moment."

He opened his own pocketbook, produced a *mille* note and laid it beside Bradley's. Presently a little exclamation broke from his lips.

"The 'i' in the last word of the inscription here is dotted," he pointed out. "It is not dotted on mine. As it is a block letter, one would not expect it."

Bradley smiled triumphantly.

"You would expect that to escape ordinary observation then?"

"Ordinary observation—yes," Thornton agreed. "I am not at all sure, however, about the people you're up against!"

Bradley glanced around the room for a moment to be sure that there was no one within hearing.

"Well, anyway, there it is," he confided. "Morris, my Marconi man, and I have spent the greater part of the day making those dots with some white ink I got and a blunted needle end. I have seen— well, the right person to see—at the Etablissement. None of the croupiers have been told the reason, but every one of the cashiers has his orders that the *mille* notes handed to croupiers for change to-night and to-morrow night will be placed in a special compartment of their boxes and examined later on."

There was an expression on Thornton's face which it was hard to classify.

"Of course, if you think it worth while to run a risk like this," he said a little stiffly, "it is no one else's business."

"It's not a question of the money," Bradley pointed out. "How do you suppose I feel about being blackmailed by this company of gangsters or cutthroats or whatever they are? It hurts a man's vanity. I haven't gone through life being any one's mug. You especially ought to be thankful, Thornton. You find the man to-night who tries to cash one of those notes—"

"And what do you suppose, Lord Bradley, may happen to you," Thornton interrupted, "if when our friends up at the Café Regent go through that bundle of bills they discover that dotted 'i'?"

"They are not likely to," Bradley scoffed. "I've tried it on a dozen people, people of experience too. I tried it on the head cashier of the principal Bank here, and the manager. Neither of them noticed it."

"All the same," Thornton said, and he spoke very earnestly and very deliberately, "it is a calm sea, Lord Bradley, and the papers are prophesying good weather. It was only yesterday you said you were ready to sail at any time. Why not to-night?"

Bradley's jaw was suddenly set. He seemed to have assumed the expression with which he was so frequently caricatured.

"I think," he confided, "I would rather stay and deal with the men who are trying to rob me of six hundred thousand francs Thornton's eyes were filled with disapproval as he watched Bradley's disappearing figure a few minutes later.

"True to type," he sighed. "It is not the loss of the money he minds but the blow to his conceit."

"I don't think it's up to us to grumble," Roger objected.

"Why not?"

"It gives us a chance, doesn't it?"

"In a way it does, of course," Thornton admitted. "But the more I think of it, Sloane, the more I'm becoming convinced that we're up against something unusually clever."

"Open up," Roger invited. "Why?"

"That faked confession of Crowley's, for one thing, and the fact that the gang were perfectly willing to commit a featureless murder in order to give the police something to pat themselves on the back for and at the same time divert suspicion from themselves."

"A dirty business that," Roger acquiesced.

"Then you must remember this," Thornton went on; "if Bradley is being watched scientifically—as seems possible from the boldness of their threats—they will know that he was shut up for three or four hours during the day with his Marconi man and they may even have an idea as to what he was doing. They will know, too, that he had an interview with the Casino authorities this morning, or has communicated with them in some way or other."

"That seems likely enough."

"I should imagine that before they are put into circulation, every one of those notes will be gone over by an expert with a magnifying glass. If so, they can't fail to find the white dot. And if they find it—well, I think that Lord Bradley would be very much safer on his way to Egypt. He may not realise it, but it was a pretty foolhardy thing to do to take this gang on."

"Maybe," Roger commented. "All the same, it would be a Simple Simon business to sit down and be robbed of a sum like that."

"If I had Bradley's millions, I should have paid the money like a bird. Are you off?"

"I'm going to change early," Roger, who had risen to his feet confided. "I played rather strenuous tennis this afternoon and I want something elaborate in the way of a bath."

Thornton glanced around. There were only two people in the room and they appeared to be of the most harmless type. The barman was gazing over their heads at the lights of a small steamer on the horizon.

"I have a fancy that one of us ought to keep an eye on the Salle Privée," he observed. "If there's nothing doing there, I may see something of you later."

* * * * *

After all, it was Roger who had the luck that evening. He was standing a little aimlessly behind the croupier at one of the roulette tables when he saw a young man seated in front of him withdraw a *mille* note from a little bundle fastened together with an elastic band and pass it up to the croupier.

"*Première douzaine*," he instructed.

The croupier glanced at the *mille* note, placed a *plaque* upon the stake, but instead of passing the note itself into the box handed it with a significant glance to the *chef*. The young man appeared to take no notice and the game proceeded. The *chef*, however, had turned his head and raised his finger. One of those silent mysterious figures who wander about the rooms with the clothes and manner of an ambassador came unobtrusively forward. The *chef* moved his head in the direction of the young man and the newcomer took up his position behind his chair. The game proceeded for several spins without incident of any sort. The representative of the hidden powers of the Casino remained a motionless, unobtrusive figure, his hands behind his back, his eyes benevolently following the play. The young man, who appeared to be in a vein of luck, noticed no one.

The time arrived, however, when he leaned back in his place and began to collect his chips. With a careless gesture he swept them into his pocket and rose to his feet.

"*Vous gardez votre place, Monsieur?*" the valet enquired.

The young man slipped a tip into his hand.

"*Finit pour ce soir.*"

He strolled away, but before he could reach the door the official who had been standing behind him touched his arm apologetically.

"A little word, Monsieur," he begged, with a glance at Roger and Thornton, who were lingering in the background.

"With me?" the young man asked.

"With you, if you please, Monsieur Froquet."

They passed into the corridor together. The young man appeared unperturbed.

"Well, what is it that you desire?" he enquired.

"Monsieur Thiers, one of the directors, would like just a word with you, if you would give yourself the trouble to step into his office," the official explained suavely. "You might perhaps be able to afford us assistance in a certain matter."

The young man appeared mystified but made no objection and walked side by side with his companion down the passage. Thornton and Roger followed behind. When they reached the director's room they were all three ushered in. The young man turned and looked with surprise at his two companions.

"What is this all about?" he demanded.

The director rose to his feet and bowed. He had recognised the young man at once.

"Monsieur Froquet," he explained. "I will not beat about the bush. There are some *mille* notes in circulation, the origin of which we desire to trace. I gather from the fact that our inspector has brought you here that one of them has come into your possession."

"That is so, Monsieur," the official affirmed. "The *chef* told me that it was handed to him by Monsieur Froquet for a stake at the roulette table."

He produced a note which the director scrutinised carefully.

"*Tiens!*" he exclaimed. "One perceives that the chef had keen eyes. It would be a great assistance to us all," he added, "if Monsieur Froquet could tell us how he came into possession of this note?"

"It is not a forgery, I hope?" the young man asked, still without any signs of undue agitation.

"Certainly not," the director assured him. "There is a slight peculiarity about it, however, which makes us anxious to discover its source."

Monsieur Froquet frowned in perplexed fashion.

"And this gentleman here, whom I do not know," he remarked, turning to Thornton. "And Mr. Roger Sloane, with whom I have once or twice exchanged civilities at the gaming table—what have they to do with it?"

"It happens to be their friend who has brought the matter before the authorities," the director explained affably. "There is no question of the note not being genuine. It is simply that we beg you to assist us, Monsieur Froquet, by telling us from whom you received it."

The young man smiled. He was very pale and thin and his hair shone almost like black varnish. He was dressed with the meticulous care of the young Frenchman of good social position.

"I find the affair a little quaint," he remarked. "However, I am pleased to be able to satisfy your curiosity. The note was given me by your barman, Jack, about half an hour ago."

The director touched a bell and spoke down the telephone. The young man seemed puzzled.

"It is not that you doubt my word, I trust?"

"Not for a moment, Monsieur," the director assured him. "We are anxious to discover with as little delay as possible, however, how the note came into the possession of our barman."

"It would appear to be treating me reasonably if you would tell me what it is all about," Monsieur Froquet observed irritably. "I answer all your questions and I arrive here at the bureau of Monsieur le Directeur without demur. Has there been a robbery, perhaps?"

"An explanation is due to you, Monsieur Froquet," the director acknowledged. "You shall have it in one moment."

The door opened. Jack, the barman, still in his white coat, came in. The director leaned across.

"Monsieur Froquet here," he said, "borrowed some money from you this evening."

"Fifteen *mille*," the barman acknowledged.

"I asked for twenty," the young man put in, "but fifteen was all Jack had at the moment."

The director concentrated upon Jack, the barman.

"Can you tell us," he demanded, "from what source you got the fifteen *mille* which you gave to Monsieur Froquet?"

The barman was obviously perplexed.

"I'm afraid not, sir," he admitted. "Not the particular fifteen *mille* you speak of. There were two *mille* Lady Harrison paid me back, directly we opened after dinner, and five *mille* Major Seddon paid back. The rest was what was left in the box since yesterday."

"May I ask a question?" Thornton begged.

The director signified his assent.

"The fifteen *mille* which you advanced to Monsieur Froquet—was any one of those notes in your possession before seven o'clock this evening?"

"Certainly, sir," the man replied. "We had an hour or so with no money coming in or going out. It has been rather a quiet day on the whole."

There was a brief silence. Thornton scribbled something on a card and passed it to the director, who nodded thoughtfully.

"I have answered your questions," Monsieur Froquet said a little curtly, "but I do not see that this matter concerns me in any way. The *mille* which I passed up to the croupier to change must have come from your bar because, as I say, I arrived with no money and went at once to Jack. The tracing of it is no concern of mine. I can do nothing more for you."

"If I may be allowed to say a word," Roger observed, "I would only like to point out to Monsieur Froquet that the note which he passed up to the croupier and which he assures us that he obtained from Jack, the barman, did not come into circulation until, at the earliest, half-past seven this evening. Jack here seems quite certain that he received no notes from any one after that time and that the notes which he handed to Monsieur Froquet had been in his possession since the afternoon."

"That is so without a doubt, sir," the man asserted positively.

There was a brief silence. Monsieur Froquet seemed in no way discomposed.

"The whole affair is very boring," he declared. "I borrowed fifteen *mille* from your barman and you find something wrong with one of the notes. I cannot help that. It is not my concern."

"You must realise, though, that it is very much our concern," Monsieur Thiers insisted, "to trace the origin of that note. And from what the barman says, it is impossible that the note you passed up to the *chef* to change was a note that came from him."

"Why impossible?"

"Because there is a mark upon it—a mark here," the director pointed out, tapping the back of the note, "a white dot. The notes bearing this mark were not put into circulation until after seven o'clock this evening."

"I had the note from the barman," Monsieur Froquet declared

brusquely. "I can say no more. If I could help you, I should be glad. As I cannot—"

He moved towards the door, but the inspector, who had remained standing in the background, a dark shadowy figure, blocked the way.

"Monsieur Froquet," the director said gravely, "you are, of course, well known to us and your reputation and the reputation of your family is above reproach. So far as I am aware, however, you are a newcomer to our Casino this season. Will you be so kind as to tell us where you are staying and your home address?"

"You can find it in the telephone book or in any directory," the young man declared angrily. "I am staying with my own people—that is all I need to say."

The director bowed.

"In that case, we will not trouble you further, Monsieur Froquet," he said. "It is evident that Jack must have been mistaken. We will examine his accounts later."

"I am at liberty then, I presume, to depart?" the young man asked, with a contemptuous smile.

"Most certainly," his inquisitor assented. "You have been kind enough to answer our questions and we offer you our thanks. The affair is a mystery. It must be investigated. *Voilà tout.*"

Monsieur Froquet turned to leave the room and no one seemed to have any intention of detaining him further. The director leaned forward in his place, frowning.

"You see, gentlemen, how it is," he pointed out. "What we have is evidence and not evidence. To me it seems a great pity that we ever interfered with the young man. It is all very well for Jack here to say that the notes which he handed to Monsieur Froquet were notes which had been in his till all the afternoon, but who is to believe it? It is not evidence. There is no proof. Money is flowing in and out all the time. It is, in my opinion, a cause for regret that we have interfered in this matter at all."

"I am surprised that you should say so," Roger answered, a little warmly. "If the evidence of your own barman is to be believed—and in my opinion Jack is absolutely honest—Monsieur Froquet is connected with the band of criminals who are going to empty the Principality of visitors and even of residents if they are allowed their way much longer."

"There is no evidence," Monsieur Thiers asserted coldly, "of the existence of any band such as you describe in the Principality."

"Two murders within the month—" Roger began.

"Nothing of the sort, sir," the director interrupted. "One

murder and a simple suicide. And both affairs promptly cleared up in satisfactory fashion by our very efficient police staff."

Roger groaned as he turned away.

"In that matter, sir," he regretted, "we are not entirely in accord."

Later in the evening Roger found Thornton seated in an easy chair in the bar. He threw himself into a vacant place by his side with a little gesture of despair.

"The Commissaire will do nothing," he announced. "He considers the evidence altogether insufficient and in any case he would require sworn information from Lord Bradley personally. The young man seems to be quite well known. He is the son of a rich jeweller in Nice but he is in disgrace with his father, owing to his gambling propensities. I wonder where he is now?"

"I think I can guess," Thornton replied. "He was talking with that atrocious little bounder from Nice—Viotti, I think you told me his name was—and they went out together along the passage. What's happened I expect is, he's gone into the Salle Privée by the private way."

"I hope to God they won't let him leave the place," Roger exclaimed anxiously. "I've squared the telephone man all right. He hasn't attempted to call any one up. If he once got away and gave the Casino people the slip, though, it might be all up with poor Bradley."

"Let's see if the yacht's still there," Thornton suggested.

They made their way into the roulette room and, drawing the blinds a little on one side, looked out on to the harbour. The *White Lady* was lying at her accustomed moorings with all her lights ablaze.

"She's there, all right," Roger observed. "I think I shall go down and let Bradley know that his scheme has gone wrong."

"We'll have a word with Monsieur Thiers first," Thornton proposed.

They made their way to the director's room. The latter looked up at their entrance and, although he was as courteous as ever, he showed no signs of pleasure at their reappearance.

"We've been wondering whether, now that you have thought the matter over," Roger said, "you might not feel disposed to ask the young man to step down to the Police Station. After all, he tried to pass a note which was obtained by blackmail."

"I fear that it is too late for that," Monsieur Thiers regretted. "Monsieur Froquet left the building a short time ago, fetched his own motor car and drove off in the direction of Nice."

58

"But what about your espionage?" Thornton demanded. "Didn't you have him followed?"

"Our espionage only exists on the premises," was the cool reply. "It is not our business to trace the movements of our clients outside. Monsieur Froquet is quite well known and would, I am sure, be available if we needed him at any moment."

The two men both stared at Monsieur Thiers, momentarily aghast. Then, without waiting to say good night to him, they made for the door. They uttered no word of reproach but their manner left him with a vague sense of discomfort which he was soon to find justified.

They were both in good condition and in less than five minutes they were halfway down the steps leading on to the quay. The yacht lay before them brilliantly lit and with the gangway aft strongly guarded. Thornton pointed downwards.

"Isn't that just like Bradley?" he groaned. "The one night when he ought to lie close—look at the fool."

Roger's eyes followed his companion's pointing finger. Bradley, his white shirt almost dazzling in the strong light, had just strolled up the companion way, smoking a cigar and stood now in plain view, leaning over the rail and looking out to sea. He had evidently left the smoking-room door open behind him, letting out a brilliant shaft of illumination. They could even see him tapping the ash from his cigar on the rail.

"Oh, my God, what fools men are!" Thornton exclaimed angrily. "I've had that sort of thing to deal with all my life. They call it courage, I suppose. A night like this! Come on."

Before they could move, however, they saw a swiftly played-out drama which they neither of them ever forgot. From somewhere thirty or forty yards away in the blackness of the harbour came a faint spit of flame and what sounded like the sharp crack of a rifle. Bradley's cigar dropped from his fingers. They saw him clutch at the rail. A moment later he had collapsed. Simultaneously from the spot whence the flame had come, they heard the sound of a powerful motor and saw a dark shape without lights making for the harbour mouth. Upon the yacht itself was pandemonium. The men guarding the gangway rushed down the deck. A procession of stewards streamed out of the top of the companionway. The captain was shouting out orders and the men were busy lowering a launch when the motor boat shot between the green and red lights and turned southwards....

The chief steward and captain met Roger and Thornton as

they hurried on deck. Both were as incoherent as even brave men can be at times.

"His Lordship, sir," the captain stammered.

"He's been shot!" the steward gasped. "Shot by some one from a motor boat without any lights."

"Send for a doctor," Roger ordered. "Tell them to telephone from the deck. Any doctor—the nearest."

"My boy has gone already, sir," the captain replied. "He climbed on to the *Maria* alongside to save a few seconds. It won't be any use, though. You can look if you want to."

They pushed their way through the awed little group of men, and Roger, summoning all his fortitude, went down on his knees. A single glance, however, was sufficient. The fatal red spot told its own story. The bullet from the night had found its way to Bradley's heart.

CHAPTER IX

Paul Viotti tapped with his fingers upon the table and the little company of men who were seated around it abandoned their whispered conversation and leaned forward.

"Pierre arrives," Viotti announced. "I heard the three honks of his horn as he turned the corner. Soon we shall have news."

The room in which they were seated was a room of silence. There was no clanging of bells from an overhead railway, no shriek of sirens from the river, none of that breathless undernote of sound which broods over a great city. Even the mistral, which was blowing outside, was unheard, for there were no windows to catch the flying leaves, or chimneys to imprison and distort the whistle of the mountain wind. Yet the room itself had a queer sort of charm. The walls, left the natural white of rough plaster, were covered with sketches, crudely executed but with the brain of a master behind their bold conception. One, of an old galleon, occupied the whole of the end wall of the room, the sails of flaming red and the sea an indigo blue. A companion picture occupied the opposite wall but this one was broken by an arch enclosing an iron door. Two electric fans were turning noiselessly, rugs were spread upon the floor and luxurious easy-chairs with deep crimson cushions gave the place an air of almost fantastic luxury. Paul Viotti sat at the head of the table with Marcus Constantine on his left. Tom Meredith, Matthew Drane and Edward Staines were all in evidence. It seemed odd that in a country where restrictions were removed and the liquor and wine were of the best there were neither bottles nor decanters to be seen, nor was any one drinking.

There was a faint sound like a single beat upon a silver gong, a blue light flashed out in the wall opposite the place where Paul Viotti was seated. He pressed something with his foot under the heavy carpet. It was at once extinguished. Marcus Constantine rose to his feet, lounged across the room and withdrew the bolts of the door. A moment afterwards it swung back on its well-oiled hinges and Monsieur Pierre Viotti, ex-Mayor of La Bastide, swaggered in. Greetings were exchanged, the door was once more secured and Pierre Viotti seated himself with the others.

"The news," he announced, "is good."

His brother rubbed his hands together.

"It is always encouraging to hear that," he said, with a slow smile. "We make no mistakes. Our enterprises are all shielded, but one likes to know that miracles have not happened."

"These are the days," Pierre Viotti declared, "of brains and common sense and not of miracles."

"Continue then, my worthy brother," Paul enjoined him.

"Twenty kilometres from land the speed boat from Monaco Harbour in the blackness of night almost collided with a fishing boat from Nice. It was a triumph of navigation that, for there were no lights. The two men from the motor boat boarded the fishing smack. In ten minutes they were wearing the clothes and boots of the *pêcheurs* Niçois. The motor boat, less its engines, was scuttled. A loss, but what would you have? The depth charge went off inside and before it had sunk a couple of feet nothing was left but fragments. Our two friends, whom you know of, are by this time in Corsica. The fishing there too is good."

"And our young friend, the jeweller's son?" his brother asked.

"He is back in Marseilles," the other announced. "He has a post as gigolo at the Café of the Seven Sisters, but he pines for other work."

"He did his job well," Edward Staines observed. "For a young man of his type he possesses nerve."

"What about the notes?" Tom Meredith demanded.

Matthew Drane drew a handful from his pocket and passed one across the table. Every one examined it. There were no signs of a white dot.

"The notes have been washed in simple acid," Paul Viotti

61

confided. "There remains not the slightest trace of the English lord's folly. To-night they go into the treasury."

"Talking of the treasury," Marcus Constantine drawled, "would this, I wonder, be an appropriate moment—"

"But when do you ever talk about anything," Paul Viotti interrupted angrily, "except money? It is always the same, and Matthew is nearly as bad. Money! Bah! Is there nothing else in the world? We speak of that presently. But listen now to what other news there is my brother brings us. Are you sap-headed, you others, or had you forgotten that this is the day our good friend Louis Lavalle of Nice is to find shelter here with his little lady friend? There may be work to do before we can place him in safety. There may be even a little trouble. The division is always a delicate matter. Let us hear what my brother has to say."

"It is the best news which I have kept till the last," Pierre Viotti declared. "Everything has gone like the striking of a clock. Barely an hour ago Louis Lavalle sat in his place like an emperor. Five, ten, fifteen *mille*—what did it matter? They were all paid. The box must be replenished. Behold Louis on his way to the head cashier. Behold him return and linger to speak for a minute with pretty Marie Louise, the ladies' *vestiaire*. Louis Lavalle and Marie Louise are drinking a glass of champagne together at the present moment in Number Fourteen."

There was that gleam in Paul Viotti's eyes from which alone one knew that he was either a very wicked or a very greedy man.

"How much?" he asked softly.

"One million, four hundred thousand francs," the *rentier* from La Bastide said unctuously. "It is money that, yes? For ten days I have rehearsed that simple walk along the Casino and down the passage. It was an affair of clockwork. There is no one there who could say how or when Louise slipped from behind her counter. There is no one there who can say which way Louis Lavalle turned when he left the Casino. Yet there they sit, drinking champagne at the expense of my hotel, and they are where no one in all Nice will dream of looking for them."

Marcus Constantine was playing with his underlip and looking speculatively at Paul Viotti.

"How much of that one million, four hundred thousand francs, dear Chief," he asked, "would it seem to you fair that Louis Lavalle, the elderly cashier, should leave behind him?"

"It seems to me," Matthew Drane murmured, "that with too large a sum, an elderly man and a young girl might easily get into trouble."

Little furrows of mirth broke up the smoothness of Paul Viotti's face. It would not be too much to say that he grinned.

"We must take care of Louis Lavalle and his little friend," he said softly. "A good beginning has been made in that direction."

"You mean—"

"They are in salon Number Fourteen."

"And that is the one—?"

"That is the one."

* * * * *

"Gentlemen," Paul Viotti asked, "my friends and companions, we are here together—it is not wise that we meet too often. For Monsieur Lavalle and his pretty *vestiaire* there is plenty of time. Let us open our hearts to one another. Is there anything to be spoken of?"

"I should like to ask a question," Meredith said. "I should like to make it two questions and to address the first to you, Boss. We've been picking up the shekels along this coast now for some two months. The treasury pans out well. What about the safety side of it?"

Paul Viotti sank down a little lower in his chair and his fingers played with his platinum and gold watch chain.

"Tom, my boy," he said, "compared to what things would be like, if we broke into similar business on the other side, this is pie. You and I, Tom, started things in Marseilles. We left the place with the best part of a million francs and I think I dare say, Tom, eh, without a stain upon our characters, without a black mark against our names?"

"Sure," Meredith agreed. "Only they weren't our own names."

"Or our own personalities," Viotti pointed out "To-day, for instance, we do not look at all as we looked at Marseilles."

"I give you Marseilles," Tom Meredith conceded graciously. "What about Cannes?"

Viotti stroked his chin.

"Cannes was difficult," he admitted. "We were obliged to use severe measures at our very first enterprise, and I think we were wise to leave by the Train Bleu for London. London meant for us Avignon and a motor ride to Nice! Nice," Paul Viotti went on, with a little roll of the head. "What a mercy that the whole world does not know of Nice!"

"When I think of those bars!" Tom Meredith murmured in ecstasy. "The tourists streaming into the casinos, the suckers everywhere!"

"You didn't seem to stay there long," Marcus Constantine reminded him.

"Nice is an Eldorado at any time of the year," Paul Viotti explained. "Monte Carlo has only a season. I pass on to Monte Carlo. Well, what have we done at Monte Carlo? I will tell you, my dear friends. We have been clever. We have been damn clever. This is what we do. We get rid of the quitter: not only do we get rid of him, but we choose the moment when he has a full wallet. Good for the treasury, yes. And then," he went on, striking the table with the palm of his hand, "more cleverness. Every one wants that the police look for the murderer of Luke Cheyne. What do we do? A great triumph. We know of Sam Crowley. We got one of his lads when Tim Rooney ran amuck and dared us on that five hundred cases of Scotch. Crowley meant having us. We killed two birds with one stone. We write a nice little confession for Sam Crowley and we make the Monte Carlo police very happy. We drop Crowley into the harbour. Very good place. Not a nice man, Crowley. Every one very happy.... Still, we look about for money. We find that English lord who talks so much. Oh, it was sad about him! What a foolish man to waste his afternoon with those *mille* notes."

"Hold on a minute," Staines admonished. "Supposing your brother's pigeon had fallen down there, we might have found a spot of trouble. The English lord was a fool, all right, and he's gone the journey fools generally go when they come up against us, but he got past us with the notes."

Paul Viotti rolled his head, smiling all the time.

"My brother, he makes no mistakes," he said. "He couldn't pick a squealer. Bad young men he knows many of, gigolos in and out of work at the casinos, bar loungers, young foreigners who have lost their money gambling and stay on. Bad enough for the knife, any of them, but not squealers. No one in this world would have got that young man to say that the notes came from anywhere but the bar, and there's no one could prove that they didn't."

"That's fine," Meredith declared. "You've come through all right with your shoes on, Chief. Now there's the other question that's been bothering me a bit. Do any of you think that that young American chap down in Monte Carlo—Roger Sloane—is getting wise to us?"

There was a somewhat impressive silence. Only Pierre Viotti was breathing heavily. There was so much that he wanted to say. Had his time come?

"Of the young man," Paul Viotti said deliberately, "I know nothing. I work from behind. Some of you others know the tricks of

64

the swell society here better than I. My brother's coming along, eh, Pierre? But I work as I did in New York—from behind."

Staines tapped with his fingers upon the table.

"I do not think that there is any immediate danger to be feared from Roger Sloane or from his friend, Lord Erskine. I can tell you this, though; they have the *will* to interfere, all right, and they have occasionally glimmerings of intelligence. They were on the spot all the time in this Lord Bradley business, and if our man in the motor boat had been a quarter of an hour later, they'd have dragged Bradley away. They are wise to the fact that there's something going on, all right, but I think I can answer for it that at present they haven't any idea where to look."

"I agree," Marcus Constantine said meditatively. "At the same time, they must be regarded as a possible danger. They are two young men with nothing to do, neither of them are gamblers, so they have little to occupy their thoughts, and they are afflicted with that youthful Anglo-Saxon impulse to thrust themselves blindly into other people's business if they think it is being conducted on lines which are contrary to their principles."

Paul Viotti moved uneasily in his chair.

"Hi, hi, hi!" he remonstrated. "Such long words. Such long sentences. I speak English good but I like my talk simple."

"Well, I'll make it simple," Edward Staines intervened. "Roger Sloane might at any time be a danger to us. He has written several stories of crime and detection and the subject evidently appeals to him. He is a born meddler. He is not worth running any risk about, for the moment, but if we could find him sitting upon his own or any one else's moneybags, we should do ourselves a doubly good turn if we—er—dealt with him. Furthermore, if he should show any disposition to hang around these premises when there is anything doing, Tom had better see that the 'Wolves' get at him."

The bell of a little squat telephone, evidently part of a private installation, tinkled musically. Paul Viotti listened at the receiver and spoke a few words in Italian. Then he rose to his feet.

"My comrades," he announced, "the affair in Number Fourteen demands our attention. Before we proceed with it, let us come to an understanding. Has any one a suggestion?"

"It's the girl that's the nuisance," Marcus Constantine observed dubiously. "Men can be made to disappear in a most miraculous fashion, especially defaulting cashiers, but there's always trouble with the women. You can't make a bargain with them, for they never keep their word."

65

"Never knew a jane in my life who knew what it was to possess a sense of honour," Meredith observed.

"No good jawing about it beforehand," Staines interposed. "Let's see how the land lies."

"Very well, my friends," Paul Viotti concluded. "Pierre and I will proceed to business."

CHAPTER X

Somewhere about the time when the little council of men had decided upon the treatment to be meted out to Roger, should he be found haunting the premises of the Hôtel du Soleil at an unpropitious moment, that young man, in mackintosh and cap, pushed open the door of the bar and entered, a little breathless from his struggle with the wind. His old acquaintance, Sam, leaned over the counter and watched his approach without enthusiasm. The welcoming smile of his class was absent from his lips, his light-coloured eyebrows were contracted in a frown, his manner was furtive, his husky tone charged with warning.

"I'm telling you, Mr. Sloane," he said earnestly, "I don't want to serve you—and that's straight. I wanted to tell you so when you called in the other day, but I thought that maybe it was an accident and I shouldn't see you again. You may have popped in by accident this evening, sure. Very well, then, pop off again. The weather isn't going to be any better and a drink here won't do you any good."

His flabby fingers, upon one of which sparkled what appeared to be a genuine diamond ring, were spread flat upon the mahogany counter. His mouth, twisted a trifle on one side, as though with the earnestness of his speech, disclosed a row of unpleasantly irregular teeth. He was a person of unattractive appearance, yet there was a ring of sincerity about his appeal. Roger, whose recollections of the man were entirely favorable, was considerably impressed. It seemed to him that he could feel the sense of danger stirring around, feel the atmosphere of it in that large, over-decorated, over-furnished barroom with its smell of freshly cut pine wood, its solid leather divans, which looked as though they had never been sat upon, its easy-chairs and stools, which all had the air of having been just removed from the factory. The place, notwithstanding the comparative extravagance of its furnishings, did not seem real or natural.... Roger pointed to the window.

"Look at that," he said.

The weather was certainly excuse enough to drive any one to seek shelter. The trees in a grove of olives on the other side of the road were bent almost double and the air was filled with floating fragments of leaves and small branches. Shrieks and moans seemed to come from the tops of the thickly growing pines, cuffed and tortured by the mistral. The freshly joined window-panes of the bar groaned and creaked and a cloud of dust and refuse from the road swept past the window.

"What are you doing up here, anyway, on a day like this?" the barman demanded.

Roger might have replied differently but it was his humour to temporise if possible. There were three remarkably unpleasant looking roadmen in the corner, who had the air of having abandoned their tasks in a hurry and who kept on whispering and casting suspicious glances towards him. There was no one else in the room except his two friends, the elderly Italian musicians.

"I'm staying at Monte Carlo," Roger explained. "For two days tennis or golf have been impossible. I wanted exercise, so I walked to La Turbie. I am now on my way back and I want a drink. Give me a whisky and soda and a glass of wine for Monsieur and Madame, and I will start off at once. Monsieur and Madame come here every day, they tell me. You can learn from them that I am a harmless person enough."

There came a chorus of words from the old couple, who understood a little English. Roger's cheeks, under other conditions, might well have grown hot with their eager praise. Monsieur was a great gentleman—the kindest-hearted and most generous of all their patrons. Their torrent of phrases was disjointed but voluble, and all the time Roger knew that there was something behind it and that that something was fear.

The barman turned unwillingly to the shelf behind and dragged down a bottle of very superior whisky. He poured a liberal portion into a tumbler, opened a bottle of Perrier and pushed both ungraciously across the counter. Then he filled two glasses with red wine and carried them to the old people. Roger laid down the money and strolled across towards them, his tumbler in his hand. The woman was now talking in rapid Italian to the barman, who shook his head sullenly.

"I ain't getting you, ma'am," he assured her. "I speak good Broadway American and no other language. Now then, Mr. Sloane,

67

down with that drink, if you please. We're not serving any more customers to-day and it's for your good that you get out of here as quickly as you can."

Roger asked the man no questions, which must have seemed strange to him. There was something wrong about the place and in his bones he knew that the sooner he was out of it the better. Nevertheless, with a queer sort of obstinacy, he lingered. He drank half the contents of his tumbler and toyed with the rest. The barman crossed the room, touched one of the three roadmen on the shoulder and whispered in his ear. With a grimace the fellow rose to his feet, turned up his coat collar and slouched towards the door. He opened it and took his leave, buffeting his way up the road. The barman remained whispering for a minute to the other two. The woman, who was seated by Roger's side, took up her guitar, strummed a few notes of an Italian song, but in the middle improvised several quavering pointed words to the familiar music.

"*Il Signore è in pericolo. Parta subito!* Go quickly away from this terrible place!"

The barman came back with his eyes fixed upon the contents of Roger's glass. The latter raised it to his lips and set it down empty, turning up his coat collar, lit a cigarette and with a farewell salute to his two old friends, moved away towards the door. He was quivering with the sense of some imminent happening but he tried his best to keep all signs of it from his tone and manner.

"Well, good night, Sam," he said. "The next time I come, I hope I shall find you in a more hospitable frame of mind."

"Shouldn't come again, if I was you," was the gruff reply. "This bar ain't going to pay and we're shutting up. There's no trade here till the summer."

Roger stepped out into the storm of wind and swung along downhill with his back to the gale. The road was a corkscrew one and before he reached the first bend he turned around. The bar itself seemed to be a sort of annex to the hotel, although in the larger building the shutters were all tightly drawn and there was no sign of life. At the top of the road, just where it diverged into the main highway, Roger could plainly see the figure of a man waiting—the man, it seemed to him, who had left the bar. He drew into the shadow of a dwarfed, but thickly growing oak tree overhanging the wall, and throwing away his cigarette, waited. Presently he heard a shrill whistle. Almost instantly men streamed out of the bar! One of them started down the road in Roger's direction, the others climbed the wall into the olive grove and in a moment or two he heard their approaching footsteps crashing through the long grass and thickets.

Suddenly the idea of the whole thing flashed upon Roger. They were beaters and he was the quarry and to make things more than ever difficult, at the last moment three other men issued from the bar and, climbing the wall by its side, started off towards the lower stretch of road.

Flight, precipitate and urgent flight, was Roger's first impulse. The sinister-looking bar, the strangely sung warning of Madame, the harsh but impressive advice of the man behind the counter—all these found swift prominence in his memory. He stole along in the shadow of the trees until he was at the bend of the road. Then, at the last moment, he formed new plans. The sound of the sticks beating their way through the grove and the memory of many a wild cock pheasant in his younger days inspired him! To continue his way downwards was madness. To deal with the one man at the corner and continue straight ahead gave him only the scantiest of chances, for there were the other three to be dealt with later on. He climbed the wall instead into the grove, cut across its last angle and in the shadow of a somewhat higher hedge turned his back to Monte Carlo and half crept, half ran up towards the main road. To his left he could hear the mumble of voices and the occasional crashing of a stick. Once or twice he caught the flash of an electric torch. He bent as low as he could and stole along at right angles to the advancing line. It was a stiff climb and, although he was in good condition, he felt the tugging of his heartstrings as he reached the top of the field. For a moment he paused here for breath. He was outside the man on the extreme left by now. He crouched more than ever, pushed his way through an irregular, straggling hedge, and after he had gained about twenty paces, looked back once more. The man on the extreme left of the line was well below him now and, as Roger had hoped, he wheeled at the end of the grove and started on his way back towards the byroad. Once he paused and began to poke about in some bushes, and Roger gave a soft whistle of relief as he saw that he was carrying an old-fashioned sporting gun under his right arm. If he had made any attempt at flight, he knew now that he would have run the risk of a pellet in his leg at any moment. Somehow or other, he had no fancy to return to that mysterious bar a wounded man.

Roger concluded his climb in leisurely fashion and reached the main road soon after the sound of the footsteps crashing downwards had ceased. He paused here for a moment to light a well-earned cigarette. Then came the question—towards Nice or Mentone? To the left or to the right? Which way should he turn? A great deal of adventure might lie to the left. Almost certain safety to be found on the right. Chance helped him to make up his mind. He realised quite suddenly that for his walk he was wearing a pair of very old shooting breeches. He clapped his hand to his pocket. He was right. He had worn them on a mountain expedition, a two day's tramp, the last time, and there in his hip pocket was a small, but very modern and useful revolver. Roger turned it out and examined it. It was fully loaded and a very adequate weapon. He turned to the left.

It took him about twenty minutes of uneventful walking to arrive at the spot where the highway branched. The light had faded now and in the semi-darkness he moved a few yards down the road and stood listening. About fifty yards below on the right was the bar and the hotel, but not a single flicker of light could he see from any one of the windows. He still waited and listened intently. He had expected to hear the distant voices or footsteps of his pursuers returning, but he heard nothing. Behind him was a fairly constant progress of motor cars and other vehicles but from the hotel itself or its immediate environments there came no sound at all. The possession of that hard little object which he drew now from his pocket lent him a courage which otherwise he might certainly not have possessed. He moved slowly through the obscurity down the lane. With every step the darkness seemed to become more intense, owing to the sharp slope on his left and the thickly growing pines which threw a shadow over the road. He reached the hotel. To all appearance it was entirely deserted. He passed on to the bar. Every light in it was extinguished. There were no signs of any movement, no sound of voices. He stepped cautiously over a low hedge and made his way around towards the back. Suddenly he stopped short and cowered beneath a mimosa tree. There were footsteps close at hand, the crash of a small gate. Some one flung open a door and a light streamed out into the darkness. He heard a rough, unfamiliar voice ask an eager question which, so far as he could understand it, referred to him.

"Any luck?"

"No."

"Blast! Half a dozen guns and you never put his light out!"

"We never saw him," a surly voice replied.

There were more oaths, more footsteps, a slamming of doors, the hum of many voices. In face of that frantically expressed wish for his decease, Roger stepped warily back into the road and, after a brief period of hesitation, returned cautiously to where it rejoined the Corniche. Here, in the lights of the motor cars flashing by every few minutes, he felt a sense of security. In the shadow of that hotel all the old presentiment that evil was afoot had seized him. The mistral was dying down. A small clump of cypresses on his right stood stark against the sky. The front of the hotel was lifeless. Was he, Roger asked himself, obeying an instinct of cowardice by resting there, or inspiration? Inspiration without a doubt. Excitement was alive again in his pulses. A slim, dark figure had emerged from the hotel and was coming towards him with incredible swiftness.

CHAPTER XI

With every flying footstep the approaching figure gained outline and distinctness. A woman! No, a girl, dressed from head to foot in black. Once she paused to look over her shoulder. Then she came on faster than ever, and from the ease of her movements and the unhampered grace of them, Roger judged that she was scantily dressed.

When she saw him, she threw up her arms and he thought that she would have screamed.

"Who are you? You are one of them!" she cried.

"I certainly am not," he assured her. "I was wondering what was going on down there."

She shivered violently and caught hold of his arm. She threw her head back and looked up at him. She was amazingly attractive in the way of the Niçoise—large soft eyes, full lips and clear complexion.

"Don't ask," she begged. "It is all horrible. Get me to Nice, I implore you. I can leave at nine for Marseilles. Oh, Monsieur, you will be kind."

Roger had no idea of being anything else and fate was certainly with him, for at that moment a P.L.M. bus, half full, came lumbering around the corner. He hailed it and half lifted her in. From the doorway he cast one glance behind. The front of the hotel and bar were still black and obscure but on the bushes and stunted trees in the garden behind shafts of moving light were playing. What was going on there, Roger wondered. The girl knew!

The girl knew—but would she tell? For the first quarter of an hour she was absolutely silent. She clung to her companion almost passionately. The people in the bus, taking them for lovers, looked away with smiles and whispers. Her fingers dug into his arm and her head was never far from his shoulder. By degrees the terror seemed to fade from her luminous eyes. Once she almost smiled at him. As the lights of Nice greeted them, she sat up, her fingers strayed around her hair and she straightened her hat. Then she returned to the shelter of Roger's arm, leaning back, somewhat to his embarrassment, as though it were her natural place.

"The good God be thanked for you!" she murmured. "You are strong and you speak French. You are my protector."

Roger coughed a little uneasily. So far as her sex was concerned, he had his own plans.

"Protect you from what?" he demanded. "What was going on in that house?"

She shuddered, but for the moment made no reply. She drew a little closer to him. He remained firm, however.

"You must tell me what is going on in there," he insisted. "Was any one being ill treated? It may be necessary to telephone to the police."

She shook her head.

"Not the police," she protested emphatically. "It is not a matter for the police."

"But I am convinced that the people in that house are a bad lot," he told her. "I blundered in and they would have shot me if they could. They evidently had some mischief on to-night. Look how terrified you were when I found you."

"I was terrified for fear I should not get away," she said simply. "Now that I have found you, I am happy. We are here amongst the lights."

"But what am I to do with you?" Roger asked. "I live at Monte Carlo. To tell you the truth, I still have a feeling that I ought to do something about that hotel."

She waved to the conductor and stopped the bus. They were at the commencement of the Promenade des Anglais, opposite a straggling line of restaurants with outside tables upon the terrace. She led the way to one of them, but she would have nothing to do with the *al fresco* portion. She passed swiftly through to the almost empty interior and chose a secluded corner table.

"Am I not terrible?" she asked, her arm stealing once more through his and her lips pouting most provocatively an inch or two away. "I am hungry. After all I have been through, I am starving."

"Come to think of it, so am I," Roger assured her, reaching for the menu.

"And I am thirsty."

Here Roger became even more enthusiastic. Afterwards he

reflected that it was seldom he had enjoyed a couple of cocktails so thoroughly, nor was his companion far behind him in appreciation. Then they washed and he telephoned for his car. The horrors of little over an hour ago seemed immensely exaggerated.

"And now," he insisted, when the sole was served and wine was in their glasses, "your name, please."

"Marie Louise. And yours?"

"Roger. Now tell me, if you please, the story of the hotel."

Her pretty face was puckered with perplexity.

"It is more difficult than I thought," she confessed.

"Why?"

"Because I am not quite sure whether afterwards you will think that I am nice. I am not really honest."

"Few people are," he reassured her.

"I was with a thief at that hotel," she confided.

"I am closely connected with the criminal world myself," he told her.

She laughed derisively.

"Anyhow, you are nice," she said, and her left hand, unoccupied for the moment, stole into his. "I shall tell you everything because I still need your help. You have not, by any chance, recognised me?"

"I have been puzzling once or twice," he admitted.

"Well, I am a cloakroom attendant at the Casino here. Are you ashamed to be having dinner with me?"

"Don't be absurd. Continue, please."

"I am so tired of young men. They are so monotonous. They want, want, want one thing. I am for the life regular. I wish for marriage."

"Quite right," Roger approved.

She was perfectly serious for the first time. She was discussing her own plans of life and to her they were the most important consideration in the world.

"A husband, a correct ménage, an automobile, a child—perhaps. As for a lover," she went on, fingering the stem of her wineglass thoughtfully, "that would depend. I think—yes. But he must not interfere with the ménage."

"Very prudent," he murmured.

She flashed a quick glance at him. Perhaps the shadow of a blush trembled at the corners of her lips and faintly stained her cheeks.

"*Voilà.* You understand. A Monsieur, elderly but *gentil*, a chef—not an ordinary croupier—approached me at the Casino. He

73

wished for marriage, but marriage with a *vieux* having the salary only of a chef! For me, you understand, *incroyable*, incroyable! I tell him so. He is almost crazy. He considers how to make money. There is only one way for such a man, of course. He must rob the Casino."

Roger gave a little start. She noticed it with surprise.

"But *mon ami*," she argued, "the Casino robs every one. Why should not some one rob the Casino? It is scarcely a crime, that. Only Henri, he alone would not have been clever enough. A short time ago he came to me very excited. He has made friends with some very clever people—*du monde serieux*—not ordinary thieves. They show him how to do it. I am to help. They have brains. They make it quite easy. The chef, carrying the *caisse* to the cashier's office, passes my cloakroom. In a moment it is in a bag. I give a ticket. It is gone. A brief visit to my retiring room. The box goes on its way, but it is empty."

"I see," Roger murmured. "How long before the box is examined?"

"One hour. It is enough. Henri's friends—I do not know who they were—rush us away in a car. We reach that hotel. They show us into a sitting room and we are gay with champagne. Then a man comes whom I have never seen before and the arrangements for division begin, I see that things are not going well. There is a violent dispute. More and more I get frightened. I have had enough. I am, as you English say, fed up. Henri does not act like a man. The other bullies him. I see that there will be little left for us, and little is not enough to marry on, with a man like Henri. *Eh, bien*, I slip away while they quarrel. I meet you. *Voilà!*"

"So you've thrown your hand in," Roger remarked. "Perhaps you were wise. But what are you going to do now?"

That insinuating little hand was creeping into his again. She leaned forward and laughed in his face.

"What do you advise, Roger?"

"Never mind what I advise," he answered severely. "I expect you have made your own plans."

"I might like yours better—if you have any," she whispered.

"Well, I haven't," he assured her. "I might do my duty, of course, and hand you over to the police. How should you like that?"

She clapped her hands gaily.

"Oh, la, la! That to me would be equal. I should have my picture in all the papers, I should have a wonderful avocat to defend me, I should be a first offender, scarcely go to prison at all, and when I came out every one would want to marry me. Of course, a *crime passionel* would make me more famous," she reflected, "but this would do."

"Well, as I am not proposing to hand you over to the police, let me hear your plans for yourself," Roger invited.

She indulged in a little grimace.

"You still come in," she warned him. "You must lend me the money to hire a car which will take me to Marseilles. There I am safe. I have friends who will take care of me."

"I will do that," he agreed. "But why not the train?"

"I should have to wait till the morning," she pointed out. "The night trains are so full and some one would be sure to recognise me. There is one at midnight—"

"What an idiot I am," he interrupted. "Of course, you would be recognised at the station. A ridiculous risk. You see that coupé out there?"

"Is it not lovely?" she sighed. "A Packard, I believe. The car I should love to own."

"Well, it's mine," he told her, "and if you like, I will send you to Marseilles in it."

She clapped her hands.

"*Merveilleuse.* But what about you?"

"I can take a taxi back to Monte Carlo."

Roger produced his pocketbook. He would have given her more but she would only take two *mille.*

"It is plenty," she assured him. "My friends have money. They will take care of me.... One more little crème de menthe, please, before I go. A packet of cigarettes, yes?"

Roger ministered to her wants.

"And now," he said, "I am going to ask you something. Tell me about that mysterious hotel."

She shook her head.

"*Mon ami,*" she regretted, "but what is there to tell? Henri did not confide in me. We were to meet the friend there who had helped him. That is all. We arrived. The place was very empty. A barman fetched a *maître d'hôtel* and he showed us into a charming sitting room. They brought champagne of the best. I was quite content but Henri was nervous. Then I was sent into the next room and told to wait. Some one came to make plans with Henri. They quarrelled. Oh, how they quarrelled! It seemed to me that the man who had helped him wished to take everything. I was frightened and I stole away. Then I met you. That is the whole story."

"The whole of it?"

"Everything."

"It isn't much," Roger declared ruefully.

"It is something to have met you," she whispered, holding his hand.

* * * * *

Somehow or other it was very nearly eleven o'clock before Roger tucked Marie Louise into his very comfortable coupé and gave the chauffeur his instructions. She suddenly leaned forward, took his face between her hands and kissed him.

"You wouldn't like to drive me to Marseilles," she whispered, her lips very close to his. "Your chauffeur could go to sleep behind!"

"The best of luck to you," he wished her. "And don't get caught."

Then Roger looked up and saw a gendarme coming quickly across the road to him, very large and imposing. His heart sank. Poor little Marie Louise!

"Your car was standing on the wrong side of the road, sir," the man said severely. "I was obliged to move your chauffeur."

Roger wiped the perspiration from his forehead, although it wasn't really a warm evening.

"Many thanks, Monsieur," he answered, as he drew the required ten-franc note from his pocket.

* * * * *

The hum of conversation directly Roger crossed the threshold of the Sporting Club bar on the following night warned him at once that something unusual had happened. His aunt Lady Julia, Erskine, Savonarilda, Thornton, the Terence Browns, Maggie Saunders—in fact, the whole crowd, were seated at the round table. They appeared to regard him as they might have done an absconding criminal who had returned to the fold.

"Where on earth have you been to, Roger?" his aunt demanded, fixing him steadily through her lorgnettes. "Where were you all day yesterday?"

He found a chair and lit a cigarette.

"I was fed up with this weather," he confided. "Two days indoors are my limit. Yesterday I went for a tramp to La Turbie, then I took a bus into Nice, had dinner there quietly—at the Pergola, if you want to know—came back latish and went straight to bed. This morning I had to be in Cannes for the tennis. Anything fresh?"

"Do you mean to say that you have not heard?" his aunt exclaimed.

76

Thornton's cold eyes never left Roger's face. The latter could only guess at the meaning of that steadfast gaze.

"I have heard nothing," he replied. "No more tragedies, I hope?"

"I wouldn't say that," Thornton observed, "but our little crowd is out of it this time, for a wonder. A croupier from Nice got away from the Casino yesterday afternoon with one million, four hundred thousand francs!"

"This sounds interesting," Roger exclaimed. "Have they caught him?"

"What happened was this," Thornton explained, his eyes once more burrowing into his opposite neighbour's—"it is the oddest thing in the world that you should be the last person to hear about it—"

"Steady on," Roger begged. "I read the *Eclaireur* from beginnng to end this morning and there wasn't a word about it."

"You should know better than to be surprised at that," Thornton remarked calmly. "It appears that there were two croupiers in the affair, or rather one croupier and a person who ranked as a chef, and a girl—that very good-looking cloakroom attendant. It was a wonderfully arranged scheme, of course, and the chef—who was the older man—and the girl got away with the money. It seems that they left in a motor car, made their way to some unknown rendezvous between Nice and Mentone, where they met some one else connected with the affair who had also come up from Nice, and one gathers that there was a grand dispute about the division of the spoils. The croupier was found this morning dying at the bottom of one of the gorges near Eze. He was just able to babble a few words of explanation before he died."

"Any clues as to his murder?" Roger asked swiftly.

Thornton shook his head.

"Not yet. There are rumours that another croupier from the Casino was concerned, but he was certainly not with them."

"And what about the money?"

"Well, it seems that the man was terribly incoherent, but in his last few breaths he tried to explain. So far as one can put the story together, it seems that when they realised that the croupier had not got it, they threw him over the precipice and rushed off to find the girl. This is where the humorous side of the story comes in. The girl had become frightened, hearing the quarrel, and had slipped away in the darkness with one million, four hundred thousand francs pinned in her chemise! According to all we can gather, no one has seen or heard of her since!"

"The girl did *what?*" Roger gasped.

"She escaped from the meeting place—it was a wild sort of night, as you may remember—made her way up on to the road and must have boarded a bus, or some vehicle or other. Anyway, she has disappeared with the whole of the stolen money, and neither she nor the young croupier have been heard of since."

Roger knocked the ash from his cigarette into a plate by his side. He thought of his car filled with red roses just back from Marseilles and the two *mille* in the scented envelope with just a single word of thanks. There was more humour in the story than even Thornton imagined!

CHAPTER XII

Lady Julia beckoned imperiously to her nephew to resume his seat. There had been a small luncheon party on the terrace of her Cap Martin villa and Roger was the last remaining guest.

"I shan't keep you five minutes," she promised. "I have a bone to pick with you, young man. What have you been doing to my little protégée?"

Roger was genuinely surprised.

"Why, I scarcely ever see her," he protested. "She works most of the daytime and, as you know yourself, she never goes out in the evening unless you take her around to show off those silly frocks. What's the matter with her?"

Lady Julia uttered a sound which could only be described as a snort.

"She's worrying about something. She always had a queer abstracted expression but lately it's worse than ever. She's in trouble of some sort, I'm sure."

"Well, it's the first I've heard about it," Roger declared. "It's rather a coincidence that you should speak about her to-day, though. I'm due to meet her in ten minutes and take her for a drive."

"If I thought," Lady Julia said severely, "that you had been playing with that child behind my back, I should have a few words to say to you, young man!"

Roger and his aunt never failed to indulge in plain speaking, and this time he did not hesitate to follow her lead.

"Don't be a fool," he enjoined. "Have you ever seen or heard of my doing that sort of thing?"

"That will do," she stopped him. "I'm quite willing to believe that you know nothing about it, but all the same she has something on her mind. I have no doubt everything is all right, Roger, but remember this. Of course you—like all these other crazy young men—are half in love with her, but if you ever let it go too far—I'm an old woman of the world, you know, but I mean it—I'll never forgive you."

"Tell me what you mean in plain words," Roger begged.

"Have you made her your mistress?"

He laughed bitterly. There was one little chapter of his past life of which his aunt knew nothing.

"I have not nor am I thinking of doing so," he assured her. "Since we are on the subject, however, what if I married her?"

Lady Julia looked at him keenly.

"Why shouldn't you?" she demanded. "Men seem to marry anything nowadays. Better Jeannine, even though she is a peasant's brat, than one of those musical comedy young women whom I can't bear the sight of. Perhaps the child's in love with you. That may be what's the matter with her."

"I wish she were!" Roger exclaimed. "She's the queerest kid I ever knew. If I thought that she really cared—"

Lady Julia reached for her novel and rang the bell.

"Well, take her for a drive, anyway," she enjoined. "Thanks for playing host for me. Dull crowd, I'm afraid, but one has to go through with a duty show now and then. See you at the Club to-night."

* * * * *

Satan or one of his phantom whelps must have induced Prétat's artist for the moment to dress Jeannine in that fawn-coloured and deep brown frock which blended so marvellously with her hair and eyes and to have designed for her head the distracting little cap which completed the toilette. At Longchamps, perhaps, at the beginning of the season, or in the Bois de Boulogne on a sunny morning one might have seen the type—not here. No wonder people's eyes followed her from every direction.... Roger brought the car to a standstill by the side of the curb at the appointed spot. He threw open the door and Jeannine, stepping in, sank down amongst the cushions by his side, a fascinating *tout ensemble* of silky wool and chiffon, silk stockings, trim patent shoes and Prétat's own perfume.

79

"So at last you really invite me to elope with you," she exclaimed. "What Paradise shall we seek?"

"Before you came," Roger replied, "I was in such a mundane mood that I actually thought of Nice. We might have an early tea there and watch the afternoon dancing at that unfortunate Casino which has just been robbed. In that case, though, you must have a coat."

"Indeed I will not," she objected. "My orders are to wear this costume for the day without a coat. You observe, however, that I have a little cape on my arm. If I am cold coming back, I will sit nearer to you, and I must be home by eight. We have no show this afternoon but at ten o'clock we exhibit evening frocks at the Hôtel de Paris."

"What a life of slavery," he murmured, as they turned upward towards the Corniche.

"It must seem so in comparison with yours."

"You have grown nimbler of tongue lately, little one," Roger told her.

"It is not that I have much practice," she sighed. "Madame Vinay speaks but seldom and then generally to grumble. Your aunt, who is always kind, is too witty for me and she speaks so much in English, which is different. And you—you are always with the grave Monsieur Thornton or the frivolous Lord Erskine or playing your games of golf or tennis."

"On the contrary, I am a working man," Roger assured her. "Only just now—"

"Oh, la, la," she interrupted, laughing gaily. "You are a working man—yes. How much since you returned to Monte Carlo?"

"Not much," he confessed. "Half a story, one article and two verses."

"People are saying," she went on, throwing her hat on to a vacant seat and leaning forward to look down at the gradually unfolding panorama, "that strange things are happening in Monte Carlo."

"They wouldn't be far out, either," he observed.

"They say that strange people are moving about undiscovered. Certainly there have been tragedies. Has it always been like this?"

"Not quite."

"A man murdered in the Sporting Club," she meditated. "Another in the harbour—or was it a suicide? A great English milord shot upon his yacht. There must be wicked people about, Monsieur Roger."

"There certainly are," he agreed.

"But amongst them all," she went on, in a graver tone, "there does not live a man so wicked as one whom you and I both know."

"Viotti—the ex-Mayor of La Bastide!" he exclaimed.

She acquiesced silently. Roger glanced towards her with a smile upon his lips.

"My dear," he protested, "Viotti is little better than a peasant. They say that he has come into a great fortune, or has a millionaire brother or something, but what can that do for him? The man is a jest."

She did not smile. She was, on the contrary, looking very serious indeed.

"Monsieur Roger," she said, "that is a man so wicked that he would be capable of anything and if you think that he has not brains, you are wrong."

"What do you know about him?" Roger asked.

She did not answer for a moment. He repeated the question.

"I do not wish for trouble," she said, "and you, Monsieur Roger, you are the kindest person I ever knew, but you have the temper of a Lucifer! I am glad that you have," she added, a little recklessly, "for the most wonderful memory I ever carry with me is the memory of one moment when there was a flame in your eyes and I was saved."

"Oh, that," Roger scoffed, "that was nothing. I was angry, of course. I hate brutality—but those days have gone."

"There is a portion of them which remains," she said calmly. "We live our lives in different places but the brute still lives in Monsieur Viotti and sometimes the fear remains with me."

"He has not dared to molest you?"

She laid her fingers softly upon her companion's arm.

"What he does is within the conventions," she declared. "There is nothing that any one can do about it. He speaks to and visits Madame Vinay. He has offered her presents. He wishes, he says, to see me with her to make friends, to speak of the past. That is useless. I could have no friendship for Monsieur Viotti."

"Presumptuous brute!" Roger muttered.

"Again I tell you something," Jeannine went on. "I wish for no friends amongst the young ladies at the *magasin*, but one there is who is all the time offering me invitations and civilities of every sort. She and the young man she calls her 'boy' took me for a motor drive on Sunday. We stayed for an *apéritif* at that new hotel between us and Eze, near where the croupier was found at the bottom of the gorge. Monsieur Viotti was there at the bar alone. It appeared that he knew my friends and he invited us to luncheon in a salon there.

My friends were angry with me that I refused but I went and sat outside and would accept nothing. You would not understand, but I have a great fear of that man, Monsieur Roger, and when you speak of these people who move about underground in Monte Carlo, to whom murder is nothing, then I think of him! I believe that he is one of them."

Roger shook his head.

"Swear, Jeannine," he begged, "that if he ever addresses or annoys you in any way, you will come to me."

"Whom else have I to go to?"

"Then put him out of your thoughts," Roger insisted. "The man is nothing but a peasant dressed up like a popinjay. He has not the brains to be anything more vicious than a village bully."

* * * * *

Nevertheless, Roger looked with more curiosity than ever before at Pierre Viotti, ex-Mayor of La Bastide, when on entering the bar of the afternoon cabaret at the Casino they saw him seated on a high stool, talking earnestly to two young men who, from the extravagance of their costume, their patent shoes and purple socks, were apparently gigolos. Roger and Jeannine sank into easy-chairs which gave them a view of the show. Roger ordered a cocktail for himself, an orange juice for Jeannine and tried to look at Monsieur Viotti with new and more critically apprizing eyes. He was dressed, as he always seemed to be, in a suit which was apparently brand-new and which was cut, as all his clothes were, a little closely to his rotund, but athletic body. His cravat was florid, his shirt and collar were of French design, but passable, his hair was smoothly brushed and the man himself curled and perfumed. His cheeks retained some of the sunburn of the fields. They were pudgy, brick red in hue and his eyes—restless, glittering eyes they were—were nevertheless of good colour and full of fire. He was stout but agile. His chin was a little pointed. There was a roll of fat at the back of his neck which should have been a warning to him, otherwise he seemed like a man of vigour. He talked with many gestures but he appeared to talk with effect. Roger glanced at the two young men who were leaning towards him and it seemed to him that there was an expression in their faces as of men who listened because they had to—men who were compelled to stay just where they were and to answer as they were supposed to answer. Roger admitted the fact with reluctance, but there was no doubt about it that those few minutes' contemplation of the man considerably changed his ideas. It was absurd to imagine that he should be one of the disorganising forces of the Principality but, on the other hand, there was something about him, beyond the pompous self-sufficiency of the suddenly enriched peasant. With all his newly acquired wealth, he was not letting himself run to seed. He was still living a life of a sort.

"Shall we dance?" Roger asked Jeannine, as the orchestra started up with a particularly promising tune.

She glanced at him with an air of surprise. Nevertheless, she rose promptly to her feet. It was just then that Monsieur Viotti, having dismissed his two companions, swung a little farther around on his stool and saw them. He was holding the rail of the bar with one hand and his glass in the other, his dark restless eyes were for an instant set in a swift and vicious stare. More than ever Roger was inclined to lean towards Jeannine's judgment. There was evil in this man and underneath some, at any rate, of the powers that dominate evil.

"You dance," Roger told his partner as they returned to their places, "like a fairy."

"And about dancing," she laughed, "I know just as much as a fairy would, if she were to come to life. Never have I danced in a public place like this before. I could not believe that you were in earnest when you asked me."

"But you must have practised somewhere," he protested.

"Sometimes in the cutting rooms," she confided, "the girls hum music and we get up. That is all I know of dancing.... Do not forget, will you, Monsieur Roger, it must be eight o'clock for me or much disgrace. Monsieur is kind but he likes punctuality. My dresses are not yet chosen. Monsieur Prétat has whims. He insists that he must see me five minutes before he makes his selection that he may decide what sort of humour I am in!"

They danced several more times and later, strolling into the baccarat rooms, watched the gambling. Afterwards they wandered in and out of the shops, loitered on the Promenade des Anglais and finally started homeward.

As they neared Monte Carlo, Jeannine drew off her gloves. Roger looked at her hands—shapely, slim, a good colour now with well-cared-for nails, but ringless.

"No ornament yet," he remarked.

She shook her head.

"They make me 'march' with the fashion and wear the jewellery that goes with the frocks," she explained. "I have begged, though, that I do not have to wear a ring and they have let me have my way. I have never worn a ring. I have never had one on my finger."

"Why not?" he asked.

She looked at him and for a single moment Jeannine of the orange tree seemed to be seated by his side instead of Jeannine the mannequin. He felt a little stab.

"Must one have a reason for everything?" she murmured.

"I am a man and I like reasons," Roger told her.

"I am a girl and it is permitted to me to prefer sentiment!" she retorted.

* * * * *

It was twenty minutes past seven when Roger and Jeannine left the Casino at Nice. The ex-Mayor of La Bastide was still seated at the bar, talking to an increasing crowd of strangely and elaborately attired young men, all with smoothly brushed hair and covetous eyes. His ugly lilac-coloured car, too, was prominent amongst the waiting automobiles, so whether Jeannine was right or wrong in her estimate of the man it could not have been he who was concerned in the strange happenings of that evening in Monte Carlo.

Roger dropped Jeannine at the futuristic-looking building—long and low, with deep cement front and blue framed windows—which was the scene of her daily labours, after which he mounted the broad steps a few yards away and entered the Sporting Club. He had no idea of playing, but from seven to eight the place was rather a rallying ground and he was hoping to plan some tennis for the next morning. Directly he entered the bar, he realised that something had happened. There was a perfect commotion of voices—every one talking eagerly, a hubbub of exclamations, everybody more or less incoherent. Savonarilda, for once without his customary lazy grin, stretched out his hand and gripped Roger's as he passed.

"You have heard?"

"I've heard nothing at all," Roger replied. "I've just got in from Nice. Nothing wrong, I hope?"

"Erskine, your friend Pips Erskine—shot in the Casino this afternoon!"

"Pips!" Roger exclaimed. "Pips Erskine! Why, it's not possible."

Savonarilda nodded. Roger had never seen him look so grave.

"He had one of those accursed letters last night. He showed it to Thornton and myself in here. You were not about or of course you

84

would have seen it too. I didn't like it, neither did Major Thornton. Erskine, however, persisted in treating it as a joke. You know how obstinate he could be when he was in the humour? Not a penny would he pay! This afternoon in the 'kitchen' of the Casino, if you please, he was shot through the shoulder blade and the heart by some one who must have been almost leaning against him."

Roger felt suddenly sick. The other tragedies had seemed terrible enough, but Erskine, Pips Erskine, who had only just come into his inheritance, steeped to the finger tips in the enjoyment of life, spending money with both hands, flirting with every woman he came across, almost savagely eager to make up for his years of privation! It was not possible!

"He is dead?" Roger faltered.

"He was dead when they picked him up," was the grave reply. "He must have been dead a few seconds after that unseen finger pulled the trigger of the pistol, or whatever fiendish weapon was used."

Roger was feeling a little giddy. He pushed on one side the drink which Savonarilda would have forced upon him. An official of the place hurried up and touched him on the shoulder.

"Monsieur the Major Thornton," he announced, "waits for you, sir, at the Casino. He is engaged with the police there."

CHAPTER XIII

Roger followed the man along that dreary carpeted way which he was beginning to loathe, mounted in the lift by the side of which Luke Cheyne had been murdered, crossed the lounge of the Hôtel de Paris, left by the swing doors and went up the steps into the Casino. Here his guide led him by a devious way to an underground floor and paused before a door guarded by a gendarme. They were allowed to pass in, however, and found Thornton engaged with one of the Monaco officials, a solemn-visaged doctor and an undertaker. Upon a mattress, raised a little from the floor and covered over with a sheet, was the victim of the tragedy. Thornton disengaged himself from the others and came over at once to Roger. It was obvious that he had received a shock, for his eyes seemed to have receded farther into his head than ever. He was very pale and had lost something of his cold equanimity of manner.

"Sloane," he exclaimed, "this is damnable!"

"I have only just heard about it," Roger groaned.

"We have been looking everywhere for you. Where the mischief have you been?"

"I dined at Cannes last night and came back late," he explained. "This morning I lunched with my aunt. Afterwards I went over to Nice and I only got back a quarter of an hour ago."

"We must have just missed you everywhere. I thought you might have been able to do something with Erskine. I don't know why, but we all had nerves. They only asked him for a hundred and eighty thousand of his winnings. I wanted him to pay and Prince Savonarilda offered to go halves. I'm afraid that rather set his back up, though."

"Where's the letter?" Roger asked.

"In my pocket. We can't do any good here. Come outside somewhere and I'll show it to you."

Roger paused for a moment, looking out of the window with his back to the room, its ghostly occupant and the little group of whispering officials. Outside were the crowds at the Café de Paris. The music was dimly audible, although the windows were closely fastened. There was something pitiless and ghastly about the gay antics of the conductor in his brilliant uniform. Roger turned back into the room and moved reverently towards the improvised bed.

"Where are you going?" Thornton asked.

"A morbid idea," Roger confessed. "I just wanted to have a look at him. Poor old Pips."

Thornton gripped the other by the arm.

"They won't let you," he warned him. "I wanted to have a last look myself. I was here when they brought him in."

"That's absurd," Roger scoffed. "He was a great friend of mine."

He moved another step towards the couch. The doctor of the Casino and a functionary with whom he had been talking blocked the way.

"The murdered man was a friend of mine," Roger explained, speaking almost under his breath. "I know all his people. I want to have just one look at him."

They both shook their heads.

"It is against the rules," the doctor regretted. "There will be another opportunity. We are waiting now for the coffin."

"What better opportunity could there be?" Roger protested.

"Monsieur does not understand, perhaps," he added, turning to the official. "Lord Erskine was an intimate friend of mine, not an ordinary acquaintance. We were at school and college together. I know some of his people. I shall be compelled to report this terrible circumstance to them. At least, they will wish to know that I paid my last respects—"

"After the coffin has arrived, if you please," the functionary pleaded. "You are the only stranger who is permitted inside this room. It is not for the public—even for the friends of the unfortunates who are brought here."

"Major Thornton is here," Roger protested.

"Major Thornton has special privileges. He has been attached to your Foreign Office and he is a member of your English police," the functionary reminded him. "We must ask you now, please, to leave."

"I think you had better come along," Thornton advised.

Roger was a little bewildered but he gave in. A man in livery let them out by a private door. They walked across the Place into the bar of the Hôtel de Paris and found two easy-chairs in a quiet corner. Neither of them thought of ordering drinks.

"Why the mischief wouldn't they let me have one last look at poor Pips?" Roger demanded.

"I can't tell, Sloane," Thornton replied. "This place is festering with rules and regulations. One is hemmed in on every side. I suppose that's why these things occur."

"Tell me more about it," Roger begged. "Did Erskine have a big win?"

"Yes, he did—a big win for him. He won about two hundred and thirty thousand early yesterday evening. Naturally he had one or two drinks and was chatty about it. It happened to be a very quiet evening over here and most of our lot, as you know, were over at Cannes and there were scarcely a dozen people in the bar when Erskine began to pull out his twenty thousand franc *jetons*. He went home, as I happen to know, quite early, because I invited him up to the Carlton and he said that he had a head. When he woke up this morning, the letter was with his newspapers and the rest of his correspondence."

"Have the police got it?" Roger asked.

"As a matter of fact, they have not," Thornton confided, thrusting his hand into his pocket. "Erskine was perfectly certain that some one was trying to get a rise out of him and left the letter with me after we had had a drink together at twelve o'clock this morning. He knew that the study of handwriting was rather in my line and he wanted me to compare it with the handwriting of any of our crowd I knew about. I think he rather suspected you. There it is."

The letter was written on the Hôtel de Paris notepaper and the envelope was addressed in plain printed characters.

LORD ERSKINE, 344 HÔTEL DE PARIS.

The contents were brief and very much to the point.

Dear Lord Erskine,

It seems hard to demand our tax on winnings so insignificant, but the fact of it is that some of your friends whom you amuse every night with your drolleries are getting rather a nuisance to us. We do not like amateur investigators. We may therefore have to remove ourselves to another sphere of activity and we are obliged to clean up pretty closely. Two hundred and thirty thousand francs is not much of a win so we will only ask you for one hundred and eighty thousand.

Get in your car to-morrow afternoon and precisely at five take a drink at the Savoy Hotel, La Turbie. When you leave there, take the short cut to Monte Carlo and slow up a little at the third bend. You will meet some one there who will relieve you of the notes.

Above all, let me beg of you not to repeat the unfortunate and ludicrous mistake of your countryman, Lord Bradley. I can promise you that the notes will be searched with a magnifying glass before they are put into circulation and there will be the equivalent of a gun in your ribs until they are passed O.K.

Do not be late. We are punctual people.

"Try to keep the letter," Roger enjoined, as he handed it back. "I fancy we may be able to work upon it better than the people out here."

"I don't intend to give it back at all, if I can help it," Thornton replied. "I don't see why I should. It was given into my keeping by Erskine himself."

The barman paused apologetically before their chairs. They gave him an order. It was past eight o'clock and Roger was due to dine in the hotel with his aunt at nine.

"Now, for heaven's sake, tell me about the shooting," Roger begged his companion. "How was it possible for Erskine to have been shot by an invisible person? I thought the Casino was always so full later in the afternoons."

"It's all very difficult," Thornton acknowledged gloomily. "Of course, not one of us was anywhere near the place. Who would have thought of Erskine, after having made a big win at the Sporting

Club, going into the 'kitchen' and playing from five o'clock on an afternoon like this?"

"I can't understand it," Roger admitted. "He always played tennis if he was not at Mont Agel. Don't you remember how he always used to say—never gamble when the sun shines?"

"He was told," Thornton reflected, "to drive in his car slowly down the road from La Turbie at six o'clock this afternoon and to have the hundred and eighty thousand francs with him. We know he didn't mean to obey, but why should he choose to abandon all his usual practices, visit the Casino and gamble in the 'kitchen'?"

"Go on and tell me about the shooting," Roger begged a little abruptly. "Speculations are interesting but I want to hear the facts. Was there no onlooker at all who saw anything of it?"

"Erskine apparently," Thornton explained, "was seated with his back to the wall, in the farthest of the suite of rooms outside the ordinary 'kitchen,' but still belonging to it, so far as regards prices and cartes. That particular room is rather cut off from the place and it would appear that no one, except people actually at the table or standing watching, was in a position to see anything. All that one has been able to gather from one of the chefs is that there was a sound like the 'plop' of a boy's toy gun with a cork in the end and Erskine, who was seated next to the croupier, was seen to lean forward. Immediately afterwards he collapsed. The police have not found any one at the table, seated or standing up, who saw or heard anything of a person with a weapon in his hand. The only witness of any consequence at all is the chef, who was close to Erskine, who declares that he felt something that was like a flash of hot air close to his cheek. The rest of the affair was just as wonderful as usual. They tell me that in less than thirty seconds poor Erskine's place was occupied by some one else, there was no sign of his body and the croupier was spinning the ball!"

"Was the table full?"

"There were only three vacant seats."

Roger swallowed the cocktail which the barman had just brought.

"Thornton," he demanded, "does it seem possible to you that a man seated at a roulette table in full view of a staff of at least six croupiers and chefs, with a dozen people seated at the table, could produce a revolver and shoot another man without being observed?"

Thornton shook his head.

"The same thing has been done before and will be again," he said. "Don't make the mistake, Sloane, of imagining that a man has to bring out his gun and brandish it before he shoots. I even know one or two of our English gunmen who can shoot through their sleeves or through their trousers with one hand, whilst doing anything you please with the other. Erskine might easily have been shot by a man behind with one hand in his pocket and the other placing a stake."

"Do you believe that he was?" Roger asked.

"I'm hanged if I know," was the despairing reply.

No one seemed to have any particular appetite that night at Lady Julia's dinner party, Erskine was popular with every one and Lady Julia herself was more disturbed than she cared to own. With her distress was mingled an anger which was almost passionate.

"I don't care," she declared, "whether this band of criminals is composed of English or Americans, Italians or Monegasques themselves. I say that it is a disgrace that they should remain undetected. I have written to tell the Prince so to-night. The Chef de la Sûreté of Paris should be invited to send some of his best men down at once. This last murder of poor dear Reggie Erskine was blatant. One might almost think that the whole Principality was in league with these people."

"It's the Principality that's going to suffer most," Terence Brown pointed out, "and a few hundred thousand francs mean nothing to them. So far, I haven't heard of any one leaving, but the place is going to have a most awful slump, if this goes on."

"And it deserves it," Lady Julia exclaimed viciously. "We seem to be without any form of protection here."

"The trouble is," Thornton intervened, "that the authorities here have got so used to covering up any unpleasant little incident that happens—and so clever at it too—that now the incidents have assumed a different aspect, they find themselves stifled before they start. All the precautions they have taken to prevent suicides or these fights that take place in the Casino getting talked about make it terribly difficult for their own police, however intelligent they may be, to deal with these new conditions."

"Then the sooner they get outside help, the better," Lady Julia snapped. "I should get the best men down from Scotland Yard and from Paris. *Amour propre* be hanged! The criminals are probably English or French, so an English or French detective would be far more likely to get at the truth than this local gendarmerie. There's no telling which of us will be the next."

"For my part," Maggie Saunders observed, "I don't think that I shall play at all, or if I do, I shall howl about my losings and keep my winnings to myself."

"That is very sensible," Savonarilda agreed. "It does not make us any the more comfortable to reflect that it has always been people who have talked about their winnings in the Sporting Club here who have met with trouble."

There was a change in the music. Every one looked up expectantly.

"It is the mannequin parade," Lady Julia announced. "Really, I don't feel that I have the heart to look at them to-night."

Roger was not well placed for seeing the nine young women who were one by one slowly threading their way amongst the tables of the ornate, magnificent room, to the strains of a slow minuet, but he was conscious almost at once of some curious emotional disturbance amongst the guests of the party, a shrinking back in their places of two of the women, an expression of fear in Lady Julia's face, something approaching horror in the deep lights of Savonarilda's Sicilian eyes. He swung his chair around to command a view of the room. He remembered what Jeannine had told him and realised the significance of the little shivering wave of unanalysable emotion which seemed somehow to be throbbing in the atmosphere of the room. It was the night for the parade of black evening frocks. One by one the young women glided amongst the tables to the open space where on gala nights there was dancing. They were clad in net, chiffon, georgette, lace—but every gown was fashioned of unadorned and unrelieved black! There was a ghostliness, indefinable and inexplicable, in their silent procession. Jeannine, who came last, though her movements were wonderful as ever, her carriage superb, the little poise of her head in itself a perfect gesture, seemed in her pallor and the strangeness of her expression like one of the wedded virgins of death. An absolute silence fell upon the room, the music and the soft fluttering of the gowns practically the only sounds. Conversation was strangled. Many of the women confessed afterwards that they had felt on the verge of hysterics. For the first time in her life Jeannine, so completely detached and impersonal in the following of her profession, looked away from vacancy as she passed Lady Julia's table and searched for Roger's eyes. He was never sure if it was fancy but she seemed to him to be calling for help almost in the same way that she had done once before, in those minutes of supreme terror. He forgot his role as onlooker, he forgot the depression from which he too was suffering, and he smiled understandingly back. He tried to send to her through the overcharged air the message of courage that he felt she needed....

"Horrible!" Lady Julia suddenly murmured.

"But don't forget that it was arranged beforehand," Mrs. Terence Brown reminded her, from the other end of the table. "I know people who came expressly to-night for this parade of black evening toilettes. A very good idea, I thought it. Of course, no one could have imagined these horrible surrounding circumstances."

The *sommelier* had an inspiration. He darted around with the wine, for which every one was grateful. In a very few minutes the mannequins had reappeared—this time wearing marvellous white evening gowns. The spell was broken. Conversation was resumed. Every one talked eloquently perhaps, but feverishly upon any subject that tumbled into their brains. By universal consent they did their best to set their heels upon that tangle of cruel memories.

Soon after midnight the first part of the enterprise which Roger had thought out step by step was safely accomplished. He had driven in his coupé on to the Moyen Corniche and when he had arrived at the corner where he had met Marie Louise, the corner where the curving, dangerous track wound its way down to Beausoleil, he turned out all his lights, descended with his engine free, his car controlled by its very excellent brakes, until he had passed the Hotel du Soleil. To all appearances, there was not a single light burning in any part of the place. Roger glided on until he reached the deep obscurity of some overhanging trees just by the first bend—very nearly the spot where once before he had paused and looked up the hill towards danger. Here he left the car, satisfied that it would start again with a touch, pulled out his revolver, examined it carefully and, keeping well on the grassy edge of the ditch, reclimbed the hill. As soon as he reached the bar, he recrossed the road. There was still not a sound to be heard but through the chinks of the closed door he realised that one light had been left on. He tried the handle but found, as he anticipated, that it was locked. The darkness was still intense but away where the moon was soon to rise it seemed to him that there was a coming break in the skies. He crept past the front and around to the side of the house. Kneeling down, he could see that there were lights in several of the windows. One of the rooms indeed must have been fully illuminated. Still, however, there was no sound, nothing but a nerve-paralysing intense silence. He leaned against the wall and tried to think out some definite plan of action. One curious discovery had brought him up here in the middle of the night on this apparently purposeless errand. How was he best to turn it to account?

The faintest breath of wind stealing round the corner of the building whispered amongst the leaves of the olive trees. Roger knew very well what that meant. In half an hour or even less there would be a rift in that bank of dense clouds and the edge of the moon would be showing. With the light would come danger. Noiselessly he stole back towards the lane. There was a vast shadow as of some shed or building which seemed to him unfamiliar. He crept towards it. Gradually it grew into shape and he realised that it was a saloon-bodied motor car. He moved on a few paces until it grew more distinct. There was no possibility now of mistake.

It was the great lilac-coloured automobile of Monsieur Pierre Viotti! It was within a dozen yards of the garage but for some reason it had been left outside.

Roger crept back towards the hotel. Another little puff of breeze came around the corner. This time it brought with it the night perfume of tobacco plant and all the fragrance of the drooping mimosas. Still no sound. There were men inside—he was sure of that. There was life—an ugly, sinister phase of life it might well be— but over it all the pall of a deep brooding silence. Roger felt then that it was inspiration indeed which had brought him but inspiration leavened with folly. To have come alone was his mistake. It was not for nothing that lights were glimmering out of half-a-dozen rooms of a building which in the daytime was reported deserted; not for nothing that Monsieur Viotti's lilac-coloured car was drawn up there in the obscurity outside the garage. The place, of course, might be just a harbourage of vice; those lights might mean nothing more than the amours of the night or some new fashion of debased orgies. Somehow or other, though, Roger did not think so. It was the silence which impressed him so much. Silence and light so seldom went together.

In the end he acted without premeditation, without common sense and without reason. He stole down to the door of the bar and hammered on it with the butt of his revolver. When he had finished, the silence appeared to be more intense than ever. All the time, though, it seemed to him that he was subconsciously aware of a world of listeners. Then a door slammed inside. He heard footsteps coming down the stairs, heard them coming along the narrow passage between the bar and the hotel. A second light flashed up inside the room. A man approached the other side of the door which at first he showed no signs of opening.

"Who's out there at this time of night making that hell of a noise? What do you want?"

"A drink," Roger answered, and he was astonished to realise how steady his voice sounded. "I need a drink. Sorry if you'd gone to bed, but now you're up, you'd better give me one."

The door was jerked open. His friend, the barman, stood there fully dressed but with tousled hair and blinking red eyes. He looked at his visitor in the blankest astonishment.

"What the hell are you doing round here again?" he demanded.

"I don't know what it is," Roger replied. "Something in the air, I suppose, but directly I get within fifty yards of your bar I'm thirsty."

The man held open the door. Roger noticed that his right hand had disappeared so he stole a march on him. He flashed out his own automatic.

"I'm not here for trouble, Sam," he said. "I don't like the way your hand is stealing around to your hip pocket. Up with them! I'd like to have a look at that diamond ring."

The man grinned and threw them both up.

"Come in and have your drink," he whispered. "If you make a noise, I promise you this—you'll sleep so hard that you won't wake in the morning. You shall have your drink, all right. That is to say if no one butts in. If they do, you're a goner. What you come nosing around for all the time, God Almighty knows, but there's trouble here for any one that wants it."

He crossed the floor towards the bar and pulled down a bottle of brandy. Roger settled himself in a chair within a yard of the door. In the mirror at the back of the counter he could see the barman watching. He brought the brandy and he brought the Perrier. He opened the latter and set it down on the table.

"Young fellow," he said, scowling, "you'd better come through with it. What the hell do you want?"

"I told you before," Roger replied, "I live on the hillside here and I get restless sometimes. This is a bar, isn't it?"

"Yes, it's a bar, but it's one o'clock in the morning and we don't expect to serve customers at that hour."

"Sam," Roger said suddenly, "why don't you go back to America?"

Sam started.

"Why should I?" he demanded. "Living here is pretty good."

"The game's up," Roger bluffed. "I've got the drop on all of you."

"You! Why, you haven't turned stiff, have you?" he asked.

"Keep your hands in front of you, Sam," Roger warned him. "I'm not a stiff. There aren't many to be met with in this part of the world. I want to warn you though—"

Here they came—flop, flop, flop—shuffle, shuffle, shuffle! They were coming along the passage. They must be now within a few yards of the door. Sam suddenly took his undesired patron by the shoulders.

"Get out of this," he ordered. "I tell you, shooting ain't in my line and there'll be a hell of a lot of it, if you stay there another minute. Get out of this and stay away."

There was something uncommonly sinister in those advancing footsteps, which perhaps helped Roger to make up his mind. Sam's clutch upon his shoulders too was the clutch of a powerful man. He stepped back on to the road and the door was slammed behind him. The light had not come yet and he had almost to feel his way as he staggered out, but more by good luck than anything else he kept in the middle of the road. He turned and ran, every moment expecting to hear the door behind him opened and to hear the hissing of bullets around him. Nothing happened. He drew nearer and nearer to the bend. Not a sound behind him! Presently the shape of his own car loomed up out of the darkness. He sprang inside, closed the door and switched on his lights. It was at that moment when he touched the contact button and at the same time released the brakes that the shock came. He very nearly let go the wheel which would probably have meant a glimpse into eternity. He recovered, though, as men do in those moments when there is no time for thought and action becomes automatic. He swung into the middle of the road, pushed his gear into third and with the car well under control turned to the figure by his side. A figure of calamity indeed, with torn clothes and blood-stained face.

"Pips!" Roger gasped. "My God, is it Pips?"

"Pips it is," the other faltered, "but I can't believe that I'm alive!"

CHAPTER XIV

Jeannine and Roger were seated in the arbour in the southwest corner of his garden, rose-wreathed now with the passing of the wisteria. Thornton, sprawling on a rock at the back of the villa was attempting a sketch.

"I want to know," Roger said, in his usual downright fashion, "exactly what is troubling you, Jeannine."

She laughed softly.

"Do I look so miserable?"

"Not at this moment, but I believe there is something the matter, all the same," he insisted. "My aunt says it is because you are growing into a woman too quickly. When I think of you a year and a half ago, doing a skirt dance before the Curé in my salon—the skirt, by the by, was almost negligible—helping yourself to apples from my dish, laughing and squealing like a happy little monkey, I ask myself sometimes whether fate has been kind to you. You've sobered down too darn quickly. Perhaps there is something at the back of your mind we don't know about."

She laid her fingers upon his arm for a moment.

"It is just foolishness," she confessed. "No one should be happier than I, because I have found such wonderful friends. Perhaps I am disturbed sometimes because I feel that they are being too good to me, because I feel that I am not exactly in my right place."

"What do you mean—not in your right place?" he asked gruffly.

"You must know," she laughed. "Remember what I looked like up in the orange tree. Sometimes I have been able to adapt myself, sometimes I have not thought about it at all, sometimes I have not felt quite comfortable."

He leaned a little closer to her.

"If you aren't talking like a silly kid!" he exclaimed. "Don't you realise that you've turned the heads of a whole colony of men?"

"I will not be made fun of," she pouted. "Now I will tell you something else. This is really why I feel unhappy and disturbed sometimes. There seems to be all the time something going on around us which I cannot understand. It is not only these strange things which have been happening to more important people, but it is I myself who am getting afraid of people, nervous when they talk to me. I feel as though there were something in the atmosphere which means harm. I even fancy that sometimes I—insignificant little Jeannine—am being watched! Not kindly—maliciously."

"Has that man Pierre Viotti been worrying you again?" Roger demanded.

She smiled, but in a forced fashion. At the mention of the man's name a momentary shiver had escaped her.

"He does not dare to speak to me, but sometimes he smiles. He sits on a stool in the Sporting Club and I have caught him watching us, even when he seemed not to be looking, and there was always that evil smile. Promise you won't do anything about it if I tell you, Roger."

"Tell me about it, anyway," he evaded. "If any one has a right to consider himself your guardian, surely I have."

"You have the right to consider yourself anything you choose," she admitted. "I speak, then, of Monsieur Viotti. He has not uttered one word to me, but he still comes to see Madame. I see that great automobile of his outside when I return home and I go away for a walk and wait until it has disappeared. When I come in, Madame looks at me curiously. She is always hinting that I should be more like other girls, that I should go to places where they dance and make acquaintances, that it is time I was fiancée. She talks like that usually after Monsieur Viotti has been there. Of course, they come from the same village—they have the right to be friends—but I believe he gives her money."

"I will have a few words with Madame," Roger said in a low tone.

Her fingers sought his arm again.

"Please do not, Monsieur Roger," she begged. "Can you not see that he has a perfect right to come? Madame and he are old friends. If I am afraid of him, it is my fault. But I am," she added, with a little burst of passion. "I hate him! When he looks at me I shiver. I know that he is a bad man. I think that I have the gift of knowing, when people come near me, if they are honest or not.... Ciel! What is this that arrives?"

Jeannine might well ask, for what was arriving was nothing less amazing than the lilac-coloured automobile of Monsieur the ex-Mayor of La Bastide! The ex-Mayor himself and his brother were seated inside. The automobile came to a standstill outside the gate.

"For the love of Mike, they're going to call on us!" Roger exclaimed.

She sprang to her feet.

"Let me go," she begged.

"Not likely," he answered, catching at her hand. "Here we stay together, here we receive them and here we finish this matter once and for all. We commence with an act of courtesy. We stand up to receive our visitors."

The two men advanced in formal fashion. They had rung the bell at the gate and Bardells himself announced them.

"Monsieur Paul and Monsieur Pierre Viotti."

By the side of Monsieur Pierre Viotti, resplendent in purple-coloured serge, with a white and yellow waistcoat, his brother looked almost distinguished. Roger, with an inward grimace, shook hands and presented his ward. Bardells placed chairs. It was Paul Viotti who took charge of the proceedings.

"Monsieur speaks French, I hope?"

"Sufficiently," Roger replied.

"That makes it easier, then," Paul Viotti remarked with a smile. "Because although I myself speak good English American, my brother understands nothing but French. It is of his affairs I wish to speak."

"I scarcely see," Roger said, "how his affairs can in any way concern me, but pray proceed."

"My brother, as you know, is your neighbour," Paul Viotti continued, "and a very successful man he has been. I myself have prospered in America and it is my wish to assist my brother in any way he may desire. I learn from him that he wishes for the hand of Mademoiselle Jeannine in marriage—"

"Then he'd better go and wish for something else," Roger interrupted bluntly, "for that he never will have."

The florid courtesy of the proceedings was somewhat marred. There was a very unpleasant light in Pierre Viotti's eyes. His brother Paul extended his hands in protest.

"My dear sir," he begged. "Why so hasty? We come to make a good offer—a very good offer. We do not demand a *dot*. On the contrary, on the day of the marriage, my brother and I will settle upon the young lady the sum of one million francs."

"One million francs," the ex-Mayor of La Bastide repeated, patting his waistcoat and looking eagerly towards Jeannine. "It is something that—yes? And the château—that you can have too. My mother and sister can find another home. You can wear beautiful clothes, you can be the belle of the village and all the villages around. It is something—yes?"

"It is a great deal," Jeannine acknowledged, smiling, "but will you permit me to say at once that nothing in the world would induce me to marry you, Monsieur Viotti. Not for one million. Not for twenty!"

There was a moment or two of silence. The ex-Mayor of La Bastide remained with his mouth open and the air of one who has heard an incredible thing. His brother, Paul, who had mixed more with the world, was perhaps less surprised. He turned to Roger.

"In your ward's best interests, Monsieur," he appealed, "can we not beg for your aid? My brother's position entitles him to consideration and money such as he speaks of is not lightly come by."

"Not a chance," was the curt reply. "As a matter of fact, Mademoiselle Jeannine has already decided to do me the great honour of becoming my wife."

All the gloss and bumptiousness and conceit seemed to pass from the unsuccessful suitor. He stood like a man withered in the sunshine. His brother preserved his dignity. He picked up his hat and rose to his feet.

"Under those circumstances, Monsieur Sloane," he said, "we offer you our regret that we have troubled you. My brother was, I am sure, unaware of this felicitous happening."

"Unaware, and I don't believe it," Pierre Viotti declared harshly. "Marriage! Bah! Rich men with villas and relations who are of the nobility do not marry village brats!"

Roger took a step forward.

"Monsieur Viotti," he said to Paul, "I once had to teach your brother a lesson. Please take him away at once before I am tempted to repeat it."

He struck the gong which stood upon the table. Bardells came hurrying out.

"Show these gentlemen to their car," Roger enjoined.

The brothers Viotti walked down the gravel path. The ex-Mayor of La Bastide was carrying his bowler hat in one hand and mopping his forehead with a handkerchief with the other.

"You will do as I ask now, Paul," he begged. "You see how he treats me—like dirt! And I must have the girl."

His brother smiled benevolently.

"The girl seems to me like many others," he said, "but, so far as I am concerned, I consent. You shall have your way with her. You shall have your way with him. He has given us trouble enough."

* * * * *

Jeannine had drawn her chair a little farther back into the seclusion of the arbour. She was sitting very upright, her fingers twisted together, undisguised tears in her eyes.

"You should not have said that," she murmured. "It was cruel of you."

"Why cruel?"

"Because you know that it is not possible."

"I don't believe anything of the sort," he replied. "You know I'm fond of you, Jeannine."

She suffered his arm around her waist unresistingly, but the hopelessness of her expression remained unchanged. She took his other hand and caressed it.

"You have been so good to me, Monsieur Roger," she said, "and now you feel that you must do this. You think so much of what

99

is right and wrong, and you know what I feel, and you are afraid that I may be unhappy. That is not what I wish in life. That I will not have."

She sprang suddenly to her feet. Roger, taken by surprise, was silent. She stood opposite to him, her eyes aflame. She was once more the gamine of the orange tree.

"You do not love me," she cried. "What you offer, you offer out of pity. You have not love in your heart—you have kindness. You have not madness in your brain—you have prudence."

"Are you gibing at me," he asked bluntly, "because I didn't take what you thought was love when you were an unformed brat?"

"You do not love me now," she faltered breathlessly.

He took her into his arms and found a very good way of ending a great deal of foolishness.

"He'll make you a good husband, my dear," Lady Julia declared later on that evening, in the salon of her villa. "His father was a good husband. I wish you could get him out of this place. I don't like it. The Princess wanted me to go to Biarritz with her this afternoon and but for you two I think I should have gone."

"Why don't you?" Roger asked. "Jeannine and I could get married. I feel I must stick it out."

"Nonsense!" his aunt protested. "When Jeannine gets married, she is married from my house. She is my ward—not yours. I am going to stick it out too. But, for heaven's sake, stop this epidemic of robbing and killing. Why doesn't your Scotland Yard man do something?"

"The poor fellow is doing his best," Roger replied, "but just think how he's handicapped. He hasn't any authority. If the Monegasque police had listened to him about the Crowley murder, I believe we should have had the gang cornered by now."

"Stay and dine," Lady Julia invited him. "I don't suppose there's much to eat, but Dalmorres is coming. He'll let you know what he thinks of you all down here."

"Thank you—not to-night," Roger refused firmly. "Jeannine and I stopped and engaged a corner table at the Sporting Club. First time I've ever dined alone with her."

"Do you mind?" Jeannine asked Lady Julia a little shyly.

"Heavens, no, my dear! Take care of him, that's all. By the by, you called to see Reggie, I suppose. How is he?"

"Better. But they won't let us see him yet. Until we can ask him a few questions, we're all at sea about the other night."

"I should stay at sea if I were you," Lady Julia advised. "I've sent all my jewels to the bank and I think I shall go to Corsica to-morrow or the next day."

"On Dalmorres' yacht?" Roger enquired with a grin.

"Scandalmonger!" his aunt exclaimed, shaking her stick at him. "If you can tear yourself away from your *dîner à deux* by eleven o'clock, I'll drink your healths up in the bar. The place has become like a news agency. You get the latest information every ten minutes. What's that, Grover?" Lady Julia went on, turning towards the butler. "Lord Dalmorres? Show him into the library. Give him a double cocktail. Curse you young people—making me late for my dinner!"

Lady Julia stumped off.

CHAPTER XV

Jeannine and Roger mounted from the dining room of the Sporting Club to the bar, arm in arm, and a riot of congratulations followed upon their entrance. Roger, however, after the first few minutes, left his companion with the Terence Browns and Maggie Saunders, and obeyed Thornton's beckoning signal. The two men seated themselves in a retired corner of the inner bar.

"Should you think I was a rotter if I chucked my hand in, Sloane?" the latter asked.

"What's wrong now?"

"I can't make any headway here," Thornton confessed. "No one wants the truth about anything. All that they want is silence. They will allow nothing to stand in the way of their routine. For instance, the pseudo Lord Erskine is already buried."

"Without being identified?"

"Without being identified. I must say, though, that they have a wonderful system in what I should call a post-mortem identification."

"What do you mean?"

"Well, before he was buried, he was weighed, measured, photographed, every item of property in his pockets was tabulated and his clothes carefully preserved. You could find out, for instance, how many teeth he had and the exact position of a small mole on his chest. On the other hand, no description of him is being circulated, no word is being sent to the police at Nice, none of the hotel proprietors in this place or anywhere else are being notified. He is just dropped into the black pool.... It's a system, all right, Sloane. I see their idea. It helps to keep this the playground of the world, but it doesn't help the public or us to fight a band of criminals. You see, I can't do myself justice, I can't work on sound methods and I think, if you don't mind, I'd rather slip out."

"Promise me one thing," Roger begged. "Don't go until Pips Erskine can talk. I have an idea that he knows something. He ought to be able to put us on the right track, anyhow. It may not be more than a few days. Certainly not more than a week."

"I'll wait until then," Thornton promised. "I warn you, though, that I'm going to take to golf. I came here for a holiday and I've been plunged into the most humiliating epoch of ineffective work the mind of man could conceive."

"That's all right," Roger agreed. "I'd play you myself but I expect I shall be busy for the next few days."

"Forgive me for being so late with my congratulations," Thornton said. "The young lady is charming."

"Glad you find her so," Roger declared enthusiastically. "She seems to have hit it up pretty strong with all the crowd around here. They'd soon spoil her if she'd let them."

"Considering what I have heard of her history," Thornton observed, "she is certainly quite a remarkable personality. Your friend Erskine summed her up, I think, when he said that she had the knack of leaving you at the end of half an hour's conversation exactly where you were when you began it."

"She's a great kid!" Roger declared happily.

"By the by," Thornton enquired after a moment's pause, "is it true that Lord Dalmorres is here?"

"Arrived this afternoon," Roger assented. "Dining alone with my aunt to-night, the old rascal."

"If he's a great friend of yours," Thornton advised, "I should give him a word of warning. Not that I think he'll need it."

"He'll hear all about our troubles from Lady Julia. In any case, he's not the man to take risks. He sleeps on his yacht and goes about generally with a whole retinue. If he got one of those letters, you'd see his smoke on the horizon in a couple of hours."

"All the same," Thornton meditated, "a word of warning wouldn't come amiss. What are his habits? Does he gamble?"

"Occasionally," Roger admitted. "But generally in the afternoon. I did see him win ten million once at baccarat about two o'clock in the morning. He came in after a big dinner party, without a cent in his pocket, and the chef put down a hundred thousand francs for him every time he nodded."

"Interesting," Thornton murmured. "A great ladies' man too, isn't he?"

"Has been," Roger smiled. "I think he prefers to talk over his past triumphs nowadays. I expect that's what he's doing with my aunt this evening, as they haven't turned up here."

"A man whom it would be interesting to meet," Thornton observed, polishing his monocle with his handkerchief. "I've heard a great deal of Lord Dalmorres in my time. He has had a wonderful career."

"If he comes in," Roger promised, "I'll introduce you."

* * * * *

The Right Honourable the Earl of Dalmorres was one of the few aristocrats who had also reached the highest honours in the legal world. He had held every office of distinction to which his profession entitled him, he had been famous for years as the most brilliant orator in the House of Lords, he had filled the position of Lord Chancellor with dignity and success, and at sixty-four years of age, on succeeding to a large fortune, he had retired altogether from public life. Lady Julia, with whom he had spent the evening exchanging many sentimental reminiscences, had once been his sweetheart, but at his age and still having the reputation of a ladies' man to keep up, he naturally lost his heart to Jeannine. He carried her away to teach her roulette, brushing on one side her objections that she was only allowed in on condition that she did not play. A nod from Dalmorres, however, to one of the supervisors was sufficient. Many laws can be strained for an English milord who can afford to play in maximums!

"Sloane, my young friend," this distinguished personage suggested, "would it be possible to induce you for ten minutes to wander away and receive the congratulations of your many friends in peace? I cannot command Mademoiselle Jeannine's attention to the game while you are in the background."

"But I do not wish him to go away," Jeannine pleaded.

"I have only been engaged to the girl an hour or so," Roger protested.

Dalmorres sighed. The situation, however, admitted of no argument. He continued to explain the game and Jeannine, with the usual beginner's luck, increased with every stake her pile of winnings. Presently, however, an interruption occurred. One of the chasseurs from downstairs approached the table and whispered in Roger's ear.

"Monsieur is asked for at the telephone," he announced.

Roger, with a word of excuse, made his way downstairs. He took up the receiver.

"Roger Sloane speaking. Who is it?"

"The matron of the hospital," a quiet voice replied. "You have a friend here—Lord Erskine."

"Yes," Roger assented. "I hope that he's not worse or anything?"

"On the contrary," the matron assured him, "the doctor reports that he is a little better. He is still in a very feverish and excited state, though. He cannot sleep and refuses to take a sleeping draught. He has an idea that he must speak with you at once whilst his memory serves him. As I daresay you know, he has been unconscious for several days and only partially conscious until this evening. Would it be possible for you to come over?"

"Rather," Sloane assented. "Do you really mean that I shall be allowed to see him?"

"I am breaking all the rules," the matron confessed, "but I think that the patient's condition justifies it. He has promised that if he is allowed to speak to you for five minutes, he will take a draught and endeavour to sleep."

"I will be there in half an hour," Roger promised.

Lady Julia made a grimace when her nephew explained.

"Just my luck," she sighed. "The little cat has stolen my man already and now she will have him for the rest of the evening. Never mind, Roger," she went on, realising for the first time the anxiety in his face, "of course I will look after Jeannine."

"You will think I'm an ass," he said, "but will you, or Madame Dumesnil, kindly see her inside her door if I am not back by half-past eleven?"

Lady Julia nodded. She had been seated at the baccarat table but she rose now to her feet.

"I will go and play roulette with them," she announced, "and I won't let Jeannie out of my sight."

Roger scarcely recognised his friend, who was sitting up in bed, awaiting his coming. Erskine had lost flesh and there was an uneasy look in his eyes, as though he were haunted by unpleasant thoughts. His expression was transformed, however, when Roger appeared.

"Good man," he murmured. "Sit down. Bring the chair up to the bedside."

104

The matron held up her finger.

"Remember," she warned them, "in ten minutes I return and in ten minutes Mr. Roger Sloane will have to go."

She took her leave with a little nod. Roger did as he had been bidden and brought a chair to the bedside.

"Jolly glad to see you looking better, Pips, old man," he said. "Tried to steal a march on those fellows, didn't you? Listen," he went on. "Don't say an unnecessary word. Just tell me what's vital. You will be strong enough to tell us the whole story in a day or two."

Erskine's fingers played nervously with the bedclothes.

"I hope so," he answered. "You know, Roger, I played the fool. I drove up to the mountains just as they told me to, but I took an automatic instead of the money, and I was idiot enough to think that I would bring down the messenger, whoever he was, and after that it would be easy to collar the gang."

"Jolly plucky," Roger murmured. "But why alone, old chap?"

"Because, of course, they would have been watching and they would have cleared out if I had brought a carload. It seemed to me the only chance was to go alone. I reached the spot and saw some one waiting for me. He was just an ordinary gigolo-looking young fellow, sitting on the wall and smoking a cigarette. He got up as I approached and I stopped the car. Between my knees there was an automatic. I got hold of it with my right hand.

"'You have something for me perhaps?' he enquired.

"'Yes, I have,' I answered. 'Come here and I will give it to you.'

"He came slowly around the bonnet of the car and stood with his foot on the running board, not two yards away from me, but just out of reach. He was a horrible-looking fellow, Roger.

"'Give me the packet,' he demanded.

"I sat looking at him and I knew at once that I should have to think quickly. He was not attempting any form of disguise. There he was, a young fellow whom I should be able to identify at any time later on. He must have known that. So must the people who sent him. I realised like a flash that I was never intended to have the chance. As soon as they had the notes, they were going to make sure of me. I whipped out my automatic.

"'Put up your hands,' I ordered.

"He put them up all right, but his eyes were horrible.

"'So that's the game,' he muttered.

"'Get into the car by my side,' I went on.

"'What for?'

"'You will soon find out,' I assured him.

"He stood with his foot still on the step and I saw something that was almost a smile on his vicious-looking face. At the same second I felt a man's breath hot upon my cheek. I can't tell you how quickly it all happened, Roger. It was like a flash. I knew I was for it and I had a murderous desire—it was murderous—to kill the man in front of me. And I did it!"

Roger held his breath. He spoke not a monosyllable. He was listening with agonised interest. Every second he feared to hear the handle of the door turn.

"You understand," Erskine faltered, "I realised that I was trapped. I felt the swish of a towel over my mouth from behind, I felt my arm knocked up and I pulled the trigger of my gun all at the same moment. I felt the pain on my arm, I was conscious of the first whiff of chloroform, and it seemed to me that I pulled the trigger at the same time, but as a matter of fact, of course, I must have pulled it a fraction of a second before. The last thing I remember, and for all I knew it was going to be my last conscious thought on earth, was the sight of the man in front of me crumpling up. I killed him, Roger."

Roger felt his forehead. The room was well aired but the perspiration was standing out in great beads.

"I can't tell you how long it was afterwards," Erskine went on, in a choked whisper, "that I opened my eyes because of the pain. I was twenty or thirty yards down that gorge where the croupier was found, and a wheel which had been torn off the car was lying on my leg, and all the clothes on my left side were ripped to pieces. Right at the bottom of the gorge—"

"They found the remnants of your car," Roger went on, hoping to save his friend speech as much as possible. "It was smashed to pieces, of course, with the wheel missing."

Erskine nodded slightly.

"Considering all things, I think I was clever. I realised vaguely what had happened. The man who had come up behind had left me in the car, pushed it down to the edge and let it go. Before it had gathered much speed, the wheel had caught one of those great boulders, been wrenched off and I must have been pitched out.... Some one might come back, I felt, at any time to be sure that everything was all right. I managed to lift the wheel and let it fall down a little cleft so that it was out of sight. Then somehow or other I pulled myself up. God knows how I did it, for I was in terrible pain. I staggered about for a time. Once I fainted. When I recovered consciousness, it was quite dark. I staggered on and suddenly I came upon your car, drawn up by the edge of the road. I got in. I just remember feeling in my pockets and realising that my money

106

and passport and cards to the *Cercle Privé* had gone, and a few other trifles. You know the state I was in when you found me!"

"Anything you could tell me to help identify the man you shot?" Roger asked wistfully.

"Nasty pale face, small eyes. His foot was on the step and I saw that he was wearing patent shoes and purple socks. I'll swear he came from Nice. I have seen—the type."

The door of the room was softly but firmly opened. The matron glanced at her patient and, turning to Roger, motioned him away.

"Quite enough for the first time," she insisted.

Erskine smiled faintly and glanced at the glass in her hand.

"I'll swallow anything you like now, Matron," he murmured.

CHAPTER XVI

The complete silence reigning in the fantastic underground apartment which had taken the place of the Manhattan clubroom, during the last sixty seconds, had become impressive. The man who sat at the end of the beautifully polished mahogany table, with its strange inlaid gilt edge, lifted the five cards which lay in front of him and dropped them face downwards, one on the top of the other. The sound of their soft patter was almost a relief. He looked across the table and there was mild reproach in his tone.

"Our friend Marcus throws bombshells to-night."

Prince Savonarilda leaned back from the table, his hands in his trousers pockets. There was a certain amount of defiance in his face and superciliousness in his tone. He was still wearing the carnation which his hostess of the gala dinner had arranged in his buttonhole a few hours ago.

"You can call them bombshells if you like," he observed, "but they contain nothing more explosive than sawdust. I simply say that we are becoming less and less cautious with every one of our enterprises. The police system here may be inferior to the police system of New York, but remember—so long as we kept within certain limits—the New York men were ours, body and soul. These fellows aren't used to our methods and they are bewildered for the moment, but if they once got after us, the Bank of France wouldn't buy them."

"We have added seven millions to the treasury," Paul Viotti murmured, with an ecstatic gesture of the hands.

"And there are three undetected murders which are still engaging the attention of the police," Savonarilda replied. "Who can tell when they may not stumble upon a clue? Supposing that, for instance," he went on, pointing to a corner of the room, "had been left upon the road and identified as an acquaintance and hanger-on of Pierre Viotti,—how should we have explained it?"

Savonarilda's finger had been directed toward a recess in the apartment where, from underneath a sheet, protruded a man's foot, a foot encased in a purple sock and shod in a patent leather shoe. It was clear enough what lay underneath.

"Who would have come to us for explanations?" Paul Viotti asked, with a smile. "We know every one of the Beausoleil police as well as the Monegasques. We know which ones operate in this direction, we can tell you even where they are. We have already taken extra precautions to meet this attack of nerves on your part, my young friend. We employ always my brother's watching squad who call themselves 'The Wolves.' We have a motor cyclist on the Nice road, one on the Mentone road, one on the Eze byway and one in the byway which passes our doors. No one could arrive here unexpectedly."

Savonarilda let his chair swing back to the table and tapped a cigarette thoughtfully.

"It is not only an affair of the police," he pointed out. "There is your compatriot—Roger Sloane. He is too honest to be thoroughly dangerous, but all the same, there is nothing of the fool about Roger. Perhaps you don't know that he has shown a great deal of curiosity concerning this little domain. He has even crept about amongst the carnations and the rose bushes which grow upon the roof of our enchanted chamber."

"And what did he find?" Paul Viotti chuckled. "Just what any one else would find, just what the cleverest detective from Police Headquarters in England, France or New York would find—just nothing at all. My brother and his Italian friend did their work too well for that. Our hiding place is undiscoverable—even by that over-curious young American."

Tom Meredith, wearing the linen coat of his assumed profession, removed the cigar from the corner of his mouth and his thumb from the armlet of his waistcoat.

"There's some men," he declared, "who are born into the world with too much curiosity. That young Sloane's one of 'em. I tell you, I don't like the way he's always nosing round. It ain't going to be good for his health if he don't quit it."

Pierre Viotti chimed in from the other end of the table.

"I think that over here you have all grown soft. Perhaps it is our sunshine and easy life. For many hours I have talked with Paul here of the way you dealt with curious people in New York. They did not live long there. Dead men are no longer dangerous."

"A bloodthirsty little gentleman for a fruit farmer, your brother," Edward Staines observed, with a melancholy smile.

Paul Viotti rubbed his hands softly together. There was a twinkle in his beadlike eyes.

"I think my brother does not like this Mr. Sloane," he confided, with a sly wink. "There has been trouble between them that need not concern us."

"Sloane," Marcus Constantine said deliberately, "is a young man whom we have to keep under observation the whole of the time. We are doing so. At present he is more useful to us than dangerous. If ever that pleasant state of things should come to an end, it will be time to deal with him. Not until then, I say. Your brother has done some useful work for us, Paul Viotti, but he is amply repaid by being made a member of our organisation. Private quarrels are not our concern."

"Quite right, Marcus, quite right," Paul Viotti assented soothingly. "The young man is useful to us. He must be watched but left alone. If the time should come when he becomes dangerous, it would be easy, very easy, to get rid of him. But not now. He has too many friends."

"And one who is an enemy," Pierre Viotti declared, with darkening face.

Savonarilda rose to his feet, crossed the room and lifted the sheet. The body of a young man lay there on a stretcher, ashen-cheeked, with closed eyes—dead. Savonarilda looked down at him curiously, without compassion, without any other sentiment, indeed, except a faint curiosity. Then he replaced the sheet with a careless gesture.

"That blundering fool of a young English lord knew how to hold his gun straight, at any rate," he remarked.

Paul Viotti shrugged his powerful shoulders.

"I think that he saved us trouble," he murmured. "The two young men were no good."

His brother groaned.

"I made a mistake," he admitted. "Dead, though, they will do nobody any harm. They will put people off the scent. The young

Englishman, if he lives, will be a hero. It is the younger one," he went on, "André, in whom I am disappointed. In Marseilles and in the old parts of Nice they call him 'The Wolf.' In Marseilles his work was good. Here he bungled and afterwards he was foolish. He should have tied Erskine in the car."

"His little expedition into the Casino," Edward Staines remarked, "was ill advised."

"The sort of fellow who got my goat," Tom Meredith muttered. "I'm glad I've seen the last of him. Drank vermouth and cassis and wanted a lump of sugar in it!"

"Took a big risk too," Matthew Drane pointed out. "If they had asked to see his card, they'd have known he wasn't Erskine, and if Erskine had been lying at the bottom of that gorge with a broken neck as he ought to have been, the young man would have found himself in Queer Street."

"It would have been even awkward for us," Edward Staines observed. "He would certainly have squealed."

"His removal," Paul Viotti pronounced, "shows that we are one bang-up organisation."

Savonarilda strolled back to his place.

"I can't think why you keep a thing like that about," he protested, pointing backwards to the body of the young man.

"Neither can I," Matthew Drane agreed, with a shudder. "Every now and then I catch a glimpse of that foot. Don't see why we need make the place look like a butcher's shop."

"Everything has to be done according to plan," Paul Viotti explained coldly. "We never fail; you must admit that. Until we were ready to dispose of it, the body had to be in a safe place. In a quarter of an hour, it will be fetched. In an hour there will be nothing but a few ashes somewhere near the small summerhouse which we call the shrine. There will be another young man less ogling the cocottes and earning their fifty francs with the old ladies at the Nice cabaret shows, but it is doubtful whether any one will even remark upon his absence. If they do, it will be too late. People disappear often from the Riviera when they have spent their money or the right finger beckons. Some are found. Those who disappear under our auspices are never found."

Matthew Drane lit a cigar and leaned back in his place.

"Our young friend, Savonarilda," he remarked, "has criticised, but he has made no suggestion. I think he has something to say to us. For my part, I think the chief's right. We have a perfect machine, running smoothly and without a flaw. It may be costing us a good deal, but on the other hand we have no Police Headquarters to take

110

care of. In short, up till now, we have had things pretty well our own way, except that this young fellow Erskine didn't cough up and we were a trifle too greedy in that Nice business. Tony has something at the back of his mind, I'm sure."

Savonarilda discarded his extinct cigarette and lit another.

"The crown jewels of Monaco," he reflected, "do not compare, of course, with other collections which Fate has brought upon the market, but there are a few good modern pieces amongst them. They are ours for the picking up."

"Such imagination!" Paul Viotti murmured, with flashing eyes. "A very Prince of Adventure!"

Savonarilda looked at him a little insolently.

"I wish you would remember sometimes, Viotti," he said, "that I do not care for my title to be banalized. My ancestors were princes when yours were scraping the soil of Corsica for a few potatoes!"

There was a curious light in Paul Viotti's eyes and his lips twitched. He remained, however, silent.

"A few nights ago," Savonarilda continued, "I dined at the Palace. The week of our arrival here, after I had paid my formal call, I lunched there. I have a complete plan of the strong room leading out of the Royal Suite where the jewels are kept, and of the two staircases leading away from it."

"They have a new American Dunster safe," Matthew Drane announced. "I heard the Princess say so."

"Tom Meredith here," Savonarilda went on, "can do anything in this world with a Dunster safe, except eat it. He can discover the combination by looking at it and the drawers fly out when he touches them. I kept guard over him at work once in the Seventh National Bank when we needed the money to buy that steamerload of whisky. I have never seen Her Royal Highness' safe, but I will back the Seventh National Bank safe against anything that ever crossed the Atlantic, and Tom opened that as though the locks were made of butter. Isn't that so, Tom?"

"I guess it didn't worry me any," was the modest reply.

Pierre Viotti beamed upon his confederates.

"The Prince has a great imagination," he murmured.

"I have more than that. I have some very useful facts," Savonarilda observed drily. "I know the number of men on guard, at what hours they are changed and where they are posted. They would be as much use against us as the golliwogs in a toyshop!"

"And the get-away?" Viotti queried.

"By sea," was the prompt reply. "One of your brother's

invaluable contributions, Viotti, was the flying motor boat. If the engines are in good shape and the new sloop is ready for use—"

"She was put in the water yesterday," Pierre Viotti announced.

"Very good," Savonarilda continued. "She must crawl around here until we are ready for her. It will not be a quick division affair, of course. All the jewels will have to go either to Amsterdam or London, and they will lose a good deal in the cutting. Even after that, I have worked it out that there ought to be twenty millions to divide."

"My friends," Viotti said joyously, "I think that our next adventure is accepted."

There was a sound like the tinkling of a musical box. Paul Viotti placed his hand under the table and produced from a ledge a small, quaintly shaped telephone. He listened, spoke down it, and added a word or two which obviously had some code significance. Then he made his way to the north wall, touched the representation of a porthole in the swaying galleon and the door swung open. Three or four men in their road-menders' garb, who were always to be seen about the outside of the place or working in the garden, entered, carrying a long, lightly built wooden box fashioned like an elongated steamer trunk. They lifted the body into it, replaced the lid and disappeared with scarcely a word. As they ascended the stairs, Viotti held open the door leading up into the bar and listened. The old man and woman were there, singing one of their Neapolitan songs.

"The requiem of the unknown victim," Savonarilda sneered.

CHAPTER XVII

The Monte Carlo world is temperamental but its spirit is resilient. After a fortnight of intermingled cold, rain and mistral, the sun suddenly shone. A flawless blue sky stretched across the heavens, a south wind stole lazily across the devastated flower fields and loitered amongst the gardens. Everybody turned suddenly cheerful. After all, Erskine had not been murdered. He had been the victim of a motor accident and was slowly recovering. The unknown person who had stolen his papers probably deserved his fate. There had been no fresh calamity. The administration breathed a sigh of relief. Something might yet be made of what was left of the season.

Roger and Jeannine who, it being Sunday, had a day's holiday, were seated with Thornton under a striped umbrella at one of the tables of the Royalty bar. There was a buzz of pleasant conversation around them, no tragedies to discuss or think about. Terence Brown went by, swinging his cane and whistling a tune from the opera of last night. Maggie Saunders was drinking cocktails with two new admirers. Prince Savonarilda, who hated cocktails and seldom entered any other bar than the Sporting Club, except under compulsion, was drinking Italian vermouth with the great Diva who had sung at the opera the night before. Every one seemed to be very content and happy.

"I asked you to meet me here," Thornton, who was the host of the party, said, "because I was not quite sure where you would like to lunch. Mademoiselle Jeannine has, perhaps, some preference?"

"None at all," she declared convincingly.

"Beaulieu?" Roger suggested.

"But it is Sunday," Jeannine reminded him. "On Sundays, Beaulieu is terribly crowded."

"Would you like," Thornton asked, "to go to a place which would be terribly empty?"

"I think that would be marvellous," Jeannine assented.

"It is a little matter which concerns Roger and me more," Thornton said, looking across at his friend, "but before I leave, I should like to pay one more visit to that quaint place, the Hôtel du Soleil. I wonder whether you would care to risk it—go up there and demand lunch? They can't do more than refuse us, and if they do, it won't take us more than twenty minutes to get anywhere."

"It is certainly an idea," Roger admitted. "I don't know what they'll say to us. Sam, the barman, has practically warned me off the premises! And I'm perfectly certain, at times, at any rate, there are some queer goings-on there. I think perhaps it would be better if we went one day when Jeannine wasn't with us."

"Sunday seemed to me such a good day," Thornton persisted, "because they must have customers for drinks, at any rate, and next Sunday I sha'n't be here."

"If you wish to go," Jeannine said, "I do not mind in the least."

"I must tell you," Thornton explained. "Mr. Sloane and I have different ideas about the place. I've been there and found it a very ordinary sort of show. He has half an idea, I believe, that it's a perfect hotbed of crime. I should like to disabuse his mind of that idea, but if either of you have the slightest objection, why, I'll take you anywhere you like."

"I think it is quite reasonable, what Mr. Thornton says,"

Jeannine approved. "If you go to-day, and all is as it should be, you will not worry about the place any more. If I go too, there will be one more to watch."

"That settles it," Roger agreed. "We lunch at the Hôtel du Soleil. Do you mind calling back at the Paris for a moment?"

Thornton smiled.

"Ridiculous," he murmured, "but I had the same idea."

Roger descended from his room about a quarter of an hour later to find Thornton at the desk. The latter held out a letter which he had just written.

* * * * *

Major Thornton, Mr. Roger Sloane and Mademoiselle Jeannine are lunching at the Hôtel du Soleil just below the Corniche. As they have some suspicions about the place, Mr. Sloane would be obliged if the Direction will communicate with the police and send some gendarmes up to the place if they have not returned by four o'clock.

* * * * *

"I'm going to give this to the concierge," Thornton explained, "tell him to keep it before him, and if we have not returned by five minutes to four, to open it and act according to its instructions."

"It's a perfectly sound idea," Roger agreed, "but somehow or other, I think that two of us—I suppose that you went to your room for the same purpose as I did—will be perfectly well able to deal with anything that may happen."

"In my profession," Thornton remarked, as they went out to rejoin Jeannine, "we learn to leave nothing to chance."

* * * * *

Roger was conscious of a genuine thrill of interest, if not of excitement, when he pushed open the door of the bar of the Hôtel du Soleil. It had changed in no respect since his last visit. Two young men, whose cycles were leaning against the wall outside, were drinking beer at one of the small tables. There was not another soul in the room except Sam, who greeted them a little surlily.

"It doesn't seem a bit of good telling you fellows that we're closed," he remarked. "I have to serve you if you come in, and then I catch it from the Governor."

"Don't you worry, Sam," Roger enjoined cheerily. "Now that the bad weather's gone, you'll have so many customers you won't want to close. What about showing us the best you can do in the way of Dry Martinis?"

The man sighed and began to juggle with the bottles. He might have been just as anxious as he seemed to discourage clients, but he was too great an artist to mix a bad cocktail. They sipped them with genuine approval.

"What about a little lunch for the three of us in the restaurant?" Thornton suggested.

The shock did not seem to be so great as they had feared. Sam sighed resignedly and lifted the flap of the counter.

"There's two or three staying in the hotel. There might be some sort of a meal. I'll enquire."

He disappeared down the passage. Thornton looked around the place carefully.

"Seems all right," he observed.

"It certainly does," Roger confessed.

Jeannine shook her head.

"It is a bad place," she declared. "I don't know why, but it is. I feel it all the time. When we have had lunch, if they give us any, I shall be glad to get away. I do not trust that barman."

"Well, he's rude enough to be honest at any rate," Thornton remarked.

Sam returned in a moment or two, followed by a *maître d'hôtel*. The latter bowed to his prospective clients and displayed none of his companion's churlishness.

"Very good luncheon just ready, lady and gentlemen," he announced. "Trout, caught near here, or an omelette, if you wish. Baby lamb or chicken and fruit."

"Ready now?" Thornton asked.

"Ready this moment."

"We'll come right along."

They followed their guide along the passage and into a plainly decorated but sufficiently attractive-looking restaurant. Two men in golfing attire were already lunching, also a man and a woman. They took their places at a corner table.

"So far," Thornton declared, as he took up the list and ordered some wine, "I don't see why you two have the creeps about this place."

"It isn't creeps with me," Roger protested. "I've told you just what actually happened, and we know for a fact, at any rate, that the beginning of that Nice drama took place here."

The trout arrived without undue delay and was certainly excellent. The baby lamb which followed was equally good. A sweet omelette which the *maître d'hôtel* offered personally was excellent. No fault could be found with the wine.

"Could we take our coffee out in the garden?" Thornton enquired.

"Wherever Monsieur wishes."

They looked about them with curiosity as they passed through the hall. There were several bags of golf clubs there and at least half a dozen fishing rods. They passed out into the garden, brilliant with flowers, and strolled along one of the paths.

"Tell me now," Thornton begged, "do you see anything suspicious about the place?"

"Not a thing," Roger admitted.

They explored the garden thoroughly, then they returned to their coffee, and the two men each drank a *Fine*. Afterwards they strolled around the garage. Through the windows, which were quite unprotected, they could see the lilac-coloured car of Monsieur Pierre Viotti and another slightly smaller Fiat. Jeannine looked at the former with a shiver.

"That man is here," she declared.

They looked simultaneously towards the upper portion of the hotel. There were no particular signs of life about the place, but the shutters of every room were thrown open.

"Any one staying here?" Thornton asked the waiter, who had just appeared with the bill.

"Pretty well as many as we can take care of, sir," the man replied. "We have three golfing gentlemen, a *pêcheur* and two artists. A fine day like this every one does not come back to lunch. If they wish, we pack it and they take it with them."

"A very reasonable arrangement. Is Mr. Viotti here to-day?"

"Not to-day, sir. His brother from America is over and they make excursions together."

"I thought he might be here," Roger suggested, "because his car is in the garage."

"They go for their excursions more often in his brother's car," the man explained. "It is a Hispano-Suiza and it travels very fast.... *Merci bien*, Monsieur."

"Stop one moment," Roger begged. "Seems to me this would be a very nice spot to spend a few days when one wanted to be quiet. Could one look at the rooms?"

"I will ask Mademoiselle."

The waiter disappeared into the hotel and returned, having in charge a florid-looking young woman who had made lavish use of her cosmetics. She welcomed her enquirers cordially.

116

"We wondered whether you happened to have a bedroom and sitting room for a few days?" Roger asked.

The girl was in despair.

"And only this morning," she confided, "a gentleman arrived with his servant and took the last rooms we have. Perhaps next week—"

"We'll enquire again next week," Roger promised.

She expatiated to them on the beauty of the view, the safety of the drains, the mid-week privacy of the place. Sunday was, without a doubt, their busiest day and the week-ends—

"Well, what would you have?" she demanded, with a gay little laugh. "They tell me that it is the same in England."

"The same the world over," Thornton declared solemnly. "By the by, I am the owner of an English illustrated paper. Can I have the names of your guests and would you like me to publish a photograph?"

"As to the photograph, with pleasure, if Monsieur has a camera to take it," the girl replied. "The names of the guests," she added, "you will find in the visitors' book."

They passed into the little hall which connected the hotel with the restaurant. Mademoiselle produced a handsome calf-bound volume which she spread open in front of Thornton. He scribbled down some names.

"Absolutely *bona fide*, all this," he observed, as they strolled down the path which led to the road. "Two young men from Norwood, with the name of their golf club—Chislehurst, I think it was. A man and his wife from Bordeaux and another man, who dares to proclaim himself a painter, from St. Paul. You must be wrong about this place, Roger. You see for yourself that there are enough guests here to take up every room in the house. I expect they get a loose lot out from Nice now and then, but they can't very well help that."

"You yourself are satisfied, then?" Jeannine demanded.

"I certainly am," Thornton replied.

"And I'm afraid I must admit that I am also," Roger added reluctantly.

"And I *not*," Jeannine declared. "I do not care that there are good and respectable people here. I do not care that there is no evil to be seen. It is there."

"Well, it doesn't seem to have touched us," Thornton observed, with one of his quiet smiles.

Mademoiselle came hurrying out to them as they were stepping into the car.

"There will be rooms free on Wednesday," she announced. "Not the corner suite with the bath, but the one next to it—Number Fourteen."

"We will telephone up to-morrow morning," Roger promised. "We have lunched excellently."

"*Au revoir j'espère*, Monsieur," Mademoiselle fluttered, with a little wave of the hand.

They glided off down the hill towards Monte Carlo. Thornton leaned forward.

"Sloane," he said, "I think after all we shall have to pass that place O.K. There isn't a thing there to take exception to. If they'd been out to do us any harm—well, first of all they could have poisoned the cocktails, they could have poisoned the food, they could have pretended to show us the rooms and locked us in. In short, we were very much at their mercy. Added to that, I haven't seen a person who looks anything like a criminal."

"The place isn't in the least like what I expected to find," Roger confessed.

"You are both of you—how do you call it in English?—boobies!" Jeannine declared. "If this hotel were being kept by a bad man for bad purposes, would he not provide himself with the means for deceiving people? On Sunday, for instance, as to-day—everything would be in order. In the week days it is different. Passers-by are few. It is easy to close up the rooms."

Thornton, an unusual thing for him, was inclined to be a little irritable.

"Mademoiselle has—what we call in England—a bee in her bonnet. You see the whole place as it stands. There is not the scope there for any deception. There is no room large enough, for instance, to be the meeting place for a gang of criminals. However, what does it matter? I, at any rate, am convinced. So is Sloane."

Roger nodded thoughtfully.

"I think that the proprietor, Monsieur Viotti, is probably in with a roughish lot of people in Nice and they use his hotel during the week for any sort of purpose they like, but I must confess," he added, as he swung around a bend of the road, "that to-day has altogether shaken my idea that the place might be the permanent headquarters of a gang of criminals. I found nothing sinister about it at all."

Jeannine sighed.

"It is useless," she declared. "How can I persist? You are clever men with brains and you judge from what you see and with your reasoning powers. I am a foolish girl and I do not care what I see or what I do not see. I am not impressed. I judge only from my feelings."

Thornton had recovered his good humour.

"Mademoiselle's attitude is not to be ignored," he said. "I can assure you that inspiration has often succeeded in our profession where brains and perseverance have failed. In this case, though," he went on, "although I agree that a man who drives about in a car painted that hideous shade of lilac, and who is altogether such an insufferable little bounder as Monsieur Viotti, might be capable of any villainy, I do not fancy that the Hôtel du Soleil shelters more than his peccadilloes."

"If the florid young lady is one of them," Roger remarked, "his tastes are at least not exotic."

"Stupid men, both of you," Jeannine lamented.

CHAPTER XVIII

It happened that Jeannine and Roger were both standing at one of the high windows of the Sporting Club, looking out across the harbour at the commencement of the strange business.

"*Ciel!*" the former exclaimed. "What is it that arrives?"

Every one was asking the same question. Behind them the croupier had paused in the act of spinning the ball. There was a general chorus of exclamations. People from all parts of the room came hurrying up to the windows. A gun from the Rock, without warning or any apparent cause, had been fired—its echoes were still reverberating amongst the hills.

"There must be a warship coming in," some one exclaimed.

They all looked out seawards but there was no sign of any lights.

"It can't be a warship," some one else pointed out. "There's not a single harbourage left in the port. There have not been so many yachts in for years. Besides, only the smaller craft would venture in, anyway."

The manager of the Sporting Club came hurrying to the window. He looked out with a blank expression upon his face.

"One could imagine trouble of some sort," he muttered, "but there is no sign of disturbance."

"There might be an outbreak of fire up at the Palace," Roger suggested. "The wind is blowing the other way and we shouldn't see any sign of it yet."

"The telephones are at work," the other man announced. "One cannot conceive—"

He broke off in his speech. A rocket went hissing into the skies from the heights on the other side of the harbour. The manager turned rapidly away.

"There is some sort of trouble," he muttered, as he hastened towards the door. "One must make preparations—"

Play was completely suspended in the room. Every one was struggling to find a place near the windows.

"It is the revolution at last," the shock-headed Monegasque shouted from the bar. "*Vive la révolution!*"

The croupiers, who were nearly all Monegasques, were gathered together in a corner of the room, whispering uneasily. For five hundred years the discharge of a single rocket had been a signal of alarm. There was, without a doubt, trouble up at the Palace, but what sort of trouble? They talked and gesticulated wildly. The discontent amongst the people was notorious. That a revolution had been threatened was well known, but that it should have come in this fashion seemed incredible. There were men there, the chef with the grey beard, for instance, who belonged to the secret council of the Monegasques and who would certainly have been called into consultation if the time had really arrived. Everything outside was once more dark and peaceful, except that at intervals a *voiture* filled with eager sightseers went by at full speed. The lights in the Palace were still in evidence and the streets were free from any sign of commotion.

"What can it mean?" Jeannine asked, clinging to Roger's arm.

"I have not the slightest idea," Roger confessed frankly. "We shall know directly. Here comes Monsieur Rignaud and he has the air of one with news."

Monsieur Rignaud, the controller of the Sporting Club, rushed into the room, his face bathed in perspiration. He mounted a chair and curiosity produced immediate silence.

"My friends," he called out, "there is no cause for alarm. What has happened is that there has been a serious robbery at the Palace. The alarm gun was fired and a rocket discharged to call back such of the gendarmerie as were on leave this evening. A robbery of jewels. There is nothing more. All croupiers will at once return to their places."

He descended from his chair. The buzz of voices recommenced, but the sense of drama seemed to have passed. A jewel robbery, after all, was an everyday happening. Thornton came up and touched Roger on the shoulder.

"Can you spare me a minute at once?" he begged.

Lord Dalmorres, chuckling with pleasure, passed his arm through Jeannine's and led her to a roulette table. Roger followed Thornton into a retired portion of the corridor.

"Sloane," he whispered, looking at him keenly out of his cold grey eyes, "I suppose you, like me, have had ideas about the doings down here which it seemed only ridiculous to put into words?"

"Sure," Roger agreed. "I'll say that I have."

"Very well, then," Thornton continued. "It might be interesting to find out who is in the Club to-night and who are absentees. You take the 'chemie' room and I'll start with the bar and work up from the far end of the trente-et-quarante and roulette until we meet."

They came together again in a quarter of an hour. Roger frankly confessed himself disappointed. Three men whom he had always vaguely distrusted—two English bookmakers and a notorious Belgian gambler—were all there in evidence at the tables. Thornton had had very little better luck. Pierre Viotti, with a half bottle of champagne before him, was seated upon a stool at the bar, talking eagerly to a Niçois friend. In his eyes was the usual expression of sly hate as he turned around to find Roger close at hand.

"Was Prince Savonarilda playing trente-et-quarante, did you notice?" Roger asked.

Thornton shook his head as he poured some Perrier into his whisky.

"I didn't see him anywhere," he acknowledged. "But look—that's odd."

Roger followed the direction of his companion's gaze. Savonarilda, looking tired and blasé as usual, was glancing languidly around the room. He nodded to the two men and lounged off down the passage.

* * * * *

"One must not miss any chance," Roger said cautiously, as they emerged from the last lift some five minutes later and made their way into the lounge of the hotel. "Can you see Savonarilda anywhere here?"

"Not a sign of him," Thornton confessed. "What do you want him for?"

121

Roger made no reply. He turned around and approached the concierge's desk.

"Is Prince Savonarilda in his room, do you know?" he enquired.

"Just gone up, sir," the man replied. "He took his key from me not a minute ago."

Roger walked towards the lift and rang the bell. Thornton looked at his companion curiously.

"What's in your mind about Savonarilda?" he persisted.

"I haven't anything in my mind," Roger confessed. "I am trying to be like Jeannine and act upon inspiration. What is Prince Savonarilda's number?" he asked the liftman, as they stepped in.

"One hundred and ninety-seven, sir," the man replied. "The Prince has just gone up."

They mounted to the second floor, walked along the corridor and Roger knocked briskly at the door of Number one hundred and ninety-seven. There was a brief delay, then Savonarilda presented himself.

"Hello!" he exclaimed, "Anything wrong?"

"Nothing at all," Roger assured him. "I tried to stop you downstairs at the lift but I was just too late. Lady Julia wants to know whether you can dine to-morrow night—just a small party? I ought to have asked you before, but I'm afraid it slipped my memory."

Savonarilda shook his head.

"Sorry," he regretted. "I always like to go to Lady Julia's parties but I'm afraid to-morrow it can't be done. I'm dining with some one or other—I forget whom."

"Bad luck! Sorry I disturbed you."

"Any news about the jewel robbery?"

"We haven't heard a thing yet. I expect in half an hour's time or so the whole story will be out."

"Ridiculous fuss about a potty lot of ornaments. There are a dozen women in this hotel whose jewels are worth a great deal more."

"Having an early night, aren't you?" Roger remarked.

"Got to, sometimes," was the languid reply. "Goodnight."

"Well, I don't see that we got much out of that," Thornton remarked, as they rang for the lift.

Roger smiled cryptically.

"I've developed a fancy for secrecy to-night," he confided, "because I want to see later on if things shape themselves the same way to you. I'll say this, though; I think before many days have passed, we're either going to bring something off or get it in the neck ourselves."

"Any facts?" Thornton asked. "Or are you still adopting Mademoiselle Jeannine's flair for inspiration?"

Roger grinned.

"I wouldn't call it that," he confessed. "One queer incomprehensible fact and a damned big guess."

* * * * *

Roger found Jeannine struggling to be polite to her temporary escort, but boring herself very much with roulette. He carried her off at once to dance at the Knickerbocker, regardless of Dalmorres' protests.

"You young engaged men are the most selfish devils on the face of the earth," the latter declared. "You seem to think because you have had the good luck to annex a most attractive young woman that for the future no one else may come near her. I think I will come to this place with you. I can at least pay the bill."

"I am in a generous frame of mind and I will bargain with you," Roger declared. "You can come on in half an hour's time. Half an hour alone I must have with Jeannine."

"One hears sometimes," Dalmorres sighed, "of the idiocy of lovers, but one scarcely expects to hear this sort of thing from men of comparatively mature years. Do you realise, young man, that you are proposing to spend the rest of your life with Jeannine?"

"Blessed thought!" Roger exclaimed. "Come on, Dalmorres, we'll take you along."

"I should think so," was the complacent reply. "My limousine is below. Perhaps you'd rather walk, Roger?"

"On the contrary, you had better come up in your limousine," Roger replied. "I'm taking Jeannine in my own little bus. Tell your man the Knickerbocker."

"Selfish pig," Dalmorres muttered, with a gleam in his eye.

Roger had brought his chauffeur and Jeannine sat very close to him as they took their places.

"You are such a darling, Roger," she murmured, when they were halfway to their destination and as soon as she had sufficient breath. "I love the way you—what is your word?—chaff Lord Dalmorres. Do all Englishmen talk to one another like that? Frenchmen would be fighting very soon."

"Dalmorres and I understand each other pretty well," Roger

confided. "He's a gay old spark and he loves to be chaffed about the girls."

"He is very attractive," Jeannine said.

"More women than you and I could count have found him so," Roger observed drily. "I rather wish he'd kept away to-night, though."

"We will dance most of the time," Jeannine suggested, "then he will get tired and he will go away."

She tripped across the pavement, her eyes dancing with happiness, very dainty and chic in the moonlight.

"'Au temps de "la fleur" ils sont tous en folie,'" she hummed. "To-night I feel like that. It is good to feel like that. I am not afraid any longer. That was silly. Monte Carlo is a good place."

Then the swing door was flung open and, with a leer on his face and a drunken lurch to his footsteps, out came Pierre Viotti, ex-Mayor of La Bastide!

Pierre Viotti was without a doubt drunk, but he was joyously and happily drunk. Never had the world seemed to him a more wonderful or delightful place. In the restaurant he was just leaving he had met with much success. He had stood drinks to all the dancing ladies and most of the men. Supper bills had been surreptitiously slipped into his hand by the *maître d'hôtel* and promptly discharged. He had danced with the principal chanteuse and when he was sober he was no mean performer. What a life! What a brother he had! What a man he was! His idea—the motor boat. Millions and millions and millions it had brought. All the champagne in the world he could drink. All the girls in the world he could have. But not this one. Well, who cared? To-night it was impossible to hate any one. He pushed aside the protecting hand of the doorkeeper, took off his hat and made a low bow.

"*Bon soir*, Mademoiselle Jeannine," he cried gaily. "It is your Mayor who salutes you."

She shrank back but it was more in scorn than from any sort of fear. A village brat, he had called her. Her poise was the poise of a princess.

"*Bon soir*, Monsieur le Maire," she said.

"*Et bon soir*, Monsieur," Pierre Viotti sang out to Roger. "You heard the little tune Mademoiselle was singing as she entered. Ask her the meaning of it and then you will not understand. It is for us French—us of a different race!"

"*Bon soir*, Monsieur Viotti," Roger answered calmly. "If you would be so kind as to stand on one side, it is our wish to enter."

Pierre Viotti crushed himself against the wall. The sound of

Roger's voice had deadened a little his alcoholic good humour. There was a cloud upon the horizon, after all. He was no longer supremely happy. He felt something hard in his pocket. If only he dared! A quick business that would make of it and no more of these arguments with Paul.

"A good place," he said, pointing backwards to the restaurant. "One amuses oneself there!"

Roger took Jeannine by the arm and passed on. Pierre Viotti would have followed them, but for the restraining arm of the doorkeeper.

"Hi!" he called out.

Roger turned his head. Something of the old malevolence was back in Viotti's face.

"Listen," he shouted. "You like my hotel. You go there sometimes. You come and see me. I show you something no one else in the world knows one little thing about. You come."

He turned away and lurched out.

"Some one seems to have drawn his fangs," Roger remarked, with a smile, as they settled themselves down at a corner table. "Perhaps we shall get a wedding present from him after all!"

"A bowl of poison perhaps," Jeannine replied. "Nothing else."

"What did he mean about showing us something no one else in the world knew anything about?" Roger speculated.

"I was wondering."

Then for a brief space of time—one hour or something like it—life became an enchantment. With them was none of the weary-footed dancing of the tired professional or the lazy effort of the dinner guest who is doing his duty. To hold Jeannine in his arms was to Roger the most amazing content, and to lean shyly against him and let her feet fly over the floor to the very seductive music was to Jeannine the last word in happiness. They drank sparingly of the champagne, but they finished the whole of an omelette and ordered another. Dalmorres strolled in long after the time he had appointed and sunk into a chair with a sigh of virtuous resignation.

"What I have denied myself!" he murmured. "Tell them, young Roger, to give me a whisky and soda and a sandwich. I have been walking in the garden sooner than disturb this idyll."

"Liar," Roger answered, as he called a waiter.

Dalmorres lit a cigarette.

"Manners must be the first thing you teach your young man, Mademoiselle Jeannine," he enjoined. "You, I am sure, will believe me. An hour ago it must have been that I looked in here and saw you two in this corner, looking so happy and so utterly content with

125

each other that I had not the courage to disturb you, and I went back again into the cold night and promenaded—in the rain too—"

"Oh, la, la!" Jeannine interrupted, with a little peal of laughter. "I will not say that you do not speak the truth, Lord Dalmorres, but the night is warm, the moon is shining, there is no rain and you have your limousine."

Dalmorres knocked the ash from his cigarette.

"It is a fact that I am dreaming," he acknowledged. "A bad habit of mine. I am too susceptible and I suffer so that it affects my memory. I think that when that whisky and soda has arrived, I shall summon up my courage and invite the blond young lady to dance with me."

"She will probably accept with pleasure," Roger remarked, "as she happens to be the danseuse of the *maison*. I gather that all the little ladies who are here to-night, though, and the men too, have been having rather a good time. A wealthy Niçois who was being armed out just as we arrived has been standing free drinks to every one in the house."

"A short rotund man with a brick-red complexion and black eyes?" Dalmorres enquired curiously.

Roger nodded. "What do you know about him?"

"I happen to have been up at a small select night restaurant on the hill, I forget the name, I was one of a party whom Miss Madge Saunders collected to visit some of the deserving institutions of Monte Carlo. Without a doubt, the same individual barged in. He embarked upon the same course of generosity there."

Jeannine leaned across.

"So you have been up the hills with Maggie Saunders to-night, since we left you!"

"For half an hour, certainly."

"And your story that you came down here and feared to disturb us?"

"Allegorical, my dear young lady," Dalmorres explained. "I told you just how I should have felt, and what I should have done, if I *had* come down here and seen you and your young man looking into each other's eyes as I did when I made my actual appearance. You follow me, I hope? I hate to be misunderstood."

Jeannine laughed softly.

"Oh, I do not misunderstand you, Lord Dalmorres," she assured him. "I think you are wonderful."

"What became of the wealthy Niçois?" Roger enquired.

Dalmorres appeared to have forgotten. A few minutes later,

however, when Jeannine's attention was engaged by some new arrivals, he leaned forward in his chair.

"Do you know the fellow, Roger?" he asked.

Roger nodded.

"In a way. I had a row with him once."

Dalmorres leaned still farther forward. He kept one eye on Jeannine.

"Look out for that little fat devil," he half whispered. "Has he got an hotel anywhere?"

"Between the two Corniches," Roger answered.

Dalmorres glanced once more towards Jeannine. She was having to speak in English to one of Prétat's patrons and the task was obviously absorbing her whole attention.

"Well, don't you go to it, that's all," Dalmorres advised. "There's something waiting for you there you wouldn't like. I couldn't make out what it was, but as soon as he got a dim idea that I was listening, drunk or not drunk, he shut up. He has an idea that you have been trying to play the amateur detective, that you have gone up there to discover his secrets, as he called them. There was one waiting there he was ready to share with you, he said, with the most malevolent grin I ever saw in my life. Take my tip, Roger; stay away from that hotel."

CHAPTER XIX

Dalmorres was perhaps a trifle indiscreet in some of his observations in the Sporting Club a few nights later. Every one was inclined to be nervy and irritated. The robbery of the royal jewels of Monaco had turned out to be a more serious affair than was at first believed. It transpired that the whole of the jewels were gone, not a portion of them; that they were valued at fifty millions and that the police were without a single clue as to the bandits. That they were a desperate gang was obvious from their methods. Two of the guards had been shot and the sentry had been stabbed to death in his own box. It was his death cry which had first given the alarm. Servants had streamed out from every direction. There was nothing but an empty safe to be seen. No motor car had been anywhere near the Palace gates. The only clue to the manner by which the thieves had made their escape was furnished by the captain of the guard, who, by throwing himself down and listening with his ear to the ground, believed that he could hear from somewhere in the black distance the rapid beating of a petrol engine driven at great speed.

"These fellows, whoever they are," Dalmorres declared, "have nerve and they have imagination. They work with one another too well to have been brought together haphazard. Neither do I believe that they are French. There's too much method and thoroughness about them."

"Where do you think they come from, then?" Mr. Terence Brown asked.

Dalmorres chuckled.

"I'm afraid you'll have to shoulder the burden, my friend," he said. "I should put them down for Americans beyond a doubt— Americans probably driven over here by the competition in the bootlegging business. That safe, for example—"

"What do you know about the safe?"

"I was up at the Palace to-day," Dalmorres confided, "and I was invited to have a look at it. I found half a dozen of the French police simply speechless with admiration. I'm perfectly certain that if the man who had done the job had turned up at that moment, they would have saluted!"

"Police headquarters of New York ought to be able to help them," some one from the edge of the circle suggested. "They generally know where their great artists are."

"The only pleasing aspect of the affair," Dalmorres remarked, "is that this time they seem to have left the visitors alone and closed in upon home products. It gives me hope that I may, after all, elude their activities."

"What they want," Savonarilda pointed out, "is a man with the actual money. You wander about the place to-night with a handful of those fifty thousand franc *jetons* and your name will soon be on the list. These fellows don't give you much grace, either. You're warned in the morning and bumped off in the evening."

"In my own case," Dalmorres said, "I should certainly prefer a little more time to settle my affairs. I have no doubt that if one approached the secretary of this organisation discreetly and pleasantly, a satisfactory arrangement could be made."

"This is the second affair," Roger Sloane reflected, "where a motor boat has been used for the get-away. Poor Bradley was shot from one to start with. The police drew a cordon around every port from Monaco to Fréjus. Not a sign has ever been seen or a thing heard of the missing boat. Now this one seems to have disappeared in the same way."

128

"Which all goes to prove," Savonarilda drawled, "that these are local fellows and not Americans at all."

"I am inclined to favour the idea of a conjunction," Dalmorres observed. "The nerve and dash of the professional criminal and the low cunning and local knowledge of some of the *indigènes*. They may have come even from so far as Marseilles."

"They are going to empty this place pretty quickly," Terence Brown grunted. "The Handleys are all going. I saw old Handley down at the P.L.M. office this morning."

"They would," Dalmorres murmured.

"They are not the only ones," Terence Brown went on. "If I were a rich man, I think I should follow suit. The local police may be, and I daresay they are, quite capable of taking care of Monte Carlo on ordinary occasions, but at the height of the season, when several thousand of the richest people in the world are here, as well as the ordinary tourists and residents, it would need a miniature Scotland Yard to deal with what we are going through. Take to-day, for instance. In addition to all the residents and visitors here, there is an American touring ship in, and at least a couple of hundred of the passengers wandering about on land."

"American tourists," Savonarilda remarked, "are not exactly like a flock of sheep waiting to be sheared."

"Perhaps not," Terence Brown agreed, "but just put yourself in their place for a moment. They land here, the drinks are good, the air is full of sunshine in the daytime and music and perfumes by night. They think they are in an earthly Paradise. What thought of evil do you think enters into their minds? None at all. They just become unsuspicious naturally."

Dalmorres tapped lightly upon the table.

"Perhaps," he suggested, "we talk without sufficient discretion of these subjects. You see who arrives, Roger?"

Sloane nodded. Bumptious, rotund, carefully dressed in the costume the hour and the place demanded, Pierre Viotti had just swaggered up to the bar. He ordered a bottle of wine, as was his usual custom, and looked around as though seeking for some one to share it. His eyes wandered wistfully past the table where the five men were seated.

"A type," Dalmorres murmured. "If I lived here or were staying here for long—especially if I were you, Roger—it would interest me to know more about that man."

"You wouldn't gain much," Roger scoffed. "He was a peasant farmer until last year and an ignorant brute of the type."

"Sometimes," Dalmorres reflected, "these fellows make up in

that very misunderstood quality—cunning—for what they lack in brains. I never saw our friend in my life until last night, but I will answer for it that he is a bad lot. He has what I call the new criminal type of face—complexion rubicund and flawless, plump cheeks, dark shifty eyes, a perpetual grin and that telltale roll of flesh at the back of his neck. That man would be a day-by-day murderer if he could take out an insurance against being found out."

Roger laughed.

"I hate the fellow myself," he admitted, "but—"

Roger never finished his sentence. They all leaned forward to watch the unusual spectacle of the august-looking doorkeeper, with the silver chain around his neck, flying past the open doors. In his silk-stockinged legs and patent shoes the sight would have been ridiculous but for the man's obvious anxiety.

"Looks like more trouble," Roger muttered.

They all rose to their feet and trooped out into the passage. Only the ex-Mayor of La Bastide, who had begun to drink his wine, remained upon his stool. Several of the attendants were gathered around the door of the Directors' room. In a moment or two Monsieur Thiers hastened out, crossed the corridor and entered the Salle de Jeu. They all crowded around a functionary from below, who appeared a moment later. He spoke a few rapid sentences and made his way towards Sloane.

"What's wrong, Henry?" the latter asked.

"An accident or something serious up at the Royalty bar, Mr. Sloane," the man answered. "They telephoned here for Doctor Grayson. He and his wife are dining with a party who have just gone into the Rooms. Monsieur Thiers has gone to fetch him."

"The Royalty!" Sloane ejaculated. "I didn't know it was open at this time of night."

He swung around and reëntered the bar. Thornton was in the act of rising to his feet. Monsieur Pierre Viotti had settled down to the pleasant task of drinking his bottle of wine alone. He was crouching over the counter with squared shoulders and feet gripping the rungs of his stool, looking very much like a toad.

"Thornton," Sloane announced, "there's trouble up at the Royalty. Do you want to come and see what it is? My car is parked just outside."

Thornton groaned.

"One of my last nights even to be broken into! Of course I'll come, Sloane. I couldn't keep away when there's anything doing, but I was giving a supper party to Miss Saunders and a few of them."

"There's a new form of entertainment in Monte Carlo these nights," Roger remarked bitterly.

Dalmorres put his head in at the door.

"Sloane," he enquired, "where's Mademoiselle Jeannine to-night?"

"Safely out of anything that may have happened, thank God," was the fervent reply. "She's dining with my aunt and two other women at the Villa. I'm going for her at half-past eleven."

Dalmorres nodded.

"Going up to the Royalty?" he asked.

"Thornton and I are off there. Come along too, if you like."

"I should like," Dalmorres consented.

Arrived at the Royalty, they found a gendarme at the entrance who passed them in at once on a signal from Francis, the proprietor, who had hurried to the doorway. They passed up the garden and into the bar itself, both rooms of which were dimly lit. In one corner, the figure of a man lay stretched upon the floor. The doctor, who had already arrived, was kneeling by his side. Roger and his companions remained just inside the door, which Francis locked.

"What's happened?" Sloane asked.

"Just as we were going to close, Mr. Sloane," Francis told him, "a gentleman from Nice, Monsieur Viotti, came in with an American gentleman from the boat. They sat down and had drinks."

"Were they sober?"

"Monsieur Viotti was quite sober. The American gentleman seemed fairly so, but after one whisky and soda he went kind of stupid. Monsieur Viotti did his best to stop him from having another. They had an argument and Monsieur Viotti got up and left him. The American was here by himself in that easy-chair over there. I didn't wish to serve him anything else, so I went up to tell him that it was time we closed the bar. He used the worst language I have ever heard! Said he would stay here as long as he liked and demanded a bottle of whisky. We didn't want any trouble, so we served him with one whisky and soda. He had a sip and when my back was turned he staggered over to the bar and filled his glass up with neat whisky. I turned around just in time to see him on his way back to his chair. I told him again that we wanted to close, but he only laughed. He began to try and tell me about the speak-easies in New York."

"Who else was in the place?" Sloane asked.

"Not a soul, sir. Alberto left at eight and the last of the waiters went off about half an hour before Monsieur Viotti and the American gentleman arrived. Then Monsieur Viotti left me alone with him and I didn't know how to get rid of him. At last I said that if he didn't go, I was very sorry but I must telephone for the police. He took out a great pocketbook and began to brandish it, asked me if I knew who he was, said he was a New York millionaire, and he had come to spend one night in Monte Carlo so as to go to the bank early in the morning. He kept on waving his great pocketbook at me. Said he had eighty thousand dollars in it, and the purser wouldn't give him the right rate of exchange, so he was going to change the whole of it here. While I was arguing with him and begging him to put his money away, the two lights I had left turned on in the place suddenly went out. I turned quickly around and I saw the shapes of two men who had entered. That was about all I could see of them. I called out but they made no answer. They came very quickly up the room and, before I could imagine what was going to happen, one of them flashed out a gun and held it to my ribs and caught me by the neck with the other hand.

"'Come this way,' he ordered me."

"Rather a nasty one for you, Francis!" Sloane remarked. "I imagine you did as you were told."

"Well, sir, I didn't see what else I could do. I went. He pushed me through the door at the back of the bar and turned the key. He must have been here before to have known there was no other way out. I heard the American gentleman shout out—

"'Turn on the lights!'

"Then I heard him shout again:

"'Come on, you fellows. I don't know who you are but have a drink!'

"After that I never heard a sound. I banged at the door and shouted, and at last I crawled through that small window and dropped into the other room, and there I got to the switches which are behind the hatstand, and turned them on. The American was lying on the floor just where his chair had been, groaning. His pocketbook was lying open by his side, absolutely empty."

"And then?" Sloane asked.

"I telephoned for the doctor and the police. Two gendarmes came. One is outside. The other has gone to fetch the chief."

The doctor came across the floor to them. He knew Roger and shook hands.

"Monte Carlo is getting as famous as Chicago," he remarked.

"Is he dead?" Roger asked, pointing up the room.

The doctor shook his head.

"No, he is not dead or likely to die, unless he has bad luck. He has been drugged, and with such a powerful drug that its effect must

132

have been almost instantaneous, and it has touched him up around the heart. I have dealt with that, though—I had something with me. I shall have to go back to the surgery—a matter of ten minutes only—and when I come back, the police had better fetch some one from the ship to look after him."

"Had he really much money on him, I wonder?" Sloane queried.

"I know nothing about that," the doctor replied.

"Last night, at that little night restaurant on the hill," Dalmorres intervened, "he was telling every one what he told Francis—that he had eighty thousand dollars which he had brought in to have changed, and was sleeping the night here, so as to get up to the bank early. No one seems to have told him that to-day was a fête day and that the bank would be closed!"

The doctor took his leave with a hasty word or two of farewell. Sloane asked the proprietor of the bar a further question.

"Tell me, Francis, if he was not absolutely drunk when he arrived here, should you have said that he had had too much to drink?"

"Certainly."

"Did he seem any worse for the drink he had with Viotti?"

Francis shook his head.

"It didn't seem to make so much difference, sir," he replied. "I saw to it that it was weak. I'm afraid it was the drink he had when he was in the corner by himself and got up and fetched the bottle of whisky, that did him the mischief, after all that he had had."

"No luck," Roger sighed. "I'm afraid that lets Viotti out."

They crossed the room and looked at the man upon the floor. The doctor had propped his head up on a cushion and, although he was a ghastly colour and his breathing was stertorous and irregular, he had by no means the appearance of a man *in extremis*. The contents of his pockets were still strewn about just as the first gendarme had left them, and rather pathetically a photograph of a woman, in a leather case, was flung scornfully on one side.

"If I might make a suggestion," Dalmorres said, "I think it would be well if we left before the commissaire arrives. He will keep us here at least two hours if he finds us upon the premises, and there isn't a single thing we can tell him."

"There's only one thing to be done," Roger put in, "I shan't tell Thornton what it is, because he would only laugh at me. Dalmorres, would you do me a favour?"

"Anything except go back to the Sporting Club and drink with Monsieur Pierre Viotti!"

"You don't need to do that," Roger assured him. "Get round to Aunt Julia's in half an hour and take Jeannine home. Take her to the Sporting Club first, if she wants to go, but don't lose sight of her."

"I'll do that with pleasure," Dalmorres promised, "but what about you?"

"I may be back about one o'clock. I won't tell you where I'm going, but if anything happens, I'll tell you both when I get back."

Thornton lit a cigarette with steady fingers. In the semi-gloom of the place, his long melancholy face seemed for a moment drawn and anxious.

"I'll come with you, if you like," he offered.

Roger led the way out.

"No, I'll go alone," he said. "If there's nothing doing, it will be awfully boring. I'll probably be back at the Sporting Club before it closes."

"You won't find me," Thornton warned him. "I'm for an early night."

Dalmorres laughed as he led his companion away.

"I've been coming to this place for forty years," he decided, "and if there's one thing I've learned to disbelieve in, it's these early nights. Let's go back to the Sporting and see if the little Niçois is still drinking his champagne."

"Why on earth should we do that?" Thornton asked, obviously surprised.

Dalmorres was returning with elaborate courtesy the salutations of two *petites dames* on their homeward way and he made no reply.

CHAPTER XX

Roger brought his car to a standstill at a place on the Corniche where the road widened a little and the wall had been recently rebuilt. He left one front lamp and the rear one burning and, buttoning up his mackintosh, walked briskly downhill until he reached the spot where the road forked. Fortunately for the success of his enterprise, the night had become cloudy and a drizzling rain was falling. In the shadow of the trees he was able to continue his progress without fear of observation until he arrived at the front of the hotel. He glanced at the luminous dial of his watch. It was five minutes to twelve. The hotel itself and the bar were in complete darkness. There was not a sound to be heard, no evidence of life in any direction. He stood still some time, listening to the patter of the rain, then, treading cautiously, he crossed the road. For the first time within his memory, the large gates leading into the courtyard of the garage and fronting the road were open. He moved stealthily on inside the yard. There was no light in the garage, but just outside the closed door was an uncertain phantomlike shape. He stole on another few paces and realised that it was a car. In its shadow he stood quite still for several minutes, every sense on the alert; then he moved cautiously forward until he reached the bonnet. He laid his hand upon the radiator and, though his nerves were well under control, his heart gave a jump and he discovered that it was hot.

Some one, then, had just preceded him. He tried to make out what he could of the car and came to the conclusion that it was a Fiat, but the darkness was so intense that he could not be sure what colour it was. He stood away from it, thinking rapidly. Some one had arrived here within the last few minutes in a Fiat which did not belong to the place and had left it out in the rain. There was not a single chink of light from the bar or any one of the rooms of the hotel, and the garage was in darkness. Where, then, was the owner of the car?

A Fiat. A coupé, to judge from what he could feel, its deep luxurious cushions already sopping wet and the rain falling with a faint sizzle upon the radiator. Whatever reckless person had left it there had been in too great a hurry even to pull up the hood. Where was he now? Roger extended his adventure. He left the garage yard and passed through the small gate which led to the walk bordering the side of the hotel. He arrived at the south front and looked eagerly along the line of windows. Not a glimmer, not a sign of life anywhere. On this side, however, with a great stretch of open country falling down to the sea, the darkness seemed less intense. Roger could discern the row of cypresses an inkier black than the darkness itself and he could even distinguish the shapes of the shrubs close at hand. Slowly he retraced his steps, once more entered the garage yard and stole up to the car. Just as it loomed up in front of him, he stopped short. Even as he had groped his way towards it, a sudden fierce line of light appeared through the keyhole, and along the hinges of the doors. Some one was in the garage. Some one who had not been there before, unless they had been content to linger there in the darkness. At any moment the doors might be rolled back and he himself, defenceless, would be bathed in the light. He caught at his shoes and tore them off; then he stole with a long lopping stride towards the gate through which he had entered, crossed the road in half a dozen paces, thanked heaven for his long legs, and stepped over the grey wall. He crouched down behind it. Almost at the same moment, what he had visualised happened. The doors of the garage, beautifully oiled and fitted, rolled noiselessly back, the open space in front was flooded with light. In another second Roger would have seen the face of the man whose footsteps he heard, then an unseen hand from inside the garage turned off the switch. Roger could hear his footsteps now as he approached the other man. The doors rolled to. Both men were apparently there at the front of the car; their smothered voices were clearly audible. Roger felt himself almost sobbing for one single flash of light.

Hearing was easy enough. Crouched behind the wall he was conscious of the squishing of the cushions soaked with rain, as some one sat down in the driving seat. Then he heard the purring of the engine and the retreating footsteps of the other man, who crossed the yard and apparently entered the hotel by the side door. The car crawled out, the figure at the wheel all the more invisible by reason of the flashing headlights. Roger ducked absolutely out of sight. Then what he had prayed might happen, happened. The car stopped in front of the café entrance. The headlights were extinguished, the bar door was opened from inside, the driver descended, was caught only for one instant in a faint oblong slant of illumination, insufficient to do more than show that he was tall, walked with a stoop and was wearing a heavy coat. Then the door closed, nothing of the light remained but a thin line at the windows. There was darkness again. Roger only smiled. The car was waiting there. Its driver would return, and when he did his back would be to those governing switches.

The watcher behind the grey stone wall was doomed to no long period of waiting. Within five minutes the door of the bar was suddenly opened. The two men lingered there and for a space of five seconds or so they stood full in the blaze from the lamps over the bar counter. Every nerve of Roger's body was tense and throbbing from the strain of keeping that cry from his lips. He was stupefied with the amazement of the moment. It was the incredible which confronted him! Even the long elegant fingers which held the briquet to the cigarette were visible. It was Prince Antonio Marcus Constantine Savonarilda, Seigneur of Savonarilda and Count of the Holy Roman Empire, who stepped into the car, and Sam the barman who in muttered words was wishing him Godspeed!

136

The Trente-et-Quarante and Roulette salons were closed when Roger, after a brief visit to the dressing room, entered the Sporting Club bar. To his surprise, it was still comparatively full. With a start he recognised Savonarilda sitting at a table alone with Terence Brown. Dalmorres, Thornton and Maggie Saunders were seated at the counter. Pierre Viotti had apparently taken his leave. There were a dozen other of his intimates scattered about the place, but no Jeannine. He made his way at once to Dalmorres.

"My little commission?" he asked.

"Faithfully and honourably executed," Dalmorres assured him.

Roger drew a sigh of relief. He turned to his favourite barman.

"A double whisky and soda, Henry," he ordered.

"Why this burst of anxiety concerning Mademoiselle Jeannine?" Dalmorres asked curiously.

"I don't know," Roger replied. "Such queer things are happening in this place all the time."

"Well, there's one thing very certain," his friend said, with a regretful sigh. "Concerning Mademoiselle Jeannine, you need have no anxiety. From what particular planet of heaven she fell I do not know, but the Lord has greatly blessed you. She has the deafest of ears to all love-making, forensic or sentimental. I, who have brought tears in my younger days to the eyes of stolid British juries, succeed in evoking nothing but ribald mirth from the lips of that young woman. What are you going to do with that enormous drink, Roger?"

"Drink it," Roger assured him and kept his word.

"You were thirsty?" Dalmorres enquired politely.

"I was thirsty," Roger confessed. "I have also been nearly wet through and I have had pretty well the shock of my life."

"Perhaps another might go to the spot," his companion suggested. "I'm taking the smaller edition myself."

"Try me," Roger begged.

The order was given. Roger leaned sideways confidentially towards him.

"You took Jeannine absolutely to her home?" he asked.

"My dear fellow, I did more than that," Dalmorres assured him. "I waited on the pavement until Madame opened the door, I introduced myself, and I saw the door closed before I took my sorrowing departure. Mademoiselle Jeannine is safe, at any rate."

"Any more news about our American friend?"

"He's gone back on the ship," Thornton announced. "It seems it doesn't sail until the day after to-morrow. The people are making

137

excursions all over the place, so he'll be able to make up his mind for himself whether he stays and tries to get back his eighty thousand dollars or leaves it to the police. From the last I heard of him, he was going to cable the President of the United States, and several Senators, the American Ambassador in Paris and a few other notabilities."

Dalmorres looked up and down the bar.

"Our little friend who was so expansive last night has left us," he observed.

Savonarilda lounged across to them.

"So for once," he remarked, "the fair ladies have not dragged you all away to dancing parties."

"There was to have been a dance at the Palace," Terence Brown, who had just joined the little group, reminded them. "The invitations were only countermanded at the last moment. Very wisely too, I think. No one wants to dance around the rooms where those two poor fellows were killed."

"Hello, Thornton! What about your early night?" Roger asked.

"I'm off directly," Thornton confided. "I should have gone hours ago, but Lord Dalmorres has been telling me stories about the law courts of his younger days, and I fell from grace."

"And Major Thornton," Dalmorres remarked, "has been telling me very interesting things too about the liaison work between the police and the foreign service. Some day you will have to write your reminiscences, Major Thornton."

The latter shrugged his angular shoulders.

"There has been too much of that sort of thing," he pronounced, with some severity. "Many things have been discussed which never should have been spoken of or written about. I have never talked of my work and I shall certainly never write about it."

"A very excellent attitude," Dalmorres approved. "I have known the sensation of sentencing criminals to the death which they richly deserved, but I should not wish to write about it. I have also known," he went on, a rare seriousness in his tone, "the experience of sentencing men to death, according to the law, but whom I did not consider morally criminals at all. Some of those cases I do not even care to think about."

"Seems to me," Terence Brown observed, lighting one of his favourite long cigars, "that crime was pretty well dying out in the world until this liquor business came along over in my country. Young fellows went into bootlegging just as their great-grandfathers went into buccaneering—for the sport of the thing—just as in England years ago all the gentry in the southwest corner of the country, when they got tired of fox-hunting and cock-fighting, used to take to smuggling."

"What's ugly to-day is this," Savonarilda suddenly affirmed, without a trace of his usual flippancy: "people are committing crimes to-day in cold deliberation where, in my country, at any rate, it was always in hot blood. They kill a man—first to get what he's got and secondly to make themselves perfectly safe. That is the ugly side of it. They do not dare to take a risk. They kill out of policy."

Thornton drew Roger a little on one side.

"I don't feel up to these abstruse discussions to-night," he admitted. "I wondered if you wanted to talk to me?"

Roger that night was a man unlike himself. Any one who was not a close observer would have thought that he was on the road to becoming drunk. His eyes were unnaturally bright, his manner detached, he was holding a half-filled tumbler in his hand, the contents of which he drained at one gulp. He passed the glass to a valet.

"Thornton," he confided, "I don't want to talk to any one to-night. I'm going to have one more drink and then I'm going home to bed."

"Did you follow out your crazy fancy?" Thornton asked him, with a shadow of that faintly disagreeable smile at the corner of his lips.

Roger also smiled, but it was a gesture of a different order. It was the smile of a man who, after stumbling about in a morass, has found solid ground beneath his feet.

"Don't think I'm bad-tempered or obstinate, Thornton, or crazy," he begged. "I'm not one of the three, I can assure you, but to-night I have nothing to say. To-morrow my head will be clear. I will meet you, and there will be things to be said and a plan to work out. I'm just going to let things lie to-night."

"Just as you please," the other replied. "I simply thought if you had discovered anything, you'd like to get it off your chest."

"What I have discovered I have not yet digested. To-night I am going to have another drink and go to bed. Savonarilda," he invited, turning back to the group at the bar, "you have many virtues but one fault—you never drink. Have a last whisky and soda with me?"

Savonarilda made a wry face.

"You flatter me with your invitation," he acknowledged, "but I do not like whisky. I will drink a *Fine* with you."

Roger gave the order. Dalmorres was watching him curiously.

"I've never seen you take three drinks in so short a time, Roger Sloane," he remarked.

"And you probably never will again," Roger assured him. "To-night I guess I'm in what they call an expansive mood. I'd like all you boys to drink with me. I feel as though it were the last night on the steamer after a three months' cruise."

"Heaven save me from such memories," Dalmorres groaned. "Every one singing national anthems and slopping tears into their tumblers over 'Should Auld Acquaintance be Forgot.' What hideous reminiscences you have evoked, Sloane!"

"I promise I'm not singing any national anthems to-night," the latter declared. "This is just a drink between myself and Savonarilda and you others chiming in. Savonarilda, I raise my glass," he added, selecting his tumbler from the counter.

There was a flash in the Sicilian's eyes as he followed suit. He had known nothing of the man cowering behind the grey stone wall when the rain was beating down on the mountainside, but he realised intuitively that something had happened, somehow or other this stubborn young American had come a little nearer the light. He felt it in his blood that this drink was a challenge. His eyes flashed as he raised his glass.

"To your very excellent health, Mr. Roger Sloane," he murmured.

CHAPTER XXI

"I do not think that I will marry you, Roger," Jeannine decided, as she helped herself with lazy fingers from a box of chocolates by her side.

"That's tough," he remarked, without undue disquietude. "And why not, please?"

"You are not obedient. I demand that you cease these dangerous expeditions up to that terrible place and come to England with Lady Julia and me. You prefer to stay. You prefer the man hunt. Is it not so?"

Roger did not answer for a moment. They were lounging after luncheon on the famous balcony of his aunt's villa at Cap Martin, from which a queen had once declared was the most beautiful view in the world. Below them flaming beds of flowers, a pergola of wisteria, a bordering hedge of hydrangeas, merged into the soft and silvery green of the olive trees and the deeper green of the pines. These fell sheer to the sea, and when the south wind fluttered up from the bay, with its incense of sea air, fluttered through the pine trees and shook the petals from the clustering roses, the place came very near being the Paradise that the guidebooks proclaimed it.

"The thing has come nearly to an end, Jeannine," he told her quietly. "To-night will probably finish it."

"You mean that you have made a discovery?"

"I have certainly discovered one thing," he acknowledged, "which has surprised me very much indeed, but it is not everything."

"I do not see why you run those risks," she protested. "You are not a gendarme. It is not for you the protection of the people. Besides, a married man should not run risks. You are fiancé, which is the same as being married. You are making me nervous so that I cannot sleep. Fancy if anything should come to disturb happiness so marvellous as this!"

He leaned over and kissed the tears from her eyes.

"You need have no fear, dear Jeannine," he assured her. "I may seem rash but I am not. Listen, you will hear this and you will forget it."

"I promise," she murmured.

"The next time I climb the Corniche and arrive at that hotel, it will not be alone. It will be with gendarmes and perhaps with soldiers. There. Now I have told you a secret."

"All the same," she persisted, with a sigh, "I wish there would be no next time."

Dalmorres sauntered out through the opened windows, a very elegant figure in white flannels and Panama hat. He sank into a chair by their side.

"We are to talk before the little one, yes?" he asked.

"Naturally," Roger replied.

"You have seen Major Thornton this morning?"

"I have been with him for two hours."

Dalmorres tapped a cigarette upon the table and lit it. For some reason or other the information did not seem to give him unalloyed pleasure.

"You persist in your idea?"

"Absolutely," Roger declared. "Until last night I had many suspicions which Thornton was perhaps the first to laugh at. To-day I have no suspicions. I deal with facts. Even Thornton is convinced."

Dalmorres grunted dubiously. He had all the time the air of keeping something back.

"After all, this is your show, Roger," he pointed out. "Why don't you make the final arrangements yourself? That fellow Thornton is a secretive sort of devil, but I fancy when he does open his mouth he talks to some purpose. Why should he have all the credit of running to earth a famous band of criminals and relieving Monte Carlo of this infernal cloud of depression? Seems to me you have done all the work, and he's been trying to put you off all the time."

"Not quite so bad as that," Roger protested. "He has made one or two very useful suggestions. Then you must remember that the police are far more likely to work pleasantly with him than with a young fellow like me, who is not in the profession at all and has just blundered into the thing. Thornton's connection with Scotland Yard entitles him to a certain amount of respect from them. They only know me as one of the crowd here."

"There's something in that, of course," Dalmorres assented. "Tell me, though, as a matter of curiosity—should you have confidence in Thornton in a crisis? Do you think he would stick it through, if you got into any real trouble?"

"Sure," Roger replied. "On the other hand, I reckon we've about finished with the risks. It's the other fellows who've got to take them now. The way we have planned it, we are going to be mostly lookers-on in this show."

"Glad to hear it," Dalmorres affirmed doubtfully. "I hope you won't change your mind. After the way I laid bare my heart to Jeannine, I should have to marry her if you left her a widowette!"

"It would be something," Jeannine sighed.

"You've not a hundred to one chance," Roger declared with unabated cheerfulness. "If you're interested to know what's going to happen, I'll tell you. My beloved aunt has given in this morning, and even Jeannine doesn't know yet. The idea of a London marriage is off. Jeannine would have no friends there and she would be miserable in a crowd of strangers. Jeannine and I are going to be married very quietly indeed, either at my own little church of La Bastide or here—before Aunt Julia goes to England."

Jeannine's eyes were shining like stars, her lips were parted.

"Roger!" she gasped.

"You have to go through with it some time or other, my dear," he told her. "As for the honeymoon, that belongs to you. We can either stay at my villa or my aunt will lend us this one. The bathing's pretty good fun. Afterwards we shall have to go over to the States, but that won't be bad—my people are dead easy."

"Roger," she begged, "do not go to that horrible place to-night. I shall lie awake trembling all the time."

He held her hand lightly in his.

"My dear," he promised, "for your sake I shall run no risk. You need have no fears. The authorities are taking over the whole business. After all that happened during the last two months, they are simply panic-stricken. When it began, they looked upon us as meddlers. To-day we are little tin gods."

"You will not forget," Jeannine begged wistfully, "that you are my *real* god."

* * * * *

For some reason or other, Pierre Viotti was spending a restless day. His lilac-coloured automobile was seen outside the doors of every bar in Monte Carlo between the hours of eleven and one. At two o'clock it stood empty in the small Place of La Turbie and Monsieur Pierre, with his napkin tucked under his chin, sat at table with his brother in a neat but unassuming little café exactly opposite. The conversation to begin with was not of serious moment.

"The affairs of the heart, my brother," Paul enquired, as he helped himself liberally to *hors d'oeuvres*. "They progress, eh?"

Pierre growled.

"They will never progress," he confided, "until—"

"Until the young man is out of the way, eh?" Paul chuckled. "Well, well, that will be not so long now."

Pierre Viotti's eyes twinkled joyously.

"It is understood, that, yes?"

"It is certainly understood. The young man knows too much. What trouble comes to him is of his own seeking."

Pierre Viotti spilled a tablespoonful of soup in his excitement.

"There is a way of disposing of him," he ventured, with tentative longing, "which would be safe, very safe indeed, Paul."

"O-ay, what is that, Pierre?"

"It is the way the young Niçois whom the English milord shot went, the way the English milord would have gone, if he had not escaped, the way Pietro went the night after he got drunk and began to talk. All tied together, he would go in the chute well like that."

Pierre Viotti frowned at his brother reprovingly.

"Pierre," he remonstrated, "you shock me. You shock me very much. You should remember that you are working now with great men, real swells; a prince amongst us, men who move in swell society. That is a low idea of yours. We kill, but we kill

143

like gentlemen. After he's dead, naturally that is the way he will go."

"You are sure of that?" Pierre asked wistfully.

Paul struck the table so that the wine rocked in their glasses.

"So like a fool you talk," he exclaimed. "This young man will see the inside of our hiding place, he will know of its secrets. More fatal than anything else, he will see our faces. Is it likely that after that a single one of us would be willing to let him live?"

Pierre nodded with slow satisfaction.

"Good words," he admitted. "Good sense. I shall see him die. That is what I wish. I shall remind him that the little Jeannine will then be mine. Ho, la! I shall skip for joy. One year and a half I shall have lost but she's all the better for that."

Paul Viotti looked curiously at his brother's rapt and lustful expression.

"You love women, little Pierre," he remarked tolerantly.

"And you not?"

"They are well in their way," Paul admitted. "For me, though, one is as good as another. I like them like ripe fruit. You shake the tree and behold—she is in your arms. No trouble. There is a café keeper's wife here, the daughter of a croupier who lives up here for his health. There are others too. Very good, very willing. It does not disturb me which I take."

An *entrecôte* arrived and Pierre attacked it vigorously with squared elbows.

"What is it that you like best in life, then, Paul?" he demanded. "When you were younger, there was trouble enough with the girls."

"There is too much trouble always about women. I will not have them in any enterprise with which I am concerned. That is why I refused to help you bring away the little Jeannine. She might have been content but she might have given trouble. Women are good but they are not worth trouble."

"What is it that seems big to you in life, then?" Pierre persisted.

Paul Viotti smiled and his face for a moment was transformed.

"This work," he confided. "Money and the joy of getting money. Robbing the rich, seeing the bank balance grow. Soon I have enough, Pierre. I shall not go back to New York. There are a few bullets that wait for me there. Somewhere near Milan I shall live. I know where."

"Have you much money, Paul?" his brother asked reverently.

"I have two million dollars, Pierre, perhaps more. You would sell many flowers and cheat your neighbours for many years in La Bastide to save that much."

"Two million dollars," Pierre repeated, moistening his dry lips and looking across the table in awed fashion. "My brother Paul too. It makes one proud."

"I might have had more," Paul went on, "but I am generous. I have spent a fortune upon your hotel, Pierre, and most of it my own. Matthew Drane, he has no money. He must live as though he had or he could bring us no news. Staines, he has little. He too has worked well. One cannot ask him for much. I am generous with them all, Pierre. You see, I do not hoard my money. I love getting it, but I love the power of spending it. The time for me has arrived now. I shall buy a farm, I shall help with the politics of the town. I shall marry and have sons. If one wife does not give me them, I shall find another. One of them may rule Italy. One of them may go to New York and become famous, as I have done."

"For me, I too shall marry," Pierre murmured ecstatically. "It would serve the little baggage right if I just put her in my house. I shall marry her, however. I am a public man and there must be no scandals. I shall buy more land. The hotel shall be made good. There are some things I shall take away. I will have a billiard table in the secret chamber and join it to the house. Oh, it will be easy, all that."

"Let us remember," Paul Viotti said, with a suddenly altered note in his tone, "that this is not the night for dreams. You are sure of the Wolves?"

"Twelve of them," Pierre replied. "They are here now. Two of them in this very café. They will be at their stations by eleven."

"Remember, also, that nothing is to be done to the young American until I give the word."

Pierre sighed.

"That is more difficult, but I obey."

Paul paid the bill and the brothers rose and left the place. They dawdled in the Place for a few minutes, exchanged civilities with the gendarme and lit cigarettes. Afterwards they entered the lilac-coloured automobile. Pierre took the wheel, Paul relapsed into the cushions.

"To the bank," the latter directed, "and drive carefully. Remember that this is a great day."

CHAPTER XXII

At a few minutes before twelve that night Roger brought his car to a standstill in the little embrasure of the Corniche where he had left it the night before. He was well out of sight, even of the turning which passed the hotel, and of the hotel itself, and he paused for a moment to collect his thoughts and smoke a final cigarette. His part in the scheme which Thornton and he had worked out was from now on an insignificant one. There were probably already two gendarmes stationed immediately below the hotel and two at the first bend past it. He himself was to take his place in the stretch of wood exactly opposite the bar, and two more gendarmes were presently to fall in and guard the spot where the road forked. At a quarter-past twelve three carloads of gendarmes with Thornton were to arrive from Monte Carlo. Half a dozen of the men were to remain in the bar and guard the hotel, the rest were to explore the garage and discover the hiding place from which Savonarilda and Sam had issued. It was all very simple, and with the score of men whom Thornton was bringing and the commissaire himself, it scarcely seemed possible that there would be any serious resistance. Roger gave a sigh of relief as he threw away his cigarette and started forward for his post. Despite his love of adventure, he was glad that this was the last night.

He followed out the plan precisely, entering the little wood where a portion of the grey stone wall had fallen away, exactly at the junction of the byroad and the Corniche. For about forty yards he made his way carefully ahead, skirting the wall but keeping inside the wood. Exactly opposite the bar door he paused, crouched down until he lay almost flat upon his stomach, and with a sigh of satisfaction blessed the clouds which were rolling down from the mountain, bringing with them almost complete invisibility. From one pocket he drew out and placed in a convenient position by his side a fully charged revolver, from another he produced an electric torch and placed it also within easy reach. Then he settled himself down to wait.

Opposite to him the bar and the hotel itself appeared to be silent and unlit. That was what he had expected. Such life as might exist within the place lay elsewhere, as he had already discovered. He felt himself pleasantly excited, thrilled even with expectation. It was the dénouement towards which he had worked. In a few hours the whole Principality would be liberated from the shadow which had been hanging over it, and he himself would be free to follow to the end this sweeter and more joyous adventure, the very anticipation of which sang in his blood by day and by night. A romantic fool he was becoming, he told himself with a half-stifled chuckle. On this one night, above all others, he must keep Jeannine out of his thoughts.

In half an hour's time, without any sensible lessening of enthusiasm, he realised that he was stiff, that his limbs were cramped, that the chill of the low-hanging mountain mists had penetrated some parts of his clothing. There had been no sign of the approach of any motor car, no lights or vehicle of any sort had climbed the hill from Monte Carlo. He looked at the two corners of the road where the outposts were to have been placed but saw no one. This in a way was understandable, because they would probably keep under cover, as he himself was doing, but the late arrival of the cars perplexed him. He felt all the sick impatience of a crisis deferred. By now he had hoped that the affair might have been almost over. He realised with a sigh that it had not even begun. There could have been no mistake. The cars, with sixteen gendarmes and four soldiers, were to mount the hill together and arrive at the strip of road fronting the hotel at a quarter past twelve. From up above in La Turbie, he heard the chiming of a clock. He listened intently. One o'clock struck. Three quarters of an hour late! Practically the whole of the time it should have taken the expedition to come from Monte Carlo.

There was still neither movement nor sound from the dark block of buildings opposite. Suddenly he forgot all his sick discomforts. There was a thin chink of light issuing from the door of the bar. He stretched out his hand cautiously and gripped his revolver. If news had arrived by telephone of the departure of the gendarmes from Monte Carlo, this might very well be some one planning to escape. Through a gap where two or three of the topmost stones had been dislodged, he had a perfect view of the place. The light increased in brilliance and he became aware that the door was being slowly opened. It was drawn back at first by an unseen hand, then a figure draped from head to foot in sombre black crept into sight. Finally the door stood wide open, and the old man who played the guitar to his wife's plaintive Neapolitan songs stepped across the threshold on to the strip of pavement outside, on which the one or two marble-topped tables were placed. He stood there quite motionless, a gaunt, strange figure, leaning forward and peering earnestly into the wood opposite. No word passed from his lips, indeed he seemed to be taking as much pains to keep silent as

Roger himself. All the time, though, Roger realised that the man was not only looking straight into the darkness, but he was looking straight at the spot where he himself was crouching.

From the road above came the sound of an automobile apparently being driven at a great pace along the main road. It was coming from the direction of Nice and had not yet reached the turn downwards. Swiftly, but with absolute silence, the door of the bar swung to and again the place relapsed into darkness. Powerful headlights illuminated the road, the honk of a horn was heard. The car flashed past the turning and swung along the curve to Mentone. The sound of it died away in the distance. Roger, crouching low in his place and almost holding his breath, watched the slow reopening of the door. Once more the musician stood there in evidence, his shambling figure bent forward, his eyes straining through the darkness. Once more he stepped out onto the pavement. Roger, still crouching low and motionless, felt a cold shiver of apprehension. There was fear in the man's face—more than fear—horror. All the time he was peering forward, he was listening backwards. He had stepped off the pavement now and was at the edge of the road, as far as he could go without passing out of the shelter of the house. Suddenly Roger realised that the man was not only conscious of his presence but, fearing to raise his voice, was making signs to him. He was evidently in a state of mortal terror, also of paralysed indecision. He shook his fist violently in the direction of that gap in the wall behind which Roger was crouching, and with his other hand pointed downwards towards where the paling lights of Monte Carlo fringed the sea. His face was distorted with some sort of emotion. Finally as though he could keep silent no longer, he broke into incoherent speech.

"*Pericolo, Signor! Partite presto!* Pericolo!"

Roger felt his heart sink. A cold wave of fear swept over him. He leaned forward to reply but remained dumb. There was the crash of a revolver behind him and he heard the swish of a bullet not far from his left ear. In front he saw the poor old musician throw up his arms, heard the gurgling in his throat, the half-stifled cry, saw him collapse as though his legs had been turned into pillars of straw. He lay doubled up upon the road, a shapeless heap, invisible save for the faint stream of light which came from the open door. He gave one more groan. Then there was silence. The door behind him was slammed. There was also darkness.

Too clever for him, Roger realised, with a groan! Curiously enough, this moment of almost certain doom brought with it more a sense of humiliation than absolute fear. He felt a sort of self-disgust

148

to think that he had been fool enough to pit his brains and his scant knowledge of this sort of man hunting against an organised band of gangsters. There were no outposts, there were no gendarmes, there was no Thornton. Somehow or other, they had dealt with these too. They had him, all right. At any moment the spit of a gun might flash out from anywhere in that wall of darkness behind. They knew very well the exact spot in which he was, from the light which had only just disappeared, and he dared make no movement, for that would equally have betrayed his whereabouts. He listened. He listened so intently that he could even hear the murmur of ground insects. Of human beings, however, he could hear nothing at all. Yet they must be near at hand. Gripping his revolver, he rose to his feet. The torch he slipped back into his pocket, for a single flash of it would have been madness. It seemed odd that he should not hear the sound of any movement or footsteps. Whoever had fired that shot must have been in the wood and only a few yards behind him. He dropped into the road and leaned against the wall, his revolver resting almost upon the top of it. Now he fancied that he could hear something! A little to the left there had been the snapping of a twig. Then again there was the sound of a stone being displaced somewhere on the right. His revolver swung down the line but he resisted the temptation to pull the trigger blindly. The idea of flight he discarded as soon as it was conceived. He had no fancy for going out of the world with half a dozen bullets in his back.

A thin and watery moon was making a brave fight to creep into evidence. Roger leaned forward, trying hard to distinguish one of the slinking forms amongst the shadows. Then indeed he realised that they were too clever for him, for without the slightest warning he was surrounded. He was in the centre of a group of men dressed like Italian road-menders, a stalwart, vicious-looking crowd. Arms were thrown around his neck from before and behind, there was a blow upon his wrist and his revolver clattered into the road. A hoarse and very unpleasant whisper reached his ears.

"Give him the cloth, quick. There's a car coming."

Whereupon Roger smelt a sickly and familiar smell, struck one blow into the air, gave one gurgle, and collapsed.

About five oclock that morning Jean Laurent, a vegetable grower in a small way upon the upper slopes of Beausoleil, discovered that he had a most unusual and magnificent crop of artichokes with which he had already, however, supplied the principal hotels of Monte Carlo. He was inspired to take his products into Nice market by the lower road, but he had scarcely travelled a hundred yards from his front gate when the sight of

149

something lying in the road caused him to apply with great delicacy and care the brakes to his old Rénault *camion*. He brought it to a standstill by the side of what seemed to be in the distance a bundle of something or other wrapped in a black shawl. The something or other, however, turned out to be the body of an elderly woman, whom he at first thought to be dead. Dead or alive, however, he saw the necessity of removing her from the middle of the road, and, lifting her frail body in his stalwart arms, he placed her in the *camion*. She rewarded him with a groan.

"*Eh, bien!*" he exclaimed, bending over her. "It is not so bad then. Madame feels better?"

The old woman opened her eyes but she was powerless to speak. Jean Laurent scratched his head. He was a strong man and a willing worker, but he knew nothing about looking after an elderly lady on the point of collapse. He suddenly thought of the flask of red wine, together with his lunch, which occupied the spare seat. He uncorked it, poured a little into a mug and forced some between her teeth. It might have killed but, as a matter of fact, it revived her. She opened her eyes.

"Jeannine," was the name she murmured. "Mademoiselle Jeannine."

"Is that your daughter or some one?" he asked. "We'll find her down in Monte Carlo perhaps."

The woman had closed her eyes as though the effort had been too much for her. Jean Laurent started up his engine and, with one arm propping up his passenger, he drove skilfully but wheezily down into Monte Carlo. Arrived there he pulled up outside the gendarmerie.

"This is what has arrived," he announced. "I have picked up an old lady in the middle of the road. Just about a hundred yards outside my gate she was. What am I to do with her?"

The sergeant looked at him keenly.

"Picked her up, eh?"

"That is what I said. She was lying in the middle of the road."

"You're sure you did not knock her down?"

Jean was strikingly eloquent for several minutes. The sergeant followed him out into the street. The old lady was beginning to groan again but she was showing more signs of vitality.

"What is the matter, Madame?" the sergeant asked. "Did this man knock you down?"

"Nobody knocked me down," she replied faintly. "I could go no farther and I fell."

"Where did you come from?"

"From the Hôtel du Soleil," she faltered. "Mademoiselle Jeannine, they have killed him."

"Killed who?"

"My husband."

"This," the sergeant remarked, "appears to be a case. Do you know who she is?"

"I had no idea," Jean Laurent answered, "until she mentioned the Hôtel du Soleil. There was an old couple always hanging about the place, the woman singing and the man playing the guitar. I believe this is the woman. Can I leave her here?" he asked. "I have the finest artichokes in the world, but they will be wasted unless I can get them into Nice market by half-past six. My name is Jean Laurent and I live at the Villa Laurent."

The sergeant copied down the name.

"Help me in with her," he assented, "and you can go."

They established her in a small room behind the bureau. The sergeant's wife made coffee for her and life came flickering back. She made a determined attempt to tell her story.

"They have killed my husband," she began. "They shot him while he was trying to warn the young American gentleman to go away."

"Who are they?"

"The Wolves of Monsieur Viotti."

The sergeant stretched out his hand for the telephone book. Without a doubt, this was a case for the mental hospital.

"They mean to kill Mr. Roger Sloane, a rich young American gentleman," she went on. "They have him up there at the Hôtel du Soleil. I can—I am the only one who can—save him. I want Mademoiselle Jeannine."

The sergeant laid down the book and rang up for the commissaire instead. The name of Roger Sloane was very well known and there had been a good deal of talk about the Hôtel du Soleil lately.

"Madame would do well to rest for a few minutes," he said, as he replaced the receiver on the hook. "Monsieur le Commissaire is coming, and he will attend to what Madame has to say."

Madame dozed peacefully for some twenty minutes, then she drank more coffee, and by the time the commissaire arrived, out of breath and temper, she was almost coherent.

"What is this I hear?" he demanded. "A woman picked up in the road who says that some one has killed her husband."

"They killed my husband before my eyes a few hours ago," the

151

woman moaned. "But it is of the living I speak now. It is a very kind gentleman, Mr. Roger Sloane—"

"We know him," the commissaire replied. "Go on."

"He is at the Hôtel du Soleil. They have him a prisoner there. They will kill him. You must send gendarmes at once."

"Name of God!" the commissaire exclaimed indignantly, "I've already sent gendarmes three times to that hotel. It is some fools' game they are playing. The place has been searched from floor to ceiling. It is owned and kept by a most respectable man who was mayor of his village. The next person who comes to me with crazy stories of the Hôtel du Soleil will go to prison for it."

The woman was stupefied at his outburst. She could do nothing but rock her head and moisten her dry lips.

"You talk too loudly," she complained. "My head is going round. If you will not help, I must find Mademoiselle Jeannine. We must get there before they kill him."

The sergeant plucked his superior by the sleeve and led him away. They whispered together for several moments. Then the commissaire returned.

"We can help you to find Mademoiselle Jeannine," he confided. "She is the fiancée of the Mr. Roger Sloane you spoke of. You had better go to her with your story."

"I am the only one who can save him," the woman moaned, "and I am so far away. Take me please, then, to Mademoiselle Jeannine."

They put her into a police automobile and they motored up to Madame Vinay's. Madame Vinay came downstairs, a little cross at being disturbed so early in the morning, but alive with interest as soon as she saw the police car and the gendarme in uniform.

"It is for Mademoiselle Jeannine," the latter announced. "We understand that she lives with you."

"Until last night," Madame Vinay announced. "Last night she moved to the villa of the aunt of the young gentleman she is going to marry—the Lady Julia Harborough at Cap Martin. There is no trouble, I hope?"

The sergeant merely saluted and they drove off. In twenty minutes they were on the terrace of the villa at Cap Martin and five minutes later Mademoiselle Jeannine appeared fully dressed.

"Tell me what is the matter, Sergeant," she implored. "Is it of Mr. Sloane you bring news?"

"It is this old lady who has brought the news, Mademoiselle," the man replied. "She was picked up in the road at Beausoleil this morning, trying to reach Monte Carlo and find you. She is telling some queer story of her husband having been murdered up there this morning."

"I will tell my story," the woman interrupted. "Mademoiselle, you came with the young American gentleman to the bar at the Hôtel du Soleil. We sang to you Neapolitan songs and my husband played the guitar."

"Of course I remember," Jeannine assented. "Tell me the news you bring, I beg of you. I am very anxious."

"Mademoiselle, they have him, that dear young gentleman, in that evil place! I know nothing else and my head is going around. They have killed my husband who tried to warn him. I left him lying there in the road."

"You hear what this woman says?" Jeannine cried, turning to the sergeant. "Mr. Sloane went there last night, I know. He believed that there were some desperate criminals hiding there. We must get together some gendarmes!"

The sergeant's attitude was noncommittal.

"You had better see the commissaire, Mademoiselle," he suggested. "To tell you the truth, I think that he has had enough of the Hôtel du Soleil. We know the place from cellar to attic and we have never found any one there who had in the least the appearance of a criminal."

Jeannine was very pale but she kept her voice steady.

"I will see your commissaire," she said. "Wait for one moment first. I must telephone."

She made her way into the room behind. Mechanically she asked for the Hôtel de Paris and mechanically she asked for Lord Dalmorres. He answered her sleepily, but when he heard the sob in her voice he was wide awake in a moment and he interrupted without hesitation her stream of incoherent words.

"I will meet you at the gendarmerie in ten minutes," he promised.

At the gendarmerie the commissaire was unexpectedly difficult.

"It is not a credible story which this poor old lady tells," he pointed out. "My belief is that she has been knocked down and that her mind is wandering. In any case, what can I do? I have one gendarme at my disposal and my sergeant here, who must remain to look after the office."

"Supposing," Lord Dalmorres asked, "you were convinced that there was a band of desperate criminals whom it was your duty to arrest up at the Hôtel du Soleil, what would you, under those circumstances do?"

"I should apply for aid to the Gendarmerie at Monaco," was the prompt reply.

Dalmorres led the way back to the car. At the gendarmerie in the Principality they had again a difficult task before them. They were received at first with the utmost coldness. Dalmorres swept all that on one side.

"I beg you to listen to me, Monsieur le Commissaire," he said. "I am Lord Dalmorres and I am the best known of all the English judges. I have been Lord Chancellor of Great Britain and am even now a member of the Privy Council. I know more about criminals and criminal life than any one in these parts. Treat me, I beg of you, with consideration."

The commissaire rose from his seat and placed chairs himself for his visitors.

"Milord Dalmorres," he said respectfully, "your name is very well known. My staff and my services are at your disposal. I will only add—if you will permit me—one little word."

"By all means go ahead," Dalmorres assented. "The only thing is, please remember that they may be doing a man to death while we hang about here."

There was a twitch of his lips which suggested that the commissaire would have smiled if he had dared. His respect for his visitor, however, kept him grave.

"Milord Dalmorres," he said, "this is all I will say. Our Principality has been cursed this season by a series of abominable crimes. I admit that we have been unable to discover their source, but at the same time I complain most bitterly that we have been impeded in our task by the well-meant but blundering efforts of certain amateurs. The young gentleman whose name you have mentioned is one of them. Three times this season on information received from him and other perfectly well-meaning people, the Hôtel du Soleil has been searched from floor to attic. On no occasion has a single suspicious circumstance been reported. The hotel is kept by a respectable Frenchman who has been mayor of his village and who is naturally indignant at our continual visits. What he will say to this last one I cannot imagine, but in the face of your request, Lord Dalmorres, nothing else counts. I will bring six gendarmes with me fully armed, and we will proceed at once, or rather I am afraid it must be in half an hour's time, to the hotel. I must request, however, that you are also there, because I tell you frankly that the blame for this last raid upon Monsieur Viotti's premises I shall place entirely upon your shoulders."

"I will accept the whole responsibility," Dalmorres declared.

"Please do not let us detain you another minute. All that we want to do is to start."

"One moment, please," Jeannine interposed. "There is something we have forgotten to ask. Had you arranged here or at the other establishment to send gendarmes up to the Hôtel du Soleil last night with Major Thornton, the Englishman?"

"We certainly had not," was the curt reply, "and if Major Thornton had applied for such assistance, we should not have dreamed of according it. We have not, if you will permit my saying so, a great opinion of Major Thornton. His position has been misrepresented to us. We have discovered that he has no connection whatever with the English Foreign Office or with Scotland Yard."

"God bless my soul!" Dalmorres groaned.

Jeannine had turned deathly pale. She would have collapsed but her companion placed his arm around her waist.

"For the love of God, hurry!" she begged.

CHAPTER XXIII

There was certainly nothing sinister or forbidding about the exterior of the Hôtel du Soleil when the three cars full of visitors drew up outside its doors at about half-past eleven that morning. The gendarmes, according to orders given on the way up, posted themselves at different points, with instructions to stop any one leaving the hotel. Lord Dalmorres, with Jeannine and the commissaire, stepped inside the bar, which presented an unusually hospitable appearance. Sam, very spruce in a clean white coat, was busy serving cocktails to two chance callers whose car was outside. One of the two golfers who had been there on the previous Sunday was taking an *apéritif* in the corner. The fisherman was dividing his attention between a mixed vermouth and the adjusting of a reel. Jeannine went straight to the counter.

"Have you seen Mr. Sloane yesterday or to-day, Sam?" she asked.

"Why, no, Miss," he answered. "Mr. Sloane hasn't been up here that I know of, since you was with him. We've been pretty busy but I should have noticed an old client, I'm sure."

"Do you happen to know a Major Thornton?" Jeannine asked.

The man shook his head.

"Never heard of the gentleman," he replied. "Can I fix you a nice Martini, Miss?" he enquired.

They all three made a pretence of drinking their cocktails. Afterwards they followed the *maître d'hôtel*, who had appeared with the luncheon menu into the restaurant. The place was half filled and Monsieur Pierre Viotti was walking around amongst his clients. He straightened himself as he recognised his three visitors, and for a single moment he flinched. The gesture, however, was scarcely noticeable. He came forward with a strained but welcoming smile.

"Mademoiselle Jeannine," he said, holding out his chubby hand, "a pleasure to see you. Monsieur Bérard, you come far too seldom. A table for three it is that you wish? I will see my *maître d'hôtel*. He will doubtless arrange something special for you."

"One moment, Monsieur Viotti," the commissaire begged. "Let me first present you to Lord Dalmorres, a very famous Englishman."

"*Enchanté*, Monsieur," Viotti murmured. "You are very kind that you honour my little hotel."

The commissaire groaned but took the plunge. They had drifted into a corner of the restaurant and were some distance from the general company.

"Monsieur Viotti, we are here at the request of this gentleman, to search your hotel."

"To search it! What for?" Monsieur Viotti demanded.

"Certain criminals," the commissaire replied, "and a young man in pursuit of them who has disappeared."

Monsieur Viotti did not appear to be angry. He was simply hurt. He held out protesting hands.

"But your gendarmes have been here before," he complained. "They have turned the place upside down, they have trampled on my beautiful carpets with their muddy feet, and they have left without spending a sou in my bar. These things are distressing, Monsieur le Commissaire."

"This, I promise you, shall be the last time," the latter declared. "Lord Dalmorres' request could not be refused, and it is an undoubted fact that the young man Roger Sloane has disappeared."

Monsieur Viotti smiled wickedly.

"I do not think that Monsieur Sloane," he said, "would pay us a visit here for any purpose. Very well, my friend Bérard, go where you will. We speak of luncheon afterwards."

"If you will permit it," was the apologetic reply.

They commenced a tour of inspection, accompanied by two of the gendarmes. They searched the lounge, the ladies' salon and they were shown over the kitchens. The flaxen-haired young woman, who seemed to appear from nowhere, showed them over the bedrooms one by one. The latter were well furnished but presented no unusual features, except that Number Fourteen, which seemed to be a suite, had double guards to the windows and was furnished rather more luxuriously than the others. They inspected the garage and all the outbuildings, then, calling in the rest of the gendarmes, they made a circular sweep of the gardens, passing over every yard of the ground. They all met together outside the front of the bar. The gendarmes stood to attention. The commissaire was saddened but triumphant. Dalmorres was frankly puzzled. Jeannine's white, drawn face alone was expressionless.

"I am inclined to believe," Dalmorres announced, "that neither Roger nor Thornton ever meant to come here. They mentioned this place only as a bluff."

"I have entered upon this task reluctantly," Monsieur Bérard said, "but I will do my duty. I will now interrogate the staff."

The commissaire, with the assistance of two of his gendarmes, held a little court in the bar. From the chef to the barman the reply was the same. No two people answering to the description of Major Thornton or Roger had been seen near the hotel. Monsieur Bérard brought the proceedings to an end.

"I have now, Lord Dalmorres," he pointed out, "as I think you will admit, done everything you asked me to do. Every inch of these premises has been searched, every one of the servants questioned. I have even gone further than I intended. I have enquired amongst the guests. The result is as you see. I venture to say that it is impossible that Major Thornton or Mr. Roger Sloane should have visited this place last night."

"I am afraid, my dear," Dalmorres said, with a sigh, "that Roger has been trying to be a little too clever with us. He didn't want any interference and he probably put us on a wrong scent. Very likely he has met with all the success he expected somewhere else and we shall hear all about it when we return."

The door of the bar was pushed open and the old woman whom they had completely forgotten came shambling in.

"They have taken Antoine away," she wailed, "and they will not tell me where. I think I know. Oh, I think I know."

The barman came from behind the counter. His face was flushed and he seemed unreasonably perturbed.

"Outside, if you please, Madame," he ordered brusquely. "You know what the boss said. You're not allowed in here any more."

"I know," she moaned. "You need not worry. I shall come no more. Without Antoine to play I shall not sing. Young lady—"

"Yes," Jeannine cried.

The barman was holding the door open.

"Outside, if you please, Madame," he repeated, stretching out his hand toward the old woman.

"Leave her alone," Jeannine ordered firmly. "What were you going to say, Madame?"

"Have you found the young gentleman?"

Jeannine shook her head. Sobs for a moment were stifling her speech. The barman leaned forward and gripped the old woman by the shoulders. Suddenly he received a surprise. Dalmorres took him by the arms and swung him away.

"We cannot find him anywhere," Jeannine sobbed.

It was a terrible sound which escaped the old woman's lips, but it was in effect a chuckle.

"You have not known where to look!" she said. "Come with me and I will show you! One cold night Antoine and I—we crept into the automobile of Monsieur le Patron. We slept there and—we saw! Follow me."

CHAPTER XXIV

Roger's return to consciousness was bewildering. He found himself lying fully undressed in a pair of strange pyjamas, in a narrow but exceedingly comfortable bunk-like bed, covered with the finest of linen and a silken coverlet. The room was in complete darkness save for a heavily shaded electric lamp burning by his side. He removed the shade and his perplexity increased. The apartment in which he found himself was no larger than a ship's cabin, and the walls appeared to be of some sort of metal. The furniture was scanty—a wardrobe of gleaming mahogany let into the wall, a large toilet basin with oxidised silver fittings, and a single chair on which were stretched the clothes he had been wearing. The room was entirely windowless, but two electric fans were revolving noiselessly. He felt very sick and he had a bad headache, but both sensations almost disappeared as, with a sudden flood of memory, he remembered the events of the preceding night. He sprang out of bed, bathed his head and his body so far as possible in cold water, and rapidly dressed. The only thing missing from amongst his belongings seemed to be his revolver. He was just completing his toilet when the door of his room opened. He gave a little gasp. Thornton stood there, looking in at him!

"Say, did they get you too?" Roger exclaimed. "What became of the men you were to bring?"

Thornton did not reply for a moment. He knocked the ash deliberately off the cigarette he was smoking and leaned against the wall.

"Where are we, anyway?" Roger went on breathlessly. "What's their game? What are they going to do with us?"

Thornton sighed.

"So far as you're concerned, Roger Sloane," he confided, "I am afraid that you are for it."

"Do you mean that they're going to kill me?"

"I am afraid so. I am, for one, in favour of it."

Roger sat quite still for a moment, his eyes fixed upon the other's face. It was hard to get this new idea into his mind.

"My God!" he cried at last. "You are one of them!"

His visitor nodded.

"It has taken you quite a long time to discover that," he remarked.

"That story about the Indian princes and Marseilles—"

"Punk," Thornton interrupted. "Good punk, but punk. There was a Major Thornton in Marseilles, but Staines my name is—Edward Staines. I came over from New York with the rest of them, except that I have been in London for a time and picked up a few things. Put on your coat and come along. The chief wants to talk to you."

Roger felt his muscles swelling. He crouched forward for the spring. Thornton only laughed. His hand seemed to go almost lazily into his pocket, but the outstretched gun was there before Roger could move.

"If I have to shoot you," Thornton confided, "it will only anticipate things by an hour or so. I shall certainly shoot if you move an inch from where you are."

Roger fought against his consuming rage. If he could have killed this man first, it seemed to him that he would have been contented to die. Not a chance.

"What do you want me to do?" he asked.

"Put on your coat and come with me. You don't need to feel such an abject fool about this, Sloane. There wasn't a single one of them there who didn't accept me just as you did. Our first spot of

159

trouble was Dalmorres. He nearly cornered me the other night, and I knew perfectly well when we parted, and he slipped away into the long writing room, that he was sending home to ask a few questions about me. Our game was pretty well up from then."

"But Terence Brown," Roger said half to himself. "Why, he was more to blame than any one. He said that he had known you in London."

"He would," Thornton replied. "You'll see him in a minute or two. Come this way."

Roger rose to his feet and followed his guide, who was walking sideways and who handled his gun as though he had grown up with it. The door of the room led straight into a much larger apartment, which had very much the appearance of a West End club smoking room, except that the ceiling was very low. It was absolutely windowless and the only ventilation appeared to come from the electric fans. Paul Viotti was seated at the head of a long table with a book bound like a ledger in front of him. By his side, a fresh carnation in his buttonhole and wearing a morning suit of wonderfully cut tweeds, was Terence Brown. Lounging in another chair was Savonarilda. Terence Brown, who was smoking a long cigar, turned his head at Roger's entrance.

"My God!" Roger exclaimed. "What have they got you for?"

Terence Brown smiled, and it didn't seem necessary for him to do anything else, for it was a smile of a particularly wicked quality. Roger's hand went up to his head.

"Where's Maggie Saunders?" he demanded, with a flickering spasm of humour.

Paul Viotti smiled.

"Ah," he said, "there we draw the line. No ladies, Mr. Sloane. When I started this new form of industry—we were bootleggers pure and simple to begin with—our one immovable decision was—no ladies. I am vain enough to think sometimes that it is through my insistence upon this that we have prospered. We have kept from trouble which others have so easily found. My brother—you remember my brother, Mr. Sloane—he has wept tears, he has pleaded with me, he has appealed to me by all the ties of old affection between us to permit him to bring the little Jeannine into our company. A day or two of seclusion and I have no doubt that she would have been amenable, but I have always refused.... Perhaps our guest would like tea or coffee. They are on the sideboard."

Roger helped himself to tea, and if his fingers were trembling it was not with fear.

"Well, I guess we know pretty well where we are now," he remarked presently. "What about Sam, the barman?"

"Sam, and our only recent election, my brother," Paul Viotti explained, "complete our little company. They are at present engaged, but they may join us later. You know us all now, Mr. Sloane. There are no more surprises for you."

Terence Brown grinned.

"I wouldn't say that," he murmured.

Roger, who had finished two strong cups of tea, was feeling better. He threw himself into an easy-chair.

"How do you expect to get away with this?" he asked Viotti. "You know as well as possible that there will be a search for me. Dalmorres, amongst others, knew that I was coming up here."

Viotti smiled.

"We have taken many precautions," he confided. "Your car has been driven into Nice and abandoned there by two men who, in dress and manner, were the exact duplicates of you and Thornton, and who took care to leave those clues the police are so fond of at various questionable haunts in the gay city. Your disappearance will always remain a regrettable mystery, but to Nice will belong the discredit of having swallowed you."

"But, first of all," Roger pointed out, "this place—I take it for granted we are not far from the hotel—will have been subjected to an inch-by-inch search. I have friends in Monte Carlo who will not be satisfied with anything casual."

"That inch-by-inch search," Terence Brown remarked, "has already taken place three times, and let me tell you this, young fellow; the police of Monte Carlo and of Nice are fed up with having to send search parties out on a fool's errand. Furthermore, I wouldn't mind betting you a box of cigars that if a dozen of the most famous detectives in the world were to go down on their hands and knees and crawl over this place for a week, they would never discover the secret of this room."

"Mr. Terence Brown is quite right in what he says," Viotti agreed. "He is quite, quite right. We had a room constructed on this principle in New York in the heart of the city. We used it for five years without the slightest trouble."

"Well, what are you going to do with me?" Roger asked bluntly.

Paul Viotti sighed.

"It is very sad," he said.

"Damned hard lines," Terence Brown echoed.

"We have spent an hour of this beautiful spring morning,"

Paul Viotti continued, "trying to discover some means whereby we could justify ourselves, establish our safety, run no risk in the future—for we are very particular about that—and yet keep you alive. Alas, we failed."

"Not a chance," Terence Brown lamented.

"You see," Paul Viotti explained, "we have been forced to deal with you as with a dangerous enemy. American by birth though you may be, you have that stupid bulldog persistence which we generally associate over in New York with the Irish and here with the Britisher. You wouldn't leave us alone here, and in time who knows what might not happen? We have dealt with so many for lesser reasons. It became obvious that you must be removed."

"You mean that you are going to kill me?" Roger demanded.

"Within ten minutes," Viotti announced. "You have only been kept alive, in case a way might suggest itself. We are ready to hear anything you have to say. Can you suggest any means by which we can assure the absolute safety of every one of us here—Mr. Terence Brown, Prince Savonarilda, and my brother Pierre particularly—and allow you to live?"

"Anything going in the shape of cigarettes?" Roger enquired. "This needs consideration."

Savonarilda threw over his case which Roger adroitly caught. He helped himself to two cigarettes and lit one of them.

"If I am on the threshold of eternity," he said, "as seems remarkably possible, would it make any difference if I asked you a few questions? I should hate to go out with a clouded mind."

Viotti looked over at his victim with a benevolent smile. He was dressed with a scrupulous care and his black satin tie was secured with a very beautiful pearl pin. He was in every respect the genial and tolerant master of ceremonies.

"Ask anything that will make that bleak passage easier," he invited. "You have," he added, glancing at his watch, "only seven minutes."

"Who killed that fellow in the Casino?"

Viotti extended his hand towards Thornton.

"A beautiful gesture," he murmured. "The young man was so terribly dangerous. Alas, my brother was to blame there. Two of his young Niçois in whom he trusted, failed us. One was not quick enough to deal with Erskine, although he had plenty of warning; the other lost his head, when he had achieved what he thought was success, and struck out on his own. He lived for an hour or two. That is as long as we permit."

"And those carefully prepared plans of ours—" Roger began, turning towards Thornton.

"They were considered in this room," Thornton expounded, "as soon as they were conceived. After all, Roger Sloane, it's level odds between the person you call the criminal and the amateur absolutely unconnected with the law, who butts in on his own account. One is the sinner and the other's the sneak. We've played our game out, hand for hand. You lost."

"Mr. Roger Sloane has derived some amusement from the enterprise, without a doubt," Viotti murmured, from the head of the table. "Your time is very close at hand now, my young friend."

"For God's sake, don't rush things," Savonarilda interposed gloomily. "This is the part of the business I do not like. I would shoot an informer, and I have done so, as easily as I would step upon a snail, and I would kill a man in a fight when it was his life or mine without turning a hair, but this cold-blooded execution of an enemy does not please me. We are five to one. It is not even a fight."

Pierre Viotti, appearing from no one knew where, suddenly struck with his fist upon the table. He was an evil-looking figure, standing in the gloomiest portion of the room, with the electric fan whirling above his head. Roger, looking in his direction, suddenly became aware of the drama by which he was surrounded. It was morning, but there was no morning. The darkness was pierced only by those artificial lights. The west wind might be blowing outside, but all the air which penetrated into the room was from the electric fans.

"It shall be a fight, if you like," Pierre Viotti grinned. "Only, as I am a fat elderly man, and he has already struck me upon the jaw, I give myself a gun. He takes his fists and I shoot when I please. Do not forget the time, Paul."

"He has four minutes to live," the latter announced suavely.

"Well, you can have the honour of killing him, for all I care," Savonarilda said. "It's a foul business, anyway. I'd get you out of this if I could, Sloane," he went on, "but you see for yourself how impossible it is. If I were to meet you in the Sporting Club to-morrow night, if you saw Terence Brown sitting there with his ears open, waiting to know who had won money, what would be your attitude? I know. You would send for the police."

"Without a moment's hesitation," Roger agreed heartily.

"*Et voilà!*" Savonarilda groaned. "What can be done with a young man so obstinate?"

"Nothing," Pierre Viotti mocked. "He might offer us millions for his liberty, he might even pay, but he would take good care to have us sooner or later. He has only three minutes of life—why do we delay? Let me be the first one to shoot. Afterwards, we will send him down the slide. I shall be the first one to push!"

It seemed to Roger then that the end had surely come. The faces of the men all turned towards him conveyed the same expression. With the exception of Pierre Viotti, there was nothing vindictive about them. They had simply made up their minds that to secure their own safety he must die. He hadn't even any arguments with which to confront them. The whole thing was so reasonable. What else could they do? He watched Paul Viotti withdraw his revolver and drop in the cartridges without even a flicker of emotion. The thing was inevitable. If he lived they died, and he was in their power.

"Two minutes, Roger Sloane," Paul Viotti said, closing the breach of his revolver. "You can sit where you are, if you please, or you can run around the room. Nothing else is possible, I fear."

"Look here," Savonarilda exclaimed, suddenly rising to his feet. "Nothing like this has ever happened before. It is a bloody business. Roger, never mind about the million. Supposing we keep you shut up safely until we have cleaned up and got away; will you hold your tongue for ever?"

"I will not," Roger answered firmly. "You're not like the others, Savonarilda, but I know they mean to kill me. Let them get on with it. Fools deserve to die and I've been fool enough, God knows. I've even been fool enough to be taken in by a blasted sneak like this."

He suddenly reached out with his long arm and struck Thornton with the palm of his hand across the cheek and mouth. He saw the blood come and he felt a swift thrill of pleasure. If these were his last moments on earth, if that was his last physical effort, it had at least brought him something. A bullet from Pierre's revolver whistled past his head. A second would certainly have followed but for the fact that Paul, his brother, had sprung suddenly to his feet and held his wrist with a grip of iron.

"Don't move, any one," he enjoined. "Listen!"

There was a sudden tense silence. A curious sound had come to them from outside, the sound of a siren which seemed as though the west wind had been driven down its mouthpiece. It flowed into the room with a strange but penetrating cadence and was followed by a renewal of the silence, deep, intense and fearful. Every one of the five men was gripping his gun. Paul Viotti leaned a little forward.

"Remember," he whispered hoarsely, "the switch was on. The

first siren would blow, even if Sam himself were to join us. If any one steps upon the third stair and the second siren blows, then there is danger. That is the time when we shall need to look to ourselves."

Almost as he finished speaking, the other siren blew—a flute-like, alluring note. Things in the room happened quickly then. First of all, four bullets whistled around the chair which Roger had known enough to vacate at the first sounds of danger, then every light in the room went out and the place was plunged in complete darkness. There was a renewal of the silence, which had about it this time a thrilling and magnetic intensity. Every one of the five men knew, and Roger himself was equally aware, that their revolvers were making a little arc, every one of them centred upon that spot from which the light must flow with the opening of that door.

A man's breath fell hot upon Roger's cheek and he was conscious of a whisper in his ear, a whisper barely audible even to him because of the droning of the electric fan overhead.

"Crawl away to the left," Savonarilda enjoined. "They may forget you."

Roger obeyed promptly. He crawled on until he reached the wall, then he lay flat upon his stomach and his whole being ached for the butt of a revolver in his hand. There were sounds which seemed as though they came from another world. Then again the silence.

"Can you hear me, Roger?"

"Yes."

Something hard touched his hand.

"I am trusting you," the voice continued, "not to use this against any of the others. That dirty little skunk, Pierre Viotti, is lying for you. If he finds out, there's your chance."

"Great fellow," Roger whispered. "I won't draw it on another soul, and not on him, if I can get my hands to his throat."

Again the silence. If indeed there were strangers outside, they were taking plenty of time before they made up their minds to attack.

"A rotten show this, all through," Savonarilda whispered contemptuously. "I never believed in it. This isn't New York. I felt that this place was a death trap from the moment they built it."

Then nothing. The absence of all sound in the room, except the low humming of the electric fans, became a terrible thing. The other four seemed to have made a little semicircle around the door, ready to shoot any one who entered. Savonarilda and Roger alone were in the background. The silence was broken at last from outside by the sound of more descending footsteps, the footsteps of stoutly shod gendarmes. Roger leaned towards his companion. The hum of the ventilating fan over their heads was still sufficient to drown his faint whisper.

"What are you going to do?" he asked.

"I'm not going to shoot any of those poor chaps. We have nothing to gain by it. I shall do the trick on myself, as soon as one is sure that no miracles are to happen. Remember, your gun is for Pierre Viotti only."

Still the footsteps descended the stairs. There must have been a small crowd on the other side of the door. Roger leaned across towards his neighbour.

"I won't use the gun on any one but Viotti," he promised. "You don't mind what else I do?"

"Not a damn. You're a brighter lad than I've ever thought you, though, if you can find a chance of getting out of here alive."

Roger kicked off his shoes and, standing up in his socks, held his breath and listened. All movement outside the door had ceased. The crowd there must have known quite well that to open it was death to the first person who showed himself, and a life in the Principality is worth as much as a life anywhere else. In his stockinged feet, Roger stole on to where he had seen the switch which governed the electric fans. He felt around it carefully, then braced himself for the effort. With a prodigious tug he pulled it down bodily. Then he dropped flat on his back just in time, for a bullet whistled over his head. Paul Viotti's voice hissed through the darkness.

"Who the hell is meddling with the switches? Turn on the light, some one."

There was no immediate move. Already the fans were slackening in speed and breathing became every second more difficult. Roger, standing upright, was once more feeling his way along the wall to the spot where he had noticed the electric light switch. He found it at last embedded in a little circle of metal, set his teeth, gripped tighter and tighter still and finally made his effort. It broke away in his grasp and he staggered back with bleeding hands into the chaos of darkness. Then Paul Viotti's voice was heard, raised this time to about ordinary talking pitch.

"The dynamo is running down," he gasped. "There'll be no air here in five minutes. Turn on the light, some one. Damn it, why don't you turn on the light? We must make sure that we put Sloane out. Staines, you're on that side, aren't you? Open the chute."

Terence Brown's quavering voice came from somewhere in the obscurity.

"The switch has gone. It's been pulled out. Oh, God, I can't breathe!"

The room was suddenly filled with the wailing cries of a man in hysteria.

"My head—bursts. Let me out! Let us open the door. I have done no wrong. This was all for Paul. Open the door! We shall die—without air—I suffocate!"

Not a soul wasted his breath in reply. The moments passed, grew into minutes. Then Pierre Viotti's voice again—fainter this time—full of the malice of a half-mad, dying beast.

"Where's Sloane? Where are you, you American dog? I'm going to kill you before the light comes. Paul—Staines—where's Sloane?"

The voice was growing nearer and nearer. They could hear him reeling towards them. Savonarilda stretched out his arm and drew Roger back.

"I'm going to kill Sloane," Pierre Viotti called out, with a sudden access of strength in his voice. "The light will come directly. I will kill him first. Where are you, Sloane? Over there—eh?"

It seemed to Roger that the crash of the revolver was almost in his ears. Three times Pierre Viotti fired into the blackness, then he paused to listen. Savonarilda peered forward. He fired one single shot and Pierre Viotti's cry of agony shivered and tore its way through the room. They heard the flop of his falling body, heard his strangled groans, what sounded to be the muttered words of a prayer and then silence.

"Sorry if I robbed you, Roger," Savonarilda whispered. "I am the only man here who can see in the dark."

Words framed themselves on Roger's lips but they failed to materialise. The minutes went on, perhaps hours. No one knew. All that they realised was that the end was coming. Then Paul Viotti made an effort. His voice had become a squeaky falsetto.

"We got—to make sure—Sloane."

Savonarilda's voice, heard by his comrades for the last time on earth, choked out his magnificent lie.

"Sloane got his—when the switch—ugh! He is lying—here—corner. I'll give him two more—make sure."

Two more shots from Savonarilda's revolver, extended towards the ceiling, rang out. Again there was a silence, another strange time-cheating interval, then Paul Viotti's voice fainter now. The words left his lips with a discordant and ghastly wheeziness.

"Pull trap door—whoever's last. The Wolves have the lorry—Pierre's dead. Better leave him—"

Footsteps pattered across the carpeted floor, swift and eager footsteps risking their way through the darkness. A moment or two later the sliding back into its place of well-oiled metal, running along a groove. Then again a silence which seemed to have in it now more of actuality. Roger, with his hand upon his chest, leaned his back against the wall and pushed his way along until he reached the door. He hammered against it, then he felt for the catch, drew it and staggered into the crowded passage, at the end of which was light and along which was sweeping life-giving air.

"Tony," he cried back to Savonarilda, as he drew in a long breath, "come along. We're through."

In his shirt sleeves, his hair in wild confusion, the blood streaming from his hands, he forced his way through the group of questioning men, he even pushed Dalmorres on one side. At the touch of his shoulder, the commissaire went staggering against the wall. Jeannine for wild seconds was in his arms, and the glory of it sent the blood singing back through his veins. Her arms were around his neck like a vice, her tears hot on his cheeks. Even then, though, he did not forget.

"Help Prince Savonarilda out," he cried. "He and I have tricked the whole lot of them. They're out by a secret way—down at the end of the garden, I should think."

Savonarilda came staggering into the light. A gendarme supported him on either side. His face, streaked with blood, was like the face of a corpse. His fingers were making feeble efforts to get at his side pocket.

"None of that, old chap," Roger called out hysterically. "Can't you see? We're safe. I'm safe and you're safe."

Savonarilda understood and abandoned his efforts. The glimmer of a smile played around the corner of his lips. Then he fainted.

* * * * *

They stumbled into the sunshine and the air and up into the waiting *camion*, which started away immediately. Terence Brown was half delirious and crying out his roulette stakes. There was blood upon Thornton's lips and deep black lines under his eyes. Paul Viotti had lost his magnificent colour and his eyes were glazed, but at the first breath of fresh air his vigour seemed to return. He tore off his clothes, drew on the trousers and jersey of an Italian workman, stuck a beret on one side of his head and lit a cigarette. The others weakly tried to follow his example.

"Be men," he begged, as he drew a jersey over Terence Brown's almost limp body. "The next few minutes will mean safety or lilies on your chests. Be men now and you can faint for the rest of your lives. Come on!"

He flogged them into some show of energy, then he crawled to the back of the vehicle, looked out and even his stout heart sank. Round the last bend they came racing—two cars full of men in uniform. He saw the glitter of the sunshine upon their waiting rifles.

"How far to Nice?" he asked the chauffeur.

"Seventeen kilometres," the man replied. "Bad tyres. No go fast."

Once more Paul Viotti glanced behind at the rapidly approaching cars. They were almost within hailing distance now and his last thought was one of self-contempt. Next time, when he started again, he would give more attention to details. The get-away *camion*, for instance, should possess a concealed seventy-horse-power engine and invulnerable tyres. Well! He scrambled through the front on to the seat by the chauffeur. With steady fingers he lit another cigarette from the stump of the old one and watched the road. They swung around another corner. The shouts of their pursuers were plainly audible now.

"Lady commit suicide here," the chauffeur muttered, pointing to the famous drop.

"No fool, that lady," Paul Viotti replied. "It's the place I've been looking for."

The chauffeur suddenly felt a hand of iron upon the wheel, wrenching it from his grasp. Then it seemed as though a thunderbolt had hit him, for Paul Viotti flung him with scarcely an effort out into the road—to live or to die, as might happen. He swung the car around to face the precipice, put his foot upon the accelerator—

"We're for it, boys!" he cried out.

They fell six hundred feet in such a manner that identification was difficult.

* * * * *

It seemed sometimes to Roger only a day or two instead of a week later that he sat once more upon the terrace of his villa with Jeannine by his side and Erskine, his arm in a sling but otherwise recovered, lounging in a chair a few feet away. The orange blossoms had long since been gathered, but there were pink and white apple

169

and peach blossoms in the orchards below, and a mass of Bougainvillæa mingled with the roses which crawled around the arbour and along the pergola. Down in the valley the bell of the little church was still clanging. Lady Julia hobbled out of the house on Savonarilda's arm.

"These French papers are disgraceful," she declared, throwing one down. "Here is a whole column devoted to the praise of the commissaire of police and the wonderful gendarmerie service which he has organised. They pat themselves on the back all the time that they have broken up the most dangerous gang of criminals who have ever visited the Principality.... Yes, that's there, all right. You can read it, if you don't believe me. They even say that it was a gang who had defied all the police of New York for years. The commissaire is to be decorated."

"Why not?" Roger demanded lazily. "He played the man at the end, anyhow."

"But it was you and Prince Savonarilda who broke up the gang," Jeannine expostulated.

Roger grinned. So, in a subtler fashion, did Savonarilda, who was spending his last day in France before returning to Sicily.

"It's hard to get these matters straightened out quite clearly sometimes," Roger observed sententiously.

Lady Julia settled herself in her chair.

"There will be changes now," she sighed, "and I hate changes. Most of all, I shall miss you, Prince. You may be a very bad man now and then, but you are capable of such splendid gestures."

The Curé came into sight, trudging up the hill. Bardells appeared, carrying a tray on which was the cocktail shaker, two bottles of champagne and sweet biscuits.

"His Reverence does not drink cocktails, sir," he confided to Roger, "and he will require a little refreshment after the ceremony. Luncheon will be ready in a quarter of an hour."

THE END

Lightning Source UK Ltd.
Milton Keynes UK
UKHW040850160720
366638UK00002B/5/J